CW00435551

# The Fractured Globe

Angela Fish

*Best wishes*

*Angela Fish*

**www.darkstroke.com**

Discover us online:
**www.darkstroke.com**

Join us on instagram:
**www.instagram.com/darkstrokebooks/**

Include **#darkstroke** in a photo of yourself
holding this book on Instagram and
**something nice will happen.**

*To the family of Fishes, with love.*

# Acknowledgements

I would like to offer sincere thanks to Laurence and Stephanie Patterson of darkstroke for making the editorial and production process swift, efficient, and supportive, and for bringing *The Fractured Globe* to life. Additional thanks to the Crooked Cat/ darkstroke community of writers for being so welcoming and informative.

Grateful thanks to my family, and to my patient friends, Diane, Ann and Jo, who have listened to my constant ramblings and 'what-ifs'; to Sam Kean for allowing me to quote from his book, *The Violinist's Thumb*, and to The British Red Cross and The British Heart Foundation for helping me with the timeline of charity shops in the UK.

Thanks to former tutor, Stephen Jenkins, for providing the prompt which started this whole process, from poem to short story to novel; the writers' group at Garth Olwg, Church Village who offered support and belief, and to readers of earlier drafts, Diane Jones, Ann Richards, Stephen Lamb and Wendy Steele.

# About the Author

Angela worked in medical research, electronic and electrical engineering, and administration. In her mid-thirties, she decided to change direction and returned to university to study Humanities, specialising in Literature and Creative Writing. She then completed an MPhil (Literature) focussing on how women writers in Wales, between 1850 and 1950, portrayed their female characters. Following this, Angela joined the staff the University of Glamorgan where, in 2000, she set up and directed The Wales Centre for Intergenerational Practice. As well as providing training and advice, she worked with local schools and communities, over a period of ten years, to improve communication between the generations. She has been in demand, nationally and internationally, as a conference presenter and an invited speaker in her field.

Her publications include non-fiction, short stories, poetry, and fiction for children. *The Fractured Globe* is her first full-length novel and explores the nature/nurture question through the lives of two single mums, their sons, and families, over twenty-five years. This debate, together with an interest in mythology and magic, has significantly influenced her writing.

Angela is a member of The Society of Authors [SoA], and the SoA Children's Writers and Illustrators Group.

She lives in south Wales.

**Find her at www.angela-fish.com**

# The Fractured Globe

*A devil, a born devil, on whose nature*
*Nurture can never stick.*
(W Shakespeare, The Tempest, 1623, 4.1.211-215)


*The more that I looked at DNA,*
*the more I realized it was nature and nurture.*
*It's how genes and your environment*
*work together to produce the person you are.*
Sam Kean, The Violinist's Thumb, 2012

# 2016

## December 1st

I don't remember much about the day my son was born. Or the day he died. I was off my head on both days. What I do remember is the snow. And the cold. And the pain. In some ways, not much has changed.

Thank God for Janet. If she hadn't helped me, I'd probably have died on the pavement. There again, maybe that would have been for the best. I know I shouldn't be here now. It's just so hard to stay away. Things could have turned out so differently but it's no good looking back. Just a few minutes. Even seeing her through the window will be enough.

I wonder how long she's been using the snow globe for the Christmas window display. It's hard to believe that something so beautiful can cause so much pain.

I remember standing right here on his birthday, in the snow, looking through the same shop window, desperate for someone to notice me. All I saw were flashing white lights, and my head felt as though it was going to split open. I can still taste the blood at the back of my throat. I remember looking at my feet. I couldn't understand why they were so red. I mean, I was freezing. Then it all went black.

When I woke up in a clean, warm bed, someone was tapping my hand. Then a nurse put a baby into my arms.

"This is your son. Do you have a name for him?"

I called him Luke.

# 1991

## December 1st

Janet McElroy pointed to the window and called out to the other two women in the shop.

"There's that girl again. She's in real state this time. No coat, black eye and a bloody nose. We can't leave her out there in this weather, poor thing."

"Wait a minute, Janet. You don't know what trouble's following her. You've seen that fellow she hangs around with. No-good layabout, if you ask me. Probably on drugs, too. I don't think Head Office would be very pleased if one of us was hurt or the place was trashed."

Janet shook her head and sighed. "You mean that we can work in a charity shop, take money off people for charity, but we can't directly help someone who obviously needs it? Sorry, I'm going out."

Janet pulled open the door as Tia slumped to the ground. The girl was wearing a thin shirt, a short black skirt and summer shoes. She lay on the pavement with her hair spread out around her, but Janet's eyes were drawn to the slashes of red on the snow beneath the girl's legs. She ran back into the shop.

"Quick! Phone for an ambulance. I think she's losing the baby. She's tiny but looks almost full term to me. Tell them she's unconscious but breathing. Where's that box of blankets that came in last week? We can't move her but I'll try to keep her a little bit warmer. I need that big umbrella as well. The snow's coming down much heavier. Can one of you help me? Now!"

***

Kay Jones screamed and was rewarded with a mask clamped over her mouth and nose.

"There now, don't fuss. Keep calm and breathe like we've told you. It'll make it easier. You're nearly there."

Kay grunted. There had been a stream of nurses over the past ten hours telling her the same thing, and now she was tired of it all. If she could have a pill to stop everything for a few hours then she'd willingly take it, but no such luck. This baby was coming out whether she liked it or not. Another contraction washed over her and she grabbed the nurse's hand.

"Don't waste your energy on me, girl. Push!" The nurse turned to one of the juniors in the room and lowered her voice. "Doesn't she have anyone with her? Doesn't seem right, her being on her own. She's only eighteen, for goodness sake."

"There's no one waiting." The junior nurse shook her head and looked through Kay's notes. "She hasn't put anyone as her next-of-kin, either. Looks like she's in one of those new council flats over Crompton way. Are Social Services involved at all?"

"Not sure. I think there's something from them at the back of her notes. She might need some extra help here. Can you see if there's a medic free?"

Kay shouted again and the nurses turned back to her. Half an hour later, after a forceps delivery, they told her she had a son. She called him Adam.

## December 2nd

I wish they'd stop asking me all these questions. First the nurses, then the doctors, now the police and Social Services. I can see by the way they keep looking at each other that they don't believe anything I've said, but if I told them the truth, they'd take Luke away before I could spit. I thought that's what I wanted but once he curled his little hand around my finger, I knew I had to keep him. I've got to find a way for us to stay together.

"Now try to remember. Where have you been living these past few months? And who was it that hurt you? We can't help you if you don't help us."

I'm so tired. I just want to sleep. I can't remember the last time I had sheets or a pillowcase. They're bringing the food trolley around now. I'm starving, but I'm afraid that I'll puke. It's been ages since I ate anything more than toast or chips.

"Come along now. I think that's enough questions for today. She's not going anywhere for a while so you can come back tomorrow. She needs to rest."

She's the only nurse who's been kind to me. Since they cleaned me up in A & E and brought me to the ward, the others have just done what they needed and left me to it. I saw a couple of them in the corner looking over at me and whispering. I know what they think and they're wrong. I've never touched anything apart from the vodka and a few pills, nothing heavy. Not like Jake and the others. I can't go back there. He'll kill me next time, that's for sure. And what about Luke? No way. There must be something I can do to keep him.

*** 

The nurse swished the curtains open and the group of people who had been questioning Tia left the ward. Kay leaned over and looked at her son. He was asleep, and she touched his face and his long, black eyelashes. She glanced across the room at Tia and saw that she was crying.

"What's the matter? Stitches? Mine hurt like bleedin' hell. Ask for some painkillers when they come around. They help a bit. I'm Kay. What's your name?"

Tia looked up and wiped her hand across her eyes. The girl in the bed opposite looked all right but Tia didn't know if she could trust her. Still, there was no one else in the room, and she could always deny everything if Kay told anyone what she'd said.

"I'm Tia. I didn't have any stitches. I'm just tired and a bit scared about what's going to happen next."

"What d'you mean? With the feeding and stuff?"

"No. I mean, I don't know if they'll let me keep him. I don't really have anywhere to live." She gulped. "My boyfriend, well, he beat me up yesterday, and I ran away."

Kay frowned. At least she had her own place, although her baby's father didn't know about him. It was going to be tough, having to look after a baby as well as herself, but she was going to try. She thought about her parents and how she'd hurt them, but she wasn't ready for any kind of reconciliation just yet.

"That's not good. Don't let on about that kind of stuff. Isn't there anyone that you could stay with? They might let you have him then, even if they keep an eye on you for a while."

"I don't have anyone at all."

Tia began to cry again and Kay slipped out of bed and crossed the room. She put a box of tissues on Tia's bed.

"Here, have those. They don't seem to have given you any. God, your face is a mess. You look like one of those paintings – you know, the ones where the nose is on the wrong bit of the face!"

Tia tried to laugh but cried even harder instead. After a few minutes she blew her nose and edged herself off the bed.

"Thanks. I haven't got anything of my own here. I don't know what happened to my clothes. Probably in the bin. Why have you got your baby in here and I haven't? You don't think they've taken him away already, do you?"

"Naaw. Probably not. I expect they thought you needed a bit more sleep. They'll bring him when it's feed time. What're you doing?"

Tia raised her eyebrows. "What?"

"Bottle or boob? I'm doing the bottle. They tried to talk me into doing it myself but no way! At least with the bottle you can get someone else to take over. If you've got someone, of course."

Tia smiled. "Bottle for me, too. But I don't know anything about babies. Maybe this is a stupid idea. Maybe he'd be better off in care. Not that it did me much good, but at least there was always food and it was warm."

Kay didn't say anything. It seemed as though Tia's past was more interesting than hers. When she saw the nurse wheeling a cot up the corridor, she climbed back into her bed.

"Look out. Here comes the friggin' night patrol! Looks like you're gonna get your first baby feeding lesson. Don't make up your mind now – about the little one. Wait until tomorrow, after you've had a sleep."

Tia nodded and her stomach began to jump about as the nurse pulled the curtain around her bed and put Luke into her arms. She wasn't even asked how she wanted to feed him. A bottle was put in her hand and the nurse turned away.

"Wait. Please. I don't know what to do."

The nurse turned and tutted. She was one of the ones who had been whispering about Tia earlier. She spent a few minutes explaining about teats and air bubbles and wind. She put a disposable nappy on the bed and told Tia to ask Kay to show her how to use it. Then she left. Tia felt like crying again but bit her lip instead and concentrated on the gurgling sounds that Luke was making. She began to count the bubbles that were racing up the side of the bottle.

"You all right there?" Kay called across the ward. "I've nearly done with this one. Just got to clean his bum, then I'll come over. Okay?"

Tia smiled. Maybe this could work after all.

## December 4th

Across the other side of town, Kay's estranged mother, Ruth, opened the front door and greeted her sister, Janet.

"Hello, love. You're early. Come in. I just need to set the next lot of washing running and then I'll make some tea."

"Hello Ruth. Not much traffic today, and they've finished the roadworks at last. You carry on. I'll make the tea."

Janet filled the kettle and sat at the table. She looked around at the neat kitchen, the clean worktops, and the spotless floor. She sighed. Sometimes she wished her life was more like her sister's, but then again maybe it was better that it wasn't.

The kettle boiled. Janet made the tea and put the cups on the table.

"Do you want to have it here or in the front room?"

Ruth turned around. "Oh, we'll stay in here if you don't mind? I've brought the decorations out and it's a bit of a mess in there."

Janet laughed. "A mess? The only room that was ever messy was Kay's!" She clamped her hand over her mouth and made a clicking noise with her tongue. "I'm so sorry, Ruth. I shouldn't have said that. Sorry."

Ruth smiled at her sister and shook her head. "Don't worry, love. It's not like she died, is it? No point pussyfooting around. That's not going to change things. It does hurt, I'll admit, but never talking about her hurts even more. Paul just walks away if I try to say anything to him."

"Is he still as bad?"

"Yes. Probably even worse. The first time she left he was really upset, but he got used to it. When she finally got in touch, and said she had a job, there wasn't much we could do about it. He calmed down a bit when she told us she was staying with one of her friends from school, but then he flared up again when she wouldn't tell us where that was."

"Did you ever find out why she wouldn't tell you?"

"No. She clammed up when we asked, so we didn't bother trying any more. When she told us last May that she was expecting, everything fell apart again. I've never seen Paul so angry. I think he was more disappointed really. She wouldn't say who the father was either, as you know, so he couldn't even take it out on him."

"Do you still think it was one of those twins she used to walk home from school with?"

"Hard to say, but I don't think so really. The younger one – well, she always called him that even though there was only ten minutes between them – he was the one she preferred, but she knew he'd be off to Uni after his A levels. Can't remember his name right now, something like Khalif, or Khalid? The older boy, well, there was something a bit wilder about him. I only spoke to them a few times, but he always seemed kind of jumpy. She called him Jazz. I remember that because I thought it suited the way he was. He was going to do some business course and was supposed to take over from the father in time. She was hanging around with him quite a bit when the other one left, but he'd told her that once he was qualified he was going to marry the daughter of the father's business partner."

"I wish I could have done more to help." Janet picked up a biscuit and dipped it in her tea. Ruth's eyebrows raised ever so slightly. The corners of Janet's mouth twitched.

"After Paul calmed down, I thought that if she came home we could work something out, but we were fooling ourselves, again." Ruth wiped the back of her hand across her eyes. Janet leaned forward and handed her a tissue.

"Come on now. I didn't mean to upset you. When I saw you all together in the summer, it looked like you had everything sorted. I couldn't believe it when you told me she'd run off again. No wonder Paul's hurt, but bottling it up won't help, though."

Ruth blew her nose quietly. "I think it hurt him more because she stole from him. She knew that the money was only here because he'd missed the bank. He never usually kept much at home."

"She must have made a quick decision to go, then? I mean, if there wasn't usually much money about?"

"I can't say, love. Maybe she was planning it anyway and it was just lucky, for her, that the cash was here. We'll probably never know. It was so unlike her. She was always stubborn but … Anyway, let's change the subject. What's happening with you? Still working at the charity shop?"

"Yes, as much as I can. I'm glad I went part-time at the hospital. It gives me more chance to do what I really want. Talking of the shop, we had a real fright the other day. You remember that girl I told you about, the one we'd seen hanging around the square? Well, she only turned up in a right state outside the shop and collapsed on the pavement. Looked like she'd been knocked about and I think she was miscarrying. The ambulance came right away and they carted her off to A & E. I did think about going with her, but I couldn't leave Marge to manage the shop. You know what a drama queen she is!"

Ruth finished her tea and put the cup down quietly. "So, what happened?"

Janet grimaced. "I don't know. I was going to go and see her later, before my shift started, but they'd taken her to St. Jude's, not Rowan Tree District. When I thought about it, I convinced myself that it wasn't a good idea to get involved. I might still go, though. What do you think?"

Ruth screwed up her mouth. "That's up to you, love, but if it was me, I'd probably stay away. More tea?"

The sisters drank a second cup almost in silence, each thinking of Kay and the impact of her disappearance on their lives. Ruth leaned forward and tapped Janet's hand.

"Before you go, there's something I want you to see. It's in the front room."

They crossed the hallway and Ruth paused for a moment before opening the door and standing back for her sister to enter. Janet blinked as the room was in darkness except for a faint glow in the far corner. She moved towards it, then drew in her breath sharply.

"You still have it."

She reached out her hand to caress a large snow globe and stood transfixed as a pale blue light flickered over the figure of Jack Frost that sat on a dead tree trunk. Everything inside the globe was made from crystals and as the snow swirled, the whole scene glistened and shimmered. Ruth flicked a switch at the base and Janet shivered as the haunting strains of *A Winter Lullaby* filled the room. She felt the hairs on her neck stiffen and realised that she was crying. Her! She wasn't ever the soppy one.

As she gazed into the globe, she remembered how Kay had been afraid of it when she was small and that it had eventually been banished to the spare room cupboard. They'd all laughed at her at first; at her insistence that Jack Frost knew what she was thinking and that he was going to take her away. Now, in the eerie stillness of the room, Janet thought she understood the little girl's fears. There was something ethereal about the globe, something unexplainable, yet she felt a more positive energy from it. It took a lot of effort for her to stop looking at it but eventually she turned to Ruth who was crying quietly.

"I couldn't bear to part with it. I never understood why Kay was so scared of it. When I plugged it in this morning, all I could see was her face in the snow. It just gives me some connection, some hope, you know?"

Janet nodded.

It was when Janet was driving home that she realised that her niece's baby was due any day, and that Ruth hadn't mentioned it. She kicked herself again.

\*\*\*

Kay's going home tomorrow. She has to have a nurse visit her for a while to check that she's doing all right, but she's really going. The kind nurse said her name was Meg and she told the doctor about the people from Social Services and he asked them to back off for a few days, but then the police came again. I was going to tell them about Jake. Not that I was living at the squat, but about him beating me up. Serve him right. But then I thought about what he'd do if he ever caught up with me, so I just said that some bloke had jumped me in the park. Didn't believe me, I could see, but what could they do?

It's still only me and Kay in here. The other two beds aren't even made up. Maybe it's a room for girls like us. Meg's been showing me how to bath Luke, how to wash his hair and to check his cord. I didn't even know what she was talking about at first. She showed me how the feeds are mixed up, even though patients aren't supposed to be in that area. She said it would be good for me to learn how to do it 'just in case'. I think she knows that the others miss me out sometimes when they're bringing around the feeds – for the babies and the mothers. It's a good job that Kay's here. She just shouts at them and calls them all spiteful bleedin' cows!

## December 5th

The ward door swung open and Kay walked in carrying her washbag. She glanced over at Tia's bed.

"Well, this is it. Nearly time to go. Just got to get dressed and see to Adam. One of my neighbours is coming to fetch me. You know, the one who's called in a few times? She's a bit of a nosey cow but means well. She told the hospital bods that she'll keep an eye on me. That's one of the reasons they're letting me go now, but I hope that doesn't mean she'll want to be in my flat all the time. What about you? Any decisions?"

Tia shook her head. "Nope. Social's coming back in a few days. I suppose I could tell them everything – well, almost everything, and ask them to help me and Luke stay together. Most likely they'll say I'm not fit to have him and they'll shove him in care, and I'll end up on the street."

Kay frowned. She wanted to get out of the hospital, with Adam, and get on with her life. She knew she'd made a mess of things, but was determined to get back on track. She didn't think her parents would be happy to see her again but hoped her Auntie Janet might help build some bridges. What she didn't need was to be involved with someone like Tia. It was all right being friendly in here – she felt sorry for Tia really, even though she was a bit of a wimp – but that was as far as she wanted it to go.

"Don't be so down. That nurse can tell them you're good with Luke, that you're learning how to look after him. She knows you're clean, and they must have tested your blood and stuff, anyway. Maybe the Social will get you into one of those homes for a while 'til they see if they can trust you. You might get a flat like me. What if you got one in my block? That would be a laugh, wouldn't it?"

Tia winced. "Yeah. We could go to clinic together like proper little mothers! Fingers crossed, eh?"

Kay pulled the curtains around her bed, dressed, packed her bag and then wrapped Adam in a pale blue blanket. She crossed the room to Tia's bed, bent over Luke's cot and kissed the top of his head.

"So long, Twinnie. Okay, time for the off. I can see Mrs Walker at the nurse's desk. I've left you a few things on my bed. I've got enough at home. Hope it all works out for you. Let me know when you're settled and come and visit sometime."

Kay laughed loudly and pushed open the ward door with her bottom before Tia could remind her that she hadn't left her address.

A few minutes later, Tia crossed the ward and looked into the corridor. Empty. She went to Kay's side of the room and took the notes from the cage at the end of the bed. The staff would be coming soon to strip the bed so she knew she had to hurry. Then she picked up the plastic bag that Kay had left. Inside were some pyjamas, slippers and a washbag. Tia started to shake and dropped into the armchair at the side of her bed. When the nurses came in, she told them she was going to have a bath and asked if she could put Luke in the nursery for a while. They just shrugged.

## December 7th

Janet slotted her car neatly into the parking bay, grabbed her bag, and hurried into the precinct. Her sister was already waiting outside *The Hot Spot*, their favourite café.

"Hello. Sorry I'm a bit late. Been here long?"

"No, only about five minutes. The bus was early. I've been looking in Cooper's window. They've got some lovely jackets."

Janet was about to reply when Ruth burst into tears.

"Whatever's the matter? Do you want to go somewhere else? Go home? What?"

Ruth gulped and shook her head. "No, I'll be all right. Sorry. I didn't mean to do that but … come on, let's go in."

She turned and pushed open the door of the café. A wave of hot air hit them and Ruth stumbled as her glasses steamed up.

"Take more water with it next time, love!"

Janet smiled at the man in the corner. "Why spoil a good

drink?"

When they'd found a table and ordered their coffee, Janet waited for her sister to start talking. She knew better than to ask too many questions.

"Sorry, love. It's just been a strange few days. I was going to tell you when you rang, but I don't think I would have made sense." She glanced at Janet. "But from the look on your face, I'm not doing much better now, am I?"

Janet shrugged. "Take your time. Whatever it is, it's obviously rattled you. Something to do with Kay?"

Ruth nodded. "When you came around the other day, I told you that I'd been sorting out the decorations, and you saw the globe. Well, Paul wasn't too happy when he came home. Said there was no point and we had a big row. I shoved everything back in the bag and was putting it in the cupboard when I bumped the globe. It only made a small crack but when I plugged it in again, it wouldn't work. I couldn't bear to put it back in the cupboard, so I put it on the dressing table. At least I can look at it when I want. Paul will probably kick off again but I don't care. I can't forget about her just like that. I know we didn't talk about it last time, but she's probably had the baby by now, or won't be far off. I can't stop thinking about it. I have a grandchild and I'll probably never see it." Ruth began to cry again.

Janet turned around and could see some of the other customers looking over to their table.

"Look, Ruth. Why don't I take you home? Too many sticky beaks in here."

"You're right, love. Come on, let's go."

***

I don't know if I can do this. It seemed like a good idea earlier. It was so quiet when I went to the bathroom. All the staff seemed to be on the wards. If someone had been on reception, I couldn't have gone into the storeroom. So much stuff! Nappies, sheets, Babygros, some of those tiny caps and socks and cot blankets. It didn't take long to roll up a pile and hide it in my locker.

There was only one nurse working in the room where they make up the feeds. Thank goodness she was called out to see to someone on the ward. I didn't have much time, but I knew where most things were kept, especially the dried milk. There was a coat hanging up behind the door. It looked a bit big for me but I still took it and stuffed it under my pillow. One of the kinder nurses was in the nursery when I went to fetch Luke and she stopped to talk to me. She's pregnant herself and finishing work after the night shift. She showed me the fluffy sleeping bag and the bath set that the staff had bought her for the baby. Lucky her! I was so tired after I'd fed Luke that I fell asleep within minutes.

## December 8th

I woke up at half past one. It was strange being on my own in the ward, but I was glad of it right then. The night nurse was doing some paperwork and didn't notice me. Everything was quiet in the nursery and I was in and out in less than minute. I took the sleeping bag and the bath stuff and went back to the ward. I checked on Luke again before creeping past the nursery to the door at the top of the stairs. Kay had told me that this was the way down to the door into the car park. There were two flights of stairs and the door to the outside was only a few steps further. It was locked, of course, but I guessed that it would be opened when the day staff came on duty.

On the way back I stopped at the first landing. The door squeaked when I opened it but no one came to check. I snuck along the corridor and began to look into the rooms. The first two were locked. Then the laundry cupboard. I thought about pinching some bedding but I knew I couldn't carry it. Bingo! The staff room. Unlocked and no one around. I'd been on enough nicking raids with Jake and the others to know what to do. Quick and quiet. Only take what you can see and carry easily. No time for rummaging.

I almost kept to the rules. Trainers, a couple of carrier bags, a sweater and a pair of jeans – all thrown about the room. But I knew that the thing I needed most would be hidden away. I tried the locker doors. Nothing opened. I tried the drawers in the table and in the little kitchen area. Nix. I opened the cupboards but there were just the usual mugs and plates and a few dusty bowls. I knew I had to get out soon, but then I saw the biscuit tin. It reminded me of one of my foster mother's habits of putting money in a tin in the kitchen for the window cleaner, or if door-to-door collectors came.

Again, I was in luck. A piece of paper with a list of names and 'coffee pot' at the top. Underneath – a load of coins and at least twenty pounds in notes. They must have liked their coffee! I did leave all the copper coins and those teeny silver ones, but the rest went into my dressing gown pocket.

When I got back to the ward, I nearly had a fit. The bitchy nurse was there standing over Luke's cot.

"Where do you think you've been? This child's been crying for over ten minutes. I should report you for this."

I told her I'd felt a bit sick and had to spend some time in the bathroom. She didn't answer me – just huffed off down the corridor. She didn't even notice what I was carrying. My heart didn't stop thumping for ages. When I looked at the clock, it was two forty.

At six thirty, Nella, the tea-lady, put a cup on my table.

"There you are, lovely. Nice cuppa for you. Going to be a beautiful day out there later. Cold, but the snow's almost gone."

I couldn't go back to sleep. I got up and drank my tea. Shit, it was awful! Luke was stirring and I knew that his bottle would be coming soon. I had to keep calm. There was still no one else in the ward. So far so good.

I fed Luke, washed and changed him, then slipped along to the bathroom. The feeding trolley was still doing its rounds and it only took a moment to filch a few extra bottles and slip them into my washbag. I knew the routine. Someone would be along very soon to do the usual checks and then the breakfast cart would come onto the ward about half past seven. After that it would go quiet for a few hours before the doctors and their tribes would be around.

I don't know how I managed to eat any breakfast, let alone keep it down. I think that Luke sensed something was different, too. He was restless and I had trouble settling him. When he finally dropped off, I checked that there was no one around and I put on the odd assortment of clothes that I'd pinched. I looked like a bag lady! The clothes were too big but at least the trainers fitted. I laid out some clothes for Luke, as well as a hat, some socks, a blanket and the sleeping bag. My stomach was turning somersaults, but I didn't dare stop. This was the first time in ages that I'd made a decision for myself and I wasn't going to back out. I owed it to Luke. I owed it to myself.

I put everything else into the carrier bags and put them on the end of the bed. Then I dressed Luke, praying that he wouldn't start crying but he'd finally zonked out. When I saw him, all wrapped up and in the sleeping bag, I felt the back of my throat start to burn and my guts cramped so bad I doubled over. I had to hang on to the bed for a second. I put on the coat – not too bad, and it had a hood – and put the money and the page from Kay's notes in the pocket. No gloves but I'd just have to put up with that. I pushed my hair into the hood and pulled it as far over my face as I could. The bruises had faded a bit, but it was best not to take chances.

The next ten minutes were the scariest ever. Nothing had made me feel the way I did as I sneaked out. I couldn't look back. I didn't dare, but every second I thought I could hear someone shouting at me. Sweat was running down my back and the blood was rushing in my ears. I thought everyone would be able to hear my heart pounding.

\*\*\*

Kay was relaxing on the settee, half listening to George Michael and Elton John's *Don't Let The Sun Go Down On Me,* when the doorbell rang. She glanced over at Adam's pushchair but he hadn't stirred. She frowned and swore under her breath. If it was Mrs Walker again, she'd scream. She knew the woman was trying to be kind but it was suffocating.

Kay opened the door and her mouth dropped open.

"Tia! What in bleedin' hell's name are you doing here? How did you find me, and how did you get through the outside door?"

Tia half smiled and dropped the carrier bags onto the floor. Her fingers were raw.

"Hi, Kay. Some woman was going out and she held the door open for me. Sorry, but I was desperate. The Social were due back today and I know what would've happened, so I legged it. Can I stay with you for a while? Just a few days until I figure out what to do?"

Kay's stomach flipped. This was all she needed, but Tia looked so small, like one of those broken dolls you see in the basket at a jumble sale or in the charity shops.

"For gawd's sake come in. Don't let Mrs W see you or we'll both be in the shit. How in hell did you get here, and where on earth did you get those clothes? You look like a friggin' scarecrow!"

Tia stumbled into the flat and lay Luke on the settee. She took off her coat and dropped down beside the baby. Her nose and cheeks were bright red. She began to shake.

"Did you have your check-up this morning? Was it all okay? You're not going to get sick on me now, are you? I can't risk anyone knowing you're here. They'll kick me out as well."

"I'm fine. Just a bit wobbly. I nicked the clothes and other stuff last night. I've got food for Luke for a while, and nappies. I got out through the car park door but I nearly got caught. I didn't think Luke would be so heavy but when I got to the door I had to stop and put the bags down. A nurse came down the corridor and asked if I was all right and why I was on my own. She wanted to know if I had my discharge papers, so I told her that my dad had them and that he'd just gone to bring the car to the door 'cos it was so cold. There was an old bloke at the far end of the car park just opening his car, so I pointed to him. She said okay but to stay in the warm until he came. Bloody hell, I was scared! As soon as she left, I scarpered."

"But how did you get here," Kay interrupted. "And how did you know where to come?"

Tia's face flushed and she hung her head so that her hair fell forward.

"I knew there was a bus stop on the other side of the car park wall. I could see the visitors getting on and off on both sides from the ward window. I didn't know which way to go, but a woman at the stop told me I'd have to go to the bus station in Alderbridge and then change for Crompton. I got your address out of your notes before they took them away. Sorry."

Kay screwed up her nose and narrowed her eyes.

"Mmm. Didn't think they had home addresses in the bed records. Thought they were just temperatures and stuff?"

"There was something in there from Social Services. Someone had clipped it in the back. Look."

Kay glanced at the sheet of paper in Tia's hand and shrugged her shoulders. She knew that she needed to think quickly if she was going to get rid of Tia and Luke before anyone found out.

## December 10th

I never thought I'd make it to Kay's. Carrying Luke and the bags nearly did me in. I only started to panic that she might not be there after I'd rung her bell. I don't know what I would have done then. When I saw her face, I thought she was going to boot me out right away. I think she was, really, but then Luke started crying. He was hot as well as wet, so she unwrapped him and changed him for me. She looked at him, then at Adam and her face changed. The tight lines around her mouth and eyes went away and then she started crying! Real big sobs, snotty nose and all. I just patted her back. Didn't even have a tissue to give her.

After that it was all right. She made us some coffee and beans on toast. I gave her most of the money I had left and promised to find a way to get more. Then we fed the kids and played with them for a bit before they went off to sleep again. She warned me about her neighbour and I had to promise to get into the bedroom with Luke as quickly as I could if the doorbell rang. She said we'd tell her I was Kay's cousin if she saw me and I was just visiting for a day or two.

I slept on the settee with Luke next to me in Adam's pushchair. Kay said we'd fix up something better for him but it would have to do for the first few nights. That sounded good. *The first few nights*. Whatever happens, at least I have somewhere safe for me and Luke for a while. I'll worry about later, well – later.

## December 14th

The rain was pounding on the windows when Kay woke. She rolled over and looked at the clock. Seven. Adam was still sleeping. She lay back and pulled the duvet up under her chin. The snow must have cleared if it was raining so heavily. She thought she'd try taking Adam out for a walk if it eased off. The main problem was Tia. It was fun having someone else around but the flat was small, and between the two of them, plus the babies and all their stuff, it was getting her down a bit. And then there was Mrs W. They'd had a lucky escape the day before. Kay shook her head. How could she have left the door on the latch? They'd been so careful with the midwife visits. She didn't stay long anyway, but Mrs W was unpredictable, and much more of a problem. They'd been even luckier when the police came knocking. Who'd have thought that they'd check up on Kay just because she'd been in the same ward as Tia for a few days. If Tia had come back from the shop ten minutes earlier, they'd have been caught. Or if the Twinnies had both started crying! There were updates on the local news about the 'missing girl and her child', and a bit in the local newspaper, but it didn't seem to be getting as much attention as some other cases. Still, it had given them a right scare and Kay had almost asked Tia to leave but changed her mind when she saw how white Tia went. It had taken a lot of persuading for Tia to cut her hair, but it did make her look different. If only there was some way to get Tia a place of her own.

The letterbox rattled and Tia stopped singing to Luke. She ran into the bedroom and shut the door as quietly as she could. Rattle, rattle. Whoever it was, they weren't going away. Luke began to grizzle and Tia rocked him, whispering into his ear any old nonsense that she could think of. Rattle, rattle. Luke relaxed and Tia sat on the edge of the bed. She started to count. Rattle, rattle. Count. Rattle, rattle. When she reached a hundred, she stopped. She laid the baby on the bed and risked a peep through the curtains. A small blue car was pulling away from the kerb, but Tia didn't know if it belonged to the person at the door. She jumped when she heard Kay's key turning in the lock.

"Oh God! I'm glad you're back. Someone was trying to get in. I don't think it was the police, but what if was the Social?"

Kay sighed. She felt better after her walk. What she didn't need was more drama or stress. Maybe it was time for Tia to go but …

"Stop bloody panicking over everything, will you? Probably only Mrs W, or one of the others." She pushed past Tia, went into the bedroom and closed the door.

An hour later, Kay opened the bedroom door and stopped dead.

"What in the name of buggery are you doing, Tia?" She looked at the bags on the floor, and at Tia and Luke, dressed for outdoors.

"I thought you'd want me to go. Sorry about before. If you could just lend me some money for the bus, I'll get out of your way." She buried her face in Luke's hair and started to cry.

"Don't be so daft. I was just a bit narked, that's all. Tired really. Get that stuff off and we'll have something to eat. I could murder a drink but – better not, I suppose. Anyway, I don't fancy going out again."

Tia half-smiled. "Sure? I didn't mean to be such a wimp but I got scared when they wouldn't go away. Sorry. And a drink? Yeah, me too, but I wouldn't trust myself."

Kay yawned and walked towards the kitchen. She smiled when she realised that Tia's face was bone dry.

The girls cleared away their dishes, went through the routine of preparing baby bottles, feeding, changing and settling the boys for the night.

"Don't know about you, but I'm knackered!" Kay flopped onto the settee and yawned. "Sit down and tell me about your dark and dirty past."

Tia sighed. "Not sure what you want to know. Nothing special about it."

"Come on! You've let drop a few things but I don't know anything about you, really. You could be a psycho for all I know!"

Tia laughed out loud. "Fool. But you're right. It's just that I've never had anyone to talk to before, so I guess I just keep things to myself. But if you really want to know …"

"Too right. Start at the beginning and don't skip things!"

"Okay, but it'll be a long night. I was told that my mother put me in care when I was about six weeks old and wouldn't sign adoption papers 'cos she said she'd be back to get me when she'd sorted out somewhere to live. Then she disappeared, and I was passed around like a parcel to foster homes for the next seven years. Don't remember much about it. Some good, some bad, but I was told I wasn't an easy child. Whatever that means. When I was eight I went to live with the Summers. For the first time it felt like someone wanted to have me around. I was desperate to call them Mum and Dad, but the social worker said that wasn't a good idea, so I called them Auntie Alex and Uncle David. I don't know how they managed it, but I stayed there for five years. They taught me how to take care of myself. They corrected me when I didn't speak properly and told me off if I swore – which I was quite good at, apparently!"

Kay laughed. "So that's why you always make faces

whenever I friggin' do it!"

Tia shook her head and grinned. "Shut up, nutter! It was great living with them. I went to Calderswell Juniors."

"Calderswell? Not the one in Winterford?"

"Yeah, that's the one. I used to tease them about where they lived. What with their name being Summers!"

"Bloody hell, Winterford! I only lived about a mile away, in The Meadows in Fieldslea. We were almost neighbours. So why didn't you come to Oakby Comp, where I was? Most of the Winterford kids did."

Tia blushed. "I went to Willow High."

Kay sat up suddenly and burst out laughing. "No way! Willow's? The private school? Ooh, real la-di-dah!"

Tia didn't think she'd heard anyone else laugh as loudly as Kay.

"Shush! You'll wake the boys. Do you want to hear the rest of this, or not?" Tia huffed.

"Sorry, yeah. It's just – Willow High! I knew a couple of kids who went there, but anyway, what happened? Why didn't you stay there?"

Tia gulped. She'd never spoken to anyone about that night. She skipped most of the details about the car crash; it was still as raw for her as when it happened.

"It was snowing and we were driving home from the pictures when a stupid junkie driver hit us. Next thing I knew, I was in hospital, the Summers were dead and the Social said I'd have to go back into care."

Kay drew in her breath and shook her head. "Bummer. Don't you remember anything at all?"

Tia shook her head. "Nope, not really. Uncle David said we could get a take-away at the shop around the corner from us. Auntie Alex and me were talking about what we were going to have and then the other car hit us. I remember the noise of the glass breaking, and then the next thing I completely remember is being in the hospital."

"God, that was crap. When did they tell you? About the Summers, I mean?"

"A few days later." Tia didn't elaborate about the

nightmares. How they reminded her of some modern art, with paint splashed about all over it, just white and red. "It was hard going back into care. They put me in Mallow Park Home in Fenlea. It's just a small village. About two miles from Alderbridge. It was the only place that would take me. I didn't like the local school and bunked off as much as I could and started hanging out with some kids in the park. There was one guy, Jake, that I really fancied. He was older than the others. He used to talk to me sometimes, but I was too dumb to answer him back. Used to nod most of the time. Must have thought I had a screw loose, or something!"

"No change there, then!" Kay poked Tia in the ribs.

"Oi, watch it! We used to buy cheap cider. Didn't like it really, but I told myself I was having fun. It wasn't long before the odd swig or two of cider became half bottles of vodka. Jake said I held my booze well. By the time I was fifteen and a half he said I was his girl and that he'd take care of me forever. I actually believed him. I legged it and moved into the squat with him and some of his mates."

"Bloody Nora. Don't do things by halves, do you? Where was this squat then? What was it like?"

Tia grinned and shrugged. "Seemed exciting at the time. Do you know the old industrial estate on the edge of town? Been derelict for years. Dunno why it was left like that but Jake and his mates found a place bang in the middle. Some kind of machine-making factory, but it had loads of storage space above it and then offices on the top floor. They'd been in there for about a year before I moved in. It was pretty grim, but I thought it was wonderful then, just cold. Always cold. Security wasn't much of a problem. Police never came around while I was there and the bloke who was supposed to patrol the place only turned up about once a week. The guys got to know when he was coming and we'd clear off for a few hours. Don't think he would have cared anyway. Fat, lazy git - 'sides, there was never any bother there. Jake saw to that."

Kay smirked. "And what about sleeping arrangements? Did he see to that too?"

Tia blushed again and looked away.

"For the first few weeks Jake set me up in one of the little offices. He had what must have been a big meeting room, or something, a few doors away. He used to sit with me and we'd just talk, at first …"

"What? Just TALK? No snogging or touchy-feely? No *show me yours and I'll show you mine* games?"

"Kay! Stop it. All right, we did kiss quite a lot but that was it for ages. Then he started wanting a bit more each night. I was scared. I'd never even kissed a boy before Jake, let alone anything else. No one had told me anything about sex. Well, only the stuff you talk about at school and most of that was bunkum. It took a couple of months before we did it. It was on my sixteenth birthday. I moved into his room and the others all knew I was his property. Stupid, when you think about it, but it made me feel good."

"Yeah, I can see why."

"Anyway, when he gave me some blues one night, I didn't hesitate. Nothing could hurt me while he was around, could it? The only thing I feel good about is that I didn't go from those to anything else. I just couldn't do it after knowing that the driver who caused the car crash was high on something, and Jake didn't force me for some reason. Probably 'cos that stuff doesn't come cheap. Funny thing is though, I don't think Jake was using half of what he made out he was. Seems like he wanted to be a bit more in control, or something."

"What were they taking? Heavy stuff?"

"Whatever they could get their hands on. Weed, LSD, Coke, one or two on snow. Depended on money more than anything else. Got worse in the time I was there, I think. Or maybe it just seemed like that 'cos I wasn't using much. Still, what I was chucking down my neck was costing plenty. I'd muddled along before – throwing in whatever I could lay my hands on, or steal, but then I got hooked on the vodka and I couldn't afford it."

Tia hesitated. She wasn't entirely sure if she wanted to share the next part of her story but she knew that her best chance of staying in the flat was to make Kay feel even more sorry for her. She took a deep breath.

"Jake came up with an idea. I wouldn't listen at first, wouldn't even consider it. I cried and he said not to worry, he'd make sure I was all right; make sure it wasn't with anyone he didn't approve of. He said that if I really loved him, I'd do it. It meant that we could stay together; otherwise I'd have to split as he couldn't afford to keep us both supplied. It wasn't easy, and I never did get used it. I never got to see any money either, just another handful of pills and a couple of bottles of booze."

Kay's eyes filled with tears and she sat with her mouth open. "Bastard!"

"Don't look at me like that, Kay. He wasn't completely to blame. I got myself into the mess."

Kay snorted.

"It went on like that for a while but then his mates moved on. I was yesterday's news and there was fresh meat waiting. It didn't stop Jake though. He'd find blokes from all over the place and if I complained I got paid with a black eye and no booze. About three months later I found out I was pregnant. I knew Jake would be mad."

"What the hell did he expect? All those blokes going through you like a train."

"Well, he used to leave packs of noddies in my room ..."

"Noddies? What did he think you were going to do? Read them a bedtime story?"

"No, you daft bugger! Noddies. Rubbers. Johnnies – whatever you call them. Most of the blokes used them. I think they were too scared of Jake not to, but when he started bringing in the last lot, they weren't having it."

"Yes, they were!"

"Kay! You know what I mean. If I complained they'd wallop me, or worse."

"What d'you mean? Worse? They didn't rape you did they?"

"Every one of them raped me, but if you mean did some of them thump me or force me to do it every which way they wanted, then yes."

Kay stretched out her hand but Tia shrugged it away.

"Didn't you worry about catching something – if they weren't using the rubbers?"

"Not really. Anyway, one of the girls was working the streets full-time and she'd found a sympathetic doctor. I guess I would have gone there if I'd needed to."

"No wonder you didn't want to tell the cops or the social where you'd been living. They'd have had Luke off you as fast as winky. I'm guessing this Jake wasn't as mad as you'd expected. Seeing as you stayed there."

Tia nodded. "He wasn't pleased, that's for sure. But there was the tiniest chance that Luke could have been his."

Kay snorted again. "You can't honestly tell me that the bastard would have had any feelings for Luke, even if he was his?"

"No, probably not. But I can't think of any other reason he let me stay. Maybe he hoped I'd lose the kid. Told me I had to move back into my own room permanently and that he'd be bringing in someone else to share with him. Said I had to get money anyway I could for my food and if I still wanted the vodka, then I had to find my own punters."

"Nice."

"The first few weeks after that were crap! I didn't know I could cry so much. I thought I'd done enough of it after the accident, but this was something else. I was puking all the time. I tried to stop the booze but couldn't quite do it. Helped me to blank out for a while."

"But what were you planning to do? About the baby, I mean. Couldn't you have seen someone about it when you first found out?"

"Kay, I knew sod all about anything. Didn't even realise I was up the duff until I was gone three months. I was so skinny that I wasn't ever regular with my monthly's. Besides, some back street dodgy woman or bloke with a knitting needle? No thanks!"

"You've been watching too many bloody films, girl. Didn't you even see a doctor?"

"Nope. Nobody. Wasn't thinking anything about the baby.

Blanked it out – it wasn't happening. Just wandered around the town looking for things to nick. That new charity shop just up from the bus station had some good pickings. Daft people used to leave the donation bags on the doorstep at night or early in the morning. Got loads of stuff for the squat and to sell down the pub. The bins at the back of the precinct were good, too. Had to be more careful there, though."

"What happened then? You just hung about town and the squat for the next six months? How did you end up in the state you were in at the hospital, as if I need to ask?"

Tia sighed. "I decided to put the baby up for adoption so he'd have a proper home, but I didn't even know how to work out when he was due. One of the girls told me she'd heard Jake telling some of the others that he was planning to use Luke for a new begging scam – getting the girls to take it in turns pretending to be homeless or just poor - around town. That's another reason I needed to get away. Jake was playing Prince bloody Charming with his new girl. I heard one of the others saying that she wasn't as easy as me. His patience gave out in the end and she was soon walking around with his trademark on her face. God knows why he started picking on me again. I looked like a scarecrow with a melon up its jumper and more often than not I smelled like a sewer. The night before Luke was born, Jake came into my room with two of his mates…"

Tia stopped suddenly and put her head in her hands. The images from that night flashed across her mind but she wasn't sure if she wanted to share them with Kay.

"It's all right, Tia. I'm sorry. I shouldn't have pushed you. You don't have to go on if you don't want to."

Tia looked into Kay's eyes and saw the tears welling up again. She felt a prickling at the nape of her neck and tasted bile at the back of her throat.

"No, it's okay. I need someone to know what happened. Someone to tell me it wasn't all my fault or that I deserved all I got – if you can."

Kay nodded.

"One of them pulled off my blanket and the other pulled

me up. I know I was crying and begging them not to hurt me, but they were all laughing. Completely trashed, all of them. Jake told me to take off my clothes, but I wouldn't. He went psycho, of course. Bloke should have been a boxer. Carried me to his room, then the others held my arms and Jake pulled out a knife."

"Oh, friggin' hell, Tia. You must have been shit-scared!"

"Understatement of the year. I thought he was going to kill me. Afterwards I wished he had. He cut off my clothes and the two blokes dragged me to his mattress." She hesitated. "They took it in turns."

"Very civilized."

"Shut up."

"Sorry. How did you get away?"

"The mates were so wasted they could barely manage the once. I was more afraid about Jake. He could always make things last forever, but even he passed out pretty quickly that time. I knew I was bleeding and had to get out of there. I grabbed some clothes from my room and hobbled through the estate to the cut-through into the back end of town. It was snowing, but I just sat on a bench in the bus station for a while. Some women kept looking at me, so I scarpered. Well, I shuffled. Next thing I remember is looking in the charity shop window. My head was banging and I was freezing. I had a pain in my guts like I'd swallowed glass. All I could see was the picture from my nightmare. Red on white. Then nothing until the hospital and Luke. You know the rest."

## December 15th

At four o'clock, the light was fading. Tia stood at the window watching people in the street below. She hoped Kay wouldn't come back too soon. It was so peaceful in the flat with just her and Luke. She smiled, then shrugged. No good thinking like that. If she'd done things properly, maybe she could have had her own place. It was beyond good of Kay to put her up. She crossed her fingers and stared out as the first flakes of snow began swirling around the streetlamps. Her stomach churned and she shuddered.

"Hello, day-dreamer! Why are you in the dark?" Kay flicked the switch and Tia blinked.

"Hi, Kay. I didn't hear you come in. Where's the buggy?"

"Left it outside. It's a bit wet. That snow's getting so thick. Lucky I was nearly home before it started. Looks like we're in for a proper storm tonight. Here, take Adam for me while I get changed. Ta."

Tia laid the baby on the settee. He gurgled at her and she laughed. He was bigger than Luke, but they had the same dark hair and brown eyes. Kay called them the Twinnies and loved to put them side-by-side. Tia sometimes felt that Kay wouldn't mind if she left Luke with her permanently, but she'd never do that, of course.

"That's better." Kay dropped down onto the settee next to Adam. "Much comfier."

"How did it go? At the doctor's, I mean."

"Fine. Friggin' receptionist is a bit of an old cow, though. Said I should have rung up to make an appointment and didn't I realise how busy they were at this time of year. Yak, yak, yak! Told her I didn't have a phone and couldn't leave Adam to go out to make the call. Made me wait for ages."

"But you did see him in the end? What did he say?"

"Nothing much. Useless really. More or less told me I was fussing, and that Adam just had a cold. Said to keep him warm, make sure he drinks, bla, bla bla. Waste of bleedin' time trudging up there."

Tia grinned. "Never mind. I made some spag bol while you were out. Do you want to eat now before the boys need feeding?"

Kay laughed. "Oooo! Get you. I hope you remembered the salt this time."

Tia punched Kay in the arm. "Oi, watch it! I haven't done the spaghetti yet – just put it ready. Won't take long, though."

Later that evening, after the girls had fed the babies, they sat on the settee. Kay put out the main light, switched on a lamp and drew back the curtains.

"I love the snow. Look, it's settling. Good job we got some stuff in yesterday, eh?"

Tia nodded. She felt a bit uncomfortable that Kay was paying for most things, but her own money had run out. She needed to get her hands on something to sell.

"I don't like it – the snow. Always make me feel queer. Don't laugh. I don't mean like that! No, it's like as if something bad's going to happen. You know, that feeling you get in your stomach? Probably 'cos of the crash. And living in the squat. It was always cold but freezing when it snowed. It's nice here, though. Safe."

Kay turned and looked at Tia. She still couldn't quite make her out. Rough start in life, then a bit of security which was snatched away. After that, some real freaky times, but it didn't seem to have toughened her up at all. She was a scaredy-cat. Afraid of her own shadow. Still, living with that bloke of hers must have worn her down. Hard to believe that she nicked all that stuff from the hospital and legged it. *Appearances, eh?*

"Come on, cheer up! We'll be fine as long as you keep your head down, but we'll have to think about things like the baby jabs. You can get away with one or two visits to the docs if you need it. Tell them the same as we told Mrs W, but I don't know about the clinic."

"When do they have to have them then?"

"The first one when they're eight weeks, I think, then some more a bit later. We'll work something out. Don't worry. Anyway, it'll be Christmas soon. We should be planning for that first."

Tia looked down at Luke and her eyes filled with tears. It had been a long time since she'd enjoyed Christmas.

"Poor Lulu. Going to be a lean time this year but I promise to make it up to you." She kissed the top of his head.

"Silly sod. You'll give that kid a complex, calling him that all the time."

"No worse that you calling them Twinnies! They look a bit samey, but..." Tia put her hand across her mouth. "Kay! Whatever's the matter? Did I say something wrong?"

Kay shook her head. "No, it's not you. It's just – well, seeing the two of them together makes me think about Adam's dad."

Tia frowned. "Eh?"

"He was an identical twin. Adam looks so like him. I know Luke's smaller, and a bit paler, but when they're together …"

"Do you want to talk about it?"

"Maybe tomorrow. I think I'll have an early night. Don't put the TV on too loud, will you? See you."

"Night." Tia frowned again. Seemed like someone else had a story to tell. As she closed the curtains, she could see the snow still swirling around the window but the gripping pain in her gut had gone. She settled Luke, put out the lamp and lay on the settee.

## December 16th

Tia had been out with Luke for the first time since she'd arrived at Kay's. The girls had worked out a system. Tia would wear Kay's coat and they would put Luke in Adam's buggy. If any of the neighbours saw her, they'd think it was Kay. If they stopped her, Tia was to tell the story of being Kay's cousin.

The snow had eased, but it was still piled up along the edge of the roads and it was bitterly cold. Tia walked as far as the shops in the next street, then turned around and headed back. As she passed the butcher's she noticed something blue in the pile of snow on the corner of the road. She left the buggy on the pavement and stepped over the pile to have a closer look. It was a purse. Tia looked around, then picked it up and pushed it into her pocket. She hurried back to Kay's but before she called the lift, she opened the purse. There was about seven pounds in loose change in one side, but when she looked in the other compartment, she gasped. She looked around again before she pulled out the wad of notes. Her hands were shaking as she tried to count the money. Sixty pounds! She was rich. There was nothing else in there. No name, address or anything. Anyone could say it was theirs if she took it back to the butcher's, couldn't they? And what would the police do with it if she took it there? Probably put it in their Christmas fund. No, it had been put in her path for a reason, and that was to help Kay with the bills, but what was she going to tell Kay? She had a feeling that although Kay came across as being a bit of a rebel, deep down she'd see this as stealing.

"Hi Kay, I'm back. I left the buggy in the corridor. Okay? It's a bit mucky."

"Yeah, that's fine. Looks like it's cold out there. Your nose is red!"

"Freezing. I only went as far as the shops, but I did have a bit of luck."

"Oh? Meet a millionaire, did you? And he fell madly in love with you at first sight?"

"Now who's been watching too many films! No, I saw an ad in the paper shop window. Someone's offering a few hours work to help clear out their mother's house. Seems like the old lady snuffed it a few weeks ago and the daughter wants the place cleared quickly so she can sell it. Nothing heavy, just sorting and packing clothes and stuff for the charity shops. I went to the phone box on the corner and spoke to her and she said I could do it. Only be a few hours on maybe two different days. I thought if you could look after Luke, then I could earn some money so I can pay you for having me here. It won't be a lot, but it'll help. What do you think?"

Kay frowned. "I don't know. Do you think you're up to it? I mean, Luke's not three weeks old yet. I don't mind having him for a few hours, but I don't want you overdoing it and getting sick on me."

Tia grinned. "That's great! I'll be fine. I told her about Luke but she said it would be better not to bring him 'cos of the dust and stuff. It won't be hard, and she only lives this side of Alderbridge. She said she'd pay me thirty quid a time."

"Bloody hell! For packing up some stuff. Okay, but let me know which days as soon as you know them so I can make sure no one's calling from the Social or anywhere, all right?"

"Yeah, well I said I'd go tomorrow, if it was all right with

36

you. She said we'd see how we got on and if she needed me again, I could go the day after."

"Oh. All right, then. That's fine."

## December 17th

God, it's so good to be outside on my own. I was going a bit stir-crazy in the flat. Money in my pocket, a full belly, and warm clothes, even if they are a bit big for me. I hope Kay doesn't find the rest of the money. Don't know how I'd explain that. Too dodgy to bring it all with me. Anyone from the squat would be after me like a leech if they thought I had any cash. Now, where to go first? Think I'll check out the charity shop by the station. On second thoughts, I'd better not. They might remember me. Perhaps the two on the high street. Buy some small things and see what I can pick up as well. Then the precinct. Too risky to nick anything in the day but I can check out that the bins are in the same places. If the snow holds off, I can come back when everything's closed up. Maybe first thing in the morning. That always used to be the best time. Guards are usually dropping off by then. I can tell Kay that the woman needs to start really early 'cos she's got to get somewhere or other. I'll have to check what time the buses start running.

\*\*\*

"Look what I've got!" Tia bustled into the living room and dumped three carrier bags onto the settee. Kay turned off the TV and put her finger to her lips.

"Shhh! The Twinnies have only just settled. I think Luke knew you weren't here. He's usually good with me, isn't he, but that's when you're around."

"Oh, sorry. Never mind. I've got some goodies for you. Look."

Tia emptied the carrier bags and Kay clapped her hands. She opened a packet of chocolate biscuits and crammed one into her mouth.

37

"Tia! This is great. Where did you get these? I haven't had chokkie biscuits for ages. What else is there?"

"I got some tinned stuff, 'cos it'll keep longer. Corned beef. Tuna. Soups, and some packet stuff, too. I didn't think I could carry any more. We can get fish and chips later if you want?"

"Bleedin' hell, yes! That would be magic, but you haven't spent all your money, have you? You need to keep some back."

"Naw. It's all right. The woman gave me a bit extra so I went into town to that shop that sells all the stuff that's nearly out of date, or dented tins and things. You know, Hypervalue. Cheaper even than Poundland! I looked at some of the clothes in C & A but I couldn't afford them, so I went to the charity shop instead. Nothing fancy and they were dirt cheap. Look."

Kay nodded. "Good. Even in my stuff you still look like a scarecrow!"

Tia laughed. "Gee thanks! Here, I want you have this." She put fifteen pounds on the table. "It'll help with the bills and perhaps you can get a bit of extra baby food and stuff from the clinic when you go."

"Tia, that's brilliant, but what about you? You must keep something for yourself. You can't have much left after buying all this."

Tia shrugged. "I'm fine. I've still got a few quid left and she wants me to go again tomorrow, if that's okay. Only a few hours again, but early. Said she's got to go home to her own place and can't hang around. I'll be back by about eleven. Is that all right? I can feed Luke and settle him before I go. It's easy money, really."

## December 18th

Bloody hell it's cold! I hope the buses are running on time. Can't stand this for long. Glad I said I was only working for two days. I hope this isn't a waste of time. Still, there's bound to be something worth having. The stuff we used to get from those precinct bins was amazing. Didn't see why we shouldn't have had it. It was only going to the dump and nothing wrong with most of it. People are too picky. Come on bus!

Not much warmer in here. Not enough people on it. Only the daft sods go out to work at this time in the morning. Still, I've got enough for some breakfast and coffee in town and for my fare home, as well as a few quid in case I really have to pay for something. It's exciting. A bit like when we used to go out from the squat, but much better 'cos I know I've got somewhere warm to go back to. And Luke.

"Ey, what yer doin? This is my patch. Clear off!"

"God, Binny! You scared the life out of me. Didn't think there'd be anyone here in this weather."

"Tia! Is tha' you, love? Haven' seen yer f'rages. Where yer bin? Still with Jako?"

"Been around, Binny. It's Jake, not Jako, and no, I'm not with him anymore."

"Bloody good job, girl. Nasty piece o' work, tha'."

"Yeah, I know now. How are you keeping, anyway? Still on the street? Must be hard."

"S'aright. Gets used to it. Cold is 'ard. Worse when it rains. I got a spot round the back o' the 'ospital now. S'not bad. Dry most o' the time. Long as I gets out before the porters open the doors, I'm a'right. Bit far outta town, but none o' the other dossers wants to walk there so I gets it to myself. I still comes down 'ere most mornin's to do a bitta divin'. Gettin' 'arder, though. Must be gettin' old. What're you doin' 'ere?

"Same as you, Binny. Trying to get by. Looking for some stuff for Christmas. Going to see what I can lift from the charity shops later. Easier there than the stores but I thought I'd give this place a go first. Guards out for count, are they?"

"Aye, lazy gits. Should be a'right for 'alf an 'our or so. Best bins for that kinda stuff are those two over the far wall. If you wants food, go for the green one and the yella one.

"Thanks, Binny. Ummm. Look, I got a few quid left. I'll let you have it if you'll do the diving for me? I can tell you what you I want. You're the expert at this, aren't you?"

"A few quid? For doin' a bit o' divin'? Show me the dosh first."

"There. I got four pounds and seventy pence. Deal?"

"Yeah. C'mon, quick!"

Well, that was handy. I'd almost forgotten how hard the bins can be. No one as good as Binny. Never thought he'd find all this stuff and most of it like new. Glad I checked over the food bags, though. Some of them looked a bit dodgy but Binny was happy enough with those. Poor sod! He'll be down the offie as soon as they open. Still, he seems happy enough. I'd better find somewhere to stash these bags. Can't go to the charity shops with this load. Going to be hard to manage it all on the bus. I wonder if I can stretch to a taxi. Good job Binny didn't see the tenner at the back of my purse.

\*\*\*

"I'm back! Sorry I'm later than I said. There was a bit more to do than we thought, and then she wanted to go the bank, so I had to go into town with her. Everything all right?"

Kay looked up from feeding Adam.

"Yeah, fine. Luke's still asleep. How d'you get on with the woman?"

"Oh, yeah, great. She was nice. She asked if I wanted anything from the house before it went in the bins and you'll never guess what was there!"

"What?"

"Wait there. I left it in the hall. Wanted to surprise you."

Tia opened the living room door and lifted in three large bags. She put them on the table. Kay laid Adam down next to Luke.

"What the hell have you got there?"

"Look." Tia tipped up the bags. "Decorations! And a tree! And lights! Almost new. We can do up the flat for Christmas after all. What d'you think?"

Kay laughed. "Bloody marvellous. You're a genius,

mate!" She picked up a bauble and hung it on her ear. "Cinderella, ready for the ball. Bit of luck, eh, having this stuff there?" She didn't notice Tia blushing.

"Too right. And after we went into town and she paid me, she took me for breakfast. She said she was gratful to have done all the clearing out and that she wanted to give me something extra 'cos she knew I was probably struggling a bit. You'll never guess what she did. Go on, guess."

"Stop messing about. Tell me!"

"She only took me to that discount baby shop and bought presents for Luke! We can share them between the boys. The clothes won't fit Adam but some of the other stuff will be okay."

"Other stuff? God, how much did she spend? Where is it, anyway?"

She wouldn't let me see the bill. We walked around the shop and she kept saying 'That's nice' and putting stuff in her basket. It's in the hall …"

"Get it. Now!"

When Tia came back with yet another three bulging carrier bags, Kay's mouth dropped open. She just stared as Tia unloaded clothes, nappies, matching sets of feeding bowls and drinking cups, cutlery, teething rings and piles of toys and rag books.

"Holy shit, Tia. She must be mental!" Tia blushed again.

"Well, it is Christmas. She said her daughter had moved to Australia after she got married and then had a baby about three months ago. Mary – that's the woman – said she'd wanted to buy all this kind of baby stuff and send it out there but her daughter told her not to. Seems like the other grandparents got there first. Anyway, I wasn't complaining! Some of the toy packaging is damaged so they'd discounted those even more. The stuff inside is all right, though."

"Yeah. We can get some wrapping paper ourselves and it'll be a proper first Christmas for the Twinnies. I feel quite excited now!"

"There's more." Tia flicked her hair back from her face.

"No, I don't believe you."

Two minutes later the table had been cleared of the decorations and the baby things, and Tia emptied out two bags of food. Kay grabbed at some of the packages.

"Oh my God! I can't believe this! She didn't buy this as well, did she? Look. Two boxes of chocolates. Tinned fruit. Custard. Stewed steak – haven't had that for ages. Tinned peas and veg. Beans. Sausage and beans. Loads of spaghetti. Pilchards? Yuk! Stuffing – ha! Appropriate. What else? Soap. Bath stuff. Baby smellies. More nappies. This'll save us a fortune! P'raps we can buy a small chicken from the butchers and get some real veg for Christmas day. What d'you think?"

Tia shrugged. "Fine by me, but you'll be doing the cooking. Apart from the spag bol that you showed me how to cook, opening a tin is about my limit! And no, she didn't pay for this. I got it from what I earned. I just picked up stuff I thought might be useful. We'll have to use some of it pretty quick but that doesn't matter. I've still got some money left over but I'll keep that if it's okay with you, in case we get a bit short later on."

Kay eyes filled up and she hugged Tia. "Thanks. Bloody thanks. This is going to be a great Christmas, I know it."

Tia stiffened. She didn't do hugging. "Yeah, right. Let's put this stuff away."

"How did you manage it all on the bus? It must weigh a ton. And that tree's got the branches all sticking out."

"Oh, yeah." Tia hesitated for just a moment. "Well, the woman – Mary – she had to pass not far from here on her way home, so she said she'd give me a lift. Least she could do!"

***

I'm knackered now. Never used to find lying so hard. Guess it didn't matter so much then. At least I won't have to think about money for a little while, and after Christmas people throw out so much stuff. A couple of early mornings before the bin men arrive and that'll be another few weeks sorted, if Slinx is still buying at the back of the pub. It's nice to see

Kay happy. Maybe she'll forget that I was only supposed to be staying for a few days.

## December 21st

Kay pulled back the curtains and peered down into the street. The lamps had just come on and were throwing an eerie yellow glare onto the pavements.

"Snowing again, Tia. Not much but I think we might have quite a bit later. Look."

Tia yawned and crossed the room to stand beside Kay. She hoped it wouldn't snow much. That meant having to stay in again tomorrow and she was beginning to feel twitchy. As much as she was enjoying the luxury of Kay's flat and all that went with it, there was still a small part of her that wanted more freedom. She watched the snow as it flickered past the streetlamps and she shuddered.

"You all right?" Kay nudged Tia's arm. "You've gone white. Sorry, it's the snow again isn't it? Sit down. I'll close the curtains and we'll have a cup of coffee. I could murder a cider, but best not."

Tia smiled. "Me too, or a vodka, but you're right, best not."

Kay made the coffee. The Twinnies were sleeping on the settee so she carried it to the table and the girls sat down. Tia looked at Adam and Luke and smiled.

"Right little angels when they're sleeping, eh? Little devils at two in the morning!"

Kay laughed. "Too right. Still …" She rubbed the back of her hand across her eyes and Tia realised that she was crying.

"What's the matter? Have I done something wrong? Or said something?" Tia stretched out her hand.

Kay shook her head. "No, it's not you. I'm just being daft. Too much time to think, that's the problem."

"Think about what?" Tia frowned.

"Everything. Most times I feel like I'm doing okay and that things will work out. Then I have a wobbly and panic that I won't cope, and I'll lose Adam, or that he'll hate me when he grows up and realises that he doesn't have a dad like the other kids."

"Should be me doing the worrying, not you." Tia grimaced. "I have to sort out how I'm going to move on. I know I can't stay here for ever but I'm really glad to have just a little time in a normal place with Luke. I couldn't do it without you."

Kay chuckled. "Normal! Are you mad?"

Both the girls burst out laughing and Adam jumped. Kay pushed his dummy into his mouth, and he settled again. She stood over him and touched his face gently.

"He's so much like his dad. It hurts every time I look at him. Yet I couldn't be without him now."

"You ever going to tell me about him, then? Adam's dad, I mean."

Kay sighed and sat down again. She twisted her coffee mug round and round, then looked up at Tia.

"All right, you win. I guess it's fair after you told me your story, but let's wait until later when the little ones are properly in bed."

Tia wondered if Kay was just stalling again but once the babies had been bathed, fed, and put to bed and the girls had eaten as well, Kay sat on the settee with Tia.

"Don't know where to begin, really. I told you that I went to Oakby Comp, didn't I?"

Tia nodded.

"Well I didn't live that far from the school, so I used to walk home. The school bus from Willow's, where you went, used to drop off some kids right next to Oakby and I got friendly with a few of them after a while."

Tia frowned. "How come? You'd have been home by the time the Willow's bus got to your school, wouldn't you?"

"Naw. Your lot finished about fifteen minutes earlier than us. When I was in the second year there were two new boys in the group, well, twins."

Tia clapped her hand over her mouth. "You mean the ones you told me about? You know, that one of them was Adam's dad? You knew him that long?"

Kay bit her lip. "Yeah, same twins, but it was complicated. We never did anything much more than walk home together for years. I saw both of them sometimes in the holidays for a game of tennis in the park or a coffee in town, but I knew things couldn't go any further really. I don't think their family approved of me."

"Why ever not? Just 'cos you went to the Comp? Bit snobbish."

Kay laughed. "No, it was more than that. Different culture; different lifestyle; different expectations. I didn't have a clue what I wanted to do but their futures were all planned out for them and that didn't include me, not even as friend, really. Jazz – he was ten minutes older than Kal – was a bit more of a rebel but they both towed the family line right then. That was all right at first, but then I started have feelings for one of them."

"Hang on a minute." Tia sat up suddenly. "What did you call them? Jazz and Kal? Not Jasveer and Kalan Khatri?"

Kay's mouth opened but nothing came out. She nodded.

Tia squeaked! "But I knew them. Well, not actually knew them. They were in my house at Willow's but about two years ahead of me, I think. They were seriously bright. All the girls fancied them, but they kept to themselves mostly. I can see now why there might have been a problem with you getting involved with either of them. Which one was it, by the way? Could you tell the difference?"

"Friggin' hell, Tia!"

"Sorry, but that's so weird. Anyway, what happened next?"

"Well, even though they were identical looking, I always fancied Kal more. He was quieter. A bit more sensitive, really. Jazz was a bit too much like me, I think. Too outspoken. A bit brash, except when he was around his parents. I got on all right with both of them but like I said, there wasn't much opportunity to take it any further."

"But you obviously did." Tia raised her eyebrows and Kay grinned.

"Yeah, well, maybe in one way it would have been better that we didn't, but I wouldn't be without Adam now."

"So, come on then. What changed?"

"It was the summer after the boys got their A level results. Kal was going to Carston Uni in the October and Jazz was

45

going to that new business college in Riverdene. He was going to be a partner in his dad's business when he finished and then take over when the old man retired. His parents' plan was that he'd marry the daughter of the other partner first. It also meant that he could stay at home, so they could keep an eye on him."

"Didn't they worry about Kal then?"

"Not really. They knew he was more sensible than Jazz, and they obviously trusted him, even if he was going to be miles away."

"Was there a plan for him as well?"

"Not quite so fixed. He'd been allowed to choose what he wanted to study but, of course, it wasn't much of a surprise that he chose medicine. I don't think there was anyone specific lined up for him to marry right then, but he knew that by the time he qualified, there'd be a list for him to choose from."

"Didn't Jazz have a choice then?"

"Not much. I think he said it was either the partner's girl or some cousin in India. Seemed to accept it, fair enough, but I soon found out that Jazz intended to have a chunk of life all for himself. And that chunk included me."

"Ah." Tia nodded.

"I don't know if the parents let the boys off the leash a bit more because they'd turned eighteen, or because Kal was going away, but that summer they were out and about a lot more than ever before. We used to meet up in the park, in town, even went to the cinema once or twice. Kal was always a bit edgy about it but he still came along! I think he liked me but there was no way on God's earth that he was going to make a move. Jazz, now, well he was different. He had a bit of a fumble in the cinema. Hand up my shirt the first time, then up my skirt the second. It was weird. No attempt to hold my hand, or snog, or anything like that. Maybe it was because Kal was there. Don't know. I'd never done anything like that before. Snogged a few lads at school dances or parties, and some of them had tried it on, of course, but I never let them do more than a quick feel of my boobs. When

Jazz got his fingers inside my pants, I nearly died!"

Tia laughed, then bit her lip. "Sorry."

"Yeah, it sounds funny now, I know, but I was scared and excited at the same time. I couldn't shout out or make a scene and, to be honest, I didn't really want to. For all his mouth, Jazz was really gentle right then. After that I didn't see them for about two weeks, then I bumped into Jazz in town and he asked if I wanted to go to the park later. I thought that Kal would be with him but when he turned up on his own, he said that the parents had taken Kal to Carston to have a look around and buy some books and stuff."

"God. Weren't you a bit scared after what happened in the cinema?"

"A bit, but I stayed, and Jazz found a spot behind some bushes, way back from the path. We had a proper snog then for ages. I wondered where he'd learned to be so good at it but then I thought, 'Who cares?' We didn't come up for air for about an hour, then we had a chat for a bit, and he said that he wanted to keep seeing me when he started college. We'd have to keep it secret, though. He couldn't risk his parents finding out. I never asked what would happen if they did. Just went along with it. I thought we were going to go home then, but he suddenly started kissing me again and …"

"Don't stop now, Madam! Come on. Tell me all of it." Tia nudged Kay's arm.

"All right, bossy cow." Kay giggled and tucked her feet up on the settee. "Well, his hands started wandering again. He unbuttoned my blouse, then undid my bra. I tried to stop it at first, but he just kept on, so I let him do it. The boobs kept him entertained for a while but then he started snogging me again and rubbing his hand up and down my leg. I knew what was going on but when he got right up under my skirt and inside my pants, I got scared and pulled away."

"What did he do then?"

"He just laughed and said not to be so bleedin' daft – that he wasn't going to hurt me or anything. When he tried again, I let him. It felt good. Even when he pushed his fingers inside me, he was slow and gentle. Part of me wanted to stop but a

47

bigger part never wanted the feeling to end. He caught hold of my hand and put it on the front of his trousers. God, he was so hard!"

Tia started to say something, then thought better of it.

"I'd never done anything like that before and didn't know what he expected. He soon showed me."

"What? You mean …"

"Exactly. So, there we were, behind the bushes in the park, me half-naked with a boy's fingers inside me while I jerked him off. Didn't take long. To be fair to him, he didn't rush off. We stayed there for ages and he never once tried to go any further."

Tia laughed out loud. "Not a lot further you could have gone!"

"Shut up, you daft bitch! You know what I mean. He said he'd meet me after school started back, outside the gates like before."

"You were going back for A levels?"

"Don't sound so surprised! I did all right in school 'til then. Anyway, he turned up like he said, but Kal was with him. I didn't know what to say to him and I felt bad 'cos it was Kal that I'd always hoped to start something with. I didn't know if Jazz had told him or not but after a while, I knew he hadn't. Kal said he'd come to say goodbye before he left for uni. We just walked back to my house and stood at the gate. I thought I'd be seeing Jazz later, but he just said he'd meet me at the school again soon. Kal waved and that was the last I saw of him for some time."

"But what about Jazz? He obviously did come back for you, and you certainly took things further but how did you end up on your own?"

Kay yawned and looked at the clock. A quarter to ten. She sat up, stretched and yawned again.

"Sorry, Tia. I'm shattered. You're right about me and Jazz but it's more complicated than that. Tell you what, let's get some sleep and I'll tell you the rest tomorrow night. Bedtime story eh?"

Tia screwed up her face but knew better than to push Kay

any further.

"Okay. Fair enough, but you don't have to tell me anything more if you don't want to."

"I know, but it feels quite good to have someone to talk to. Never thought I'd say that. Might be 'cos I know you'll understand – what with you having had a rough time as well."

Tia switched on the television but after ten minutes of *The Morecambe and Wise Christmas Show,* she turned it off and settled down for the night.

***

Fancy that! Kay and the Khatri twins. Would never have put them together. Wonder what happened after she found out she was pregnant. Can't imagine Jazz's family would have been pleased. No question of them making a go of it, but what about her folks? Sounded like they were all right. Maybe it was 'cos of who the baby's dad was. Some people are funny like that. Still, it's not that obvious. Adam's a bit darker skinned than Luke, but Kay's no English rose. Her hair's as dark as mine and her eyes are brown. She must have got that from her parents, so why did they think the baby would be that different? Maybe it was something else.

I hope she doesn't cop out of telling me the rest. She right – it's good to be able to talk to someone. It's weird but I feel like I can trust her. Still, better keep on my guard. Have to watch what I say – don't want to piss her off. No way I can manage if she chucks me out. Have to think about some more money as well. The bit I kept back won't last much longer. I could check out the bins in Maple Avenue first thing in the morning. Posh houses all along there and they were chucking out some good stuff last week. Probably a bit close to Christmas though and I can't see Slinx buying much off me right now, but it's worth a try. Might risk a trip to town and try the begging box trick. Shoppers are more generous at this time of year but it's always a bit dodgy with the law about. I'll see what the weather's like – then I'll decide.

# December 22nd

Adam was grizzling in his cot and Kay rolled over, stretched out her arm and put his dummy in his mouth. She looked at the clock. Ten past six. She yawned noisily and snuggled back under the duvet, praying that the baby would settle, even for half an hour. He'd been sleeping well over the past week and hadn't been waking until almost eight o'clock. Maybe something had disturbed him. She listened but couldn't hear any movement from the living room. She shrugged. Didn't matter. Adam had quietened down and Kay was soon drifting off herself. She didn't hear the faint whir of the lift doors or the even fainter clunk of the outer door closing.

Tia hurried along the street and into the lane behind the shops. The predicted heavy snow fall had not materialised and there was just a thin layer covering the roads and pavements. She kept her gaze on the floor, ever-hopeful of another lucky find but, apart from a ten pence coin, there was nothing. At the end of the lane she crossed the small patch of open ground that the locals called 'the park' and turned into the top of Maple Avenue. There were about twenty houses either side of the road. All were well-cared-for, bay-fronted semis with small gardens at the front and driveways to the side leading to the garages. All but a few had put out their rubbish for collection and Tia made straight for the first house, keeping close to any walls or hedges and well away from the glare of the streetlamps. She moved systematically down the road, looking for anything within easy reach that she might be able to use or, more importantly, sell. It didn't take her long. Most of the rubbish was just that – rubbish, and she wasn't interested in poking through people's left-over food, newspapers and such stuff. At one or two houses she found a box or a bag that was separate from the bins. That was more like it. A pair of leather shoes – a bit scuffed but good enough. A travel clock in a case. The clasp didn't work but might make a few quid. A handbag – nothing in it though!

Just over half an hour later Tia had worked her way back to the top of the road. She turned the corner, sat on the low wall that ran around the end house, looked through her finds, and repacked them into the carrier bags that she'd brought with her. She knew she'd have to find some way to hide them, and then get them out of the flat quickly. One disadvantage of not having her own room was a lack of privacy! She picked up the bags and began to cross the road back into the park, when she noticed that the garage door of the end house was slightly open. This was just too tempting. It only took a moment to check out the street. No-one about. A quick slide over the wall and Tia was in the driveway. She left her bags next to the wall and crouched down before moving towards the garage. She checked again for any signs of life, but all was still.

Tia put her hand into the gap and pulled the door towards herself very gently. No squeaks or creaks so she pulled a bit harder and the door opened easily. She slipped inside and stood still, listening and waiting for her eyes to adjust to the darkness. There was no car. None on the drive, either. Maybe the people were away? Better and better. Tia's heart was racing, and she felt incredibly warm despite the frosty patterns on the windowpanes. She moved forward one step at a time, making sure that she didn't knock anything over or trip herself up. She kept glancing back to the door – her only escape route. All was fine.

At the far end of the garage was a door into the house. Tia was tempted to try the handle, but she decided to ransack the garage first and put anything useful with the bags she'd left outside. That way, if she was disturbed, she'd have some chance of getting away and taking some of the stuff with her.

There was the usual clutter of paint tins, tools and garden equipment, plus a spare car tyre, two pushbikes, a few deckchairs and some boxes of old magazines. She worked her way down the garage checking out everything. Nothing of much use except the bikes, but how she could get them into town to sell? Maybe not. She decided to try her luck with the door. What was it Jake used to say when they went for a risky raid? *Shit or bust!* Yeah, that was it. She hesitated for just a moment as an image of Luke came to her mind. What would happen to him if she got caught? Maybe Kay would keep him? Nobody knew he was there. Nobody really knew he existed so unless Kay gave him up he wouldn't have to go into care. Would he? And Kay did love him. Didn't she?

Tia pulled the door handle down as slowly as she could. It made a loud clicking noise and she froze. Nothing happened. She tried again and pulled on the door. Bugger! It was locked. She bent down and squinted through the keyhole, then she grinned. Stupid people had left the key in the lock. It only took a moment to rummage through the tools to find a long screwdriver and then she took a magazine from one of the boxes. Fingers crossed that there was a big enough gap under the door for the key to slide through.

A few minutes later Tia stepped into a small passageway that lead into the kitchen. There was hardly a sound in the house, just the groaning of the fridge. No heating kicking into life, no water running. Tia convinced herself that the occupants of this particular house really were away, but she knew from experience that she had to be very careful. Would it be better to check the whole house quickly before looking for sellable things, or should she start downstairs and take what she could to her outside stash? She stood perfectly still for a few minutes to calm herself, but she knew that she'd have to start moving soon. She couldn't risk still being around when the streetlights went out. That gave her about thirty to forty minutes. Enough – as long as there was no-one here. She decided to make sure.

Tia crept through the kitchen into the hallway and put her head around the door into the living room. No-one. On the other side of the hall was the dining room. Quiet. The stairs creaked a few times as she climbed up, but she didn't pause. On the landing she looked around and counted five doors. One had a sign on the front, 'bathroom', and two of the others had drawings pinned to them. 'Maxine' and 'Stephen'. The kids' rooms. Tia decided to check them out first. If they were empty, then the chances were that all the others would be as well. It was risky though, as they might be likely to wake easily. Still …

Stephen's door opened silently. The light from the street shone right in and Tia could see an empty cot. A baby's room! She looked around at all the toys, clothes and other baby things and felt her eyes filling up. She scooped up a blanket from the cot, spread it on the bed and began to pile it up with anything that caught her eye.

Maxine's room was darker, but also empty, as were the other two. Just to be absolutely sure, Tia checked out the bathroom, but it was empty and cold. She returned to the main bedroom and sat on the edge of the bed. She was shivering and pulled her coat around her more tightly. Now, where to begin? Even though there was a chance of picking up some jewellery or money in the parents' room, she decided to begin downstairs. She thought that the kitchen was her best starting point. The possibility of finding loose change was high and it was also her escape route.

Tia retraced her steps until she was standing in front of the kitchen window. As it was at the back of the house, she risked opening the curtains to let in a little light. If only she'd brought a torch. Maybe there was one in the garage? She started to walk towards the door, but remembered Jake's advice about speed, and changed her mind. She looked around for any obvious items and picked up a few pound coins that were next to the telephone. She decided to chance looking through the drawers and cupboards but apart from being well-stocked with food, there was little of any value. She was just about to move on to the living room when she spotted the notice board next to the fridge. Of itself it was nothing remarkable, but what she learned from it made her heart start pounding again.

Pinned to the board was a twenty-pound note attached to a piece of paper.

*Helen.*

*We've decided to leave a few days early. The weather forecast isn't great and we can't risk not making it to Mum's for Christmas. We'll be back on January 3rd about 6pm.*

*There's not a lot to do right now, so if you'd prefer to come in the day before we get back, that's fine. Can you put the heating on for us – usual settings – and get in some bread and milk? We'll pick up anything else we need later. Hope you and your family have a good Christmas and thank you for everything. Please take the £ for yourself – I'll pay you for the cleaning when I get back.*

*Sarah.*

*p.s. I forgot to call in to the paper shop to pay our December bill. I've put an envelope on the hall table. Would you be an angel and drop it off for me? Thanks x.*

*p.p.s! There's a carrier bag in the fridge with some veg and other odds and ends that were too good to throw out, and two unopened cartons of milk. Please take what you want and bin the rest.*

Tia laughed. This was proving to be a very profitable raid! She went into the hall, picked up the envelope and gasped when she saw how much was there. Must do a lot of reading in this house. She stuffed the envelope into her pocket and went back to the kitchen. She thought about taking the cleaner's money but knew that would give the game away too quickly, so she tore off the paper after 'Sarah' and then re-pinned the rest of the note and the money. *Clever me!*

Tia had taken longer than she intended in the kitchen. She realised that she didn't know when the cleaner was due or even what time of day she started work. As it was only a few days until Christmas, she guessed that it would be today or tomorrow that the woman was due. What to do? Take what she could now and come back or risk staying longer and getting a bit more? She decided to leave and was just about to open the door into the garage when she recalled what she'd seen in the hallway, next to the front door. She retraced her steps and stood looking at a pram that could only have been a few years old. It would be perfect for Luke! He could even sleep in it for a few months – it would be better than the old baby basket that Kay had found in the second-hand store, and it meant that Tia could take him out anytime she wanted. She wondered if the cleaner would notice that the pram was missing but convinced herself that the woman would probably think it had been packed up along with all the other baby things or stored in the garage. She released the brake and wheeled the pram through the house. She took a few tins and packets of baby food from the kitchen cupboards, plus the carrier bag and milk from the fridge, and pushed them under the pram cover, along with her haul from the baby's room. She locked the door, pocketed the key and moved quietly to the garage door, but she stopped in her tracks when a car's headlights illuminated the whole of the garage. She heard a car door slam shut, a loud curse as someone tripped in the driveway, then a rattling of the letterbox. *Guess someone forgot to cancel the papers, as well!* A few minutes later the car pulled away and Tia risked a peep around the garage door. Coast clear. Just time to collect her stash near the wall.

Fifteen minutes later Tia was strolling past the shops at the end of Kay's street. The convenience store was the only one open and Tia stopped to look in the window. She saw the display of Christmas cards and chocolates. Could she risk a few things? Would Kay believe her? Seemed odd to spend her money on sweets instead of booze, but it felt good. Well why not? Might be the only time – who knew?

As Tia neared the flats she started to worry again about how to explain her sudden good fortune. Finding such a good quality pram, plus buying the chocolate treats would stretch Kay's trust to the limit. There had to be a way to make it believable.

Tia slid the key into the lock very carefully. She hoped that Luke and Adam had slept through, and that Kay would still be in bed so that she wouldn't have any explaining to do. She held her breath as the door swung open. Complete silence. Brilliant! She just had time to drop her coat on the chair, replace Kay's keys on the hook, and put the kettle on before Kay emerged from her bedroom.

"Morning. Sleep all right?"

Kay yawned. "Yeah, great. Adam stirred about six, but he went right back. How about you?"

Tia nodded. "Good. I woke about half past seven and was going to make some coffee, but we didn't have a lot of milk, so I popped down the shop to get some."

"Aww, that was good of you. Thanks."

"S'all right. Want some?"

The girls sat at the table and watched the sun climbing higher in the sky while they chatted about the babies and Christmas and what the future might hold. Later, after Luke and Adam had been fed, washed and dressed, Kay decided to go for a walk.

"I won't be long, Tia. Just going to get some air. Shall I see what the butcher's charging for his chickens? Might be cheaper to get it in the Co-op."

"That's true. Never thought I'd be talking about the price of chickens, though! God, what a difference a couple of weeks can make. You're a good influence on me, Kay Jones."

"Shut up you silly cow. I'll see you later." Kay laughed as she opened the front door.


Kay returned at half-past eleven and Tia put her plan into action.

"Kaaaay?"

Kay laughed. "What do you want? I know that tone of voice, and that look. Don't try playing the innocent with me, lady! Come on, spit it out."

"Well, when I went to the shop for the milk, I heard these women talking about some kind of sale in that new church hall near town. You know the one?"

"Yeah, I think so but don't tell me you're getting bleedin' religious now!"

Tia snorted. "Don't be so daft. No, I wondered if you'd keep an eye on Luke so I can go? It's too far for us to walk with only the one pushchair. One of the women said that her daughter had given some of her baby stuff and the other one said she's given a basket of food. Thought I might be able to pick up a few bargains. I've still got a bit of money left, unless you need it?"

"What you gave me and what you bought was great. We'll

be all right 'til after Christmas anyway. What kind of sale is it? Like a jumble sale?"

"Something like that but it sounded like it was to raise money for some charity. From what they were saying, some of the stuff might be quite good. What do you think? If you want to go instead, I'll stay here with the Twinnies." She crossed her fingers behind her back.

Kay thought for a moment, then glanced out of the window.

"No, you go. Looks like it might piss down soon, so don't get yourself soaked. Can't risk getting ill, you know. How long d'you think you'll be?"

"Not sure." Tia shrugged. "Depends on what's there. I won't hang around if it's rubbish. Anything you want me to look out for?"

Kay shook her head.

Half an hour later Tia bought some chips and walked to the park. She found a bench that was relatively dry and sat down to eat and to make some more plans. She congratulated herself on her quick thinking when it came to hiding the pram after her early morning 'walk'. Not many of the residents at the block of flats used the communal storage area but Kay had shown it to her one day when she'd left her pushchair in there to dry off. Tia had put the pram as far away from the door as she could and had pulled some empty cardboard boxes in front of it. The sale that she was supposed to be going to wasn't entirely fictional. She had seen a notice about something happening at the church hall, but it was a good cover, anyway. She could explain away the pram and the food, but what about the other things from the 'bin raid'? Maybe it would be best to leave them in the storeroom. After all, she now had access to much richer pickings than that discarded stuff. Question was, when should she go back to the house and how much could she risk taking? She knew that she'd have to think hard about finding plausible reasons for the appearance of the goods or money she was planning to steal. There was plenty from the house that she could keep, plus food, but she had to think about making some money as well. Maybe it was worth a trip into town to see if Slinx or any of the others who dealt in stolen goods were around. If she knew what they were after or what they knew they could sell on, she could be more selective. Probably a bit late for Christmas stuff but as long as what she took was small, she could keep it for later. The guys always knew someone who wanted something.

Three hours later Tia jumped off the bus and walked as quickly as she could towards Kay's flat. At the end of the street she stopped and checked that Kay wasn't looking out of the window. Nope. All in darkness. Probably having a nap.

"Hello! I'm back. What're you doing in the dark?"

"Just dossing. The Twinnies were a bit cranky after their feed so I got them off to sleep in my bed. They'll probably wake up soon, but we can have a coffee if you like?"

"Great. I got some chokkie biscuits as well. D'you want one?"

"You bet I do. Haven't been spending your money on treats again, have you? How was the sale?"

Tia blushed slightly. "I didn't think it was going to be much good, but it was great! I nearly didn't go in 'cos the woman on the door said I had to pay, but I could see that there was loads of stuff on the tables, so I handed over my fifty pence and it was so worth it."

"Why? What did you get? Where is it?"

"Well, I got these biscuits and some tinned stuff and packets. They'd put up bags of mixed goodies for just a few quid. And you'll never guess what else they had – a few bags of vegetables! I don't know if I've got the right stuff or even if we like them, but I thought it would be great for Christmas. I didn't know if I'd be able to carry them all on the bus, but then I saw something that made my eyes pop out, and it would help me get the groceries home. It meant walking back, but it was worth it."

"What? A shopping trolley? A go-cart?" Kay laughed.

"Silly sod! No. It was a pram. Must have been what the old dear was on about this morning. Honest to God, I was shaking when I saw it. There wasn't any price on it, but a woman saw me looking at it and said it was supposed be ten quid but that if I wanted it, I could have it for a fiver 'cos they weren't going to stay open much longer. She said that all the non-foodstuff that was left over was going to the charity shop but that the woman who was coming to collect it said they couldn't take the pram. She told me to have another quick look around and if there was anything that I wanted, she'd reduce the price for me."

"Blimey, that was lucky. Good thing you didn't go too early then."

"Yeah. Well, I had to check how much money I had left, and I wanted to keep a bit back – we've still got to get the chicken! Anyway, I told her I definitely wanted the pram, and then I just went through all the baby things. Wasn't much else worth looking at. All the women's clothes were massive or fuddy-duddy – real *House of Fraser* stuff. I made up a pile of things and asked her to tell me the cost, so I could see what I could afford. I think she felt sorry for me 'cos she said I could have the lot for another fiver! I nearly died. Some of the clothes are going to be too big for Luke, but I thought that Adam could have them, then when Luke's big enough, you could pass them on. OK?"

Kay smiled. Tia was making a lot of assumptions about staying.

"Sounds good to me but what did you get for Luke?"

"Oh, a pillow and blanket, a couple of pram toys, and there was someone from the local chemist there with a stall and she was selling baby milk on offer, so I got a couple of packs of that as well. The lady who sold me the pram helped me to pack the stuff in then she asked if I wanted a cup of tea before they emptied it out. She said I could have the tea and a cake for ten pence. I didn't really want to talk to anyone much, just in case they might recognise me, but she started chatting while she was clearing up. There was another woman in the kitchen area who'd been doing sandwiches and stuff and she asked Sadie –"

"Who's Sadie?"

59

"The pram woman – keep up! Well, she asked her if she wanted to have any of the leftovers. Said there was some ham and cheese, salad things and a bit of fruit, and some cake. Sadie didn't want it, but I think she must have seen my face when the sandwich woman said she'd bin it all, 'cos she went into the kitchen, put it all in a bag and pushed it into the pram. Never said a word – just winked at me!"

"What! Sounds like we won't have to spend too much for Christmas after all. So where is it?"

"In the corridor. Shall I bring it in?"

"Too bleedin' right, girl."

After Kay had admired the pram and agreed that Tia could use it as a bed for Luke, and squealed over the food and clothes, the girls spent a little time rearranging the furniture and making plans for Christmas. Tia was disappointed that Kay didn't want to continue her story that night but she made her promise that she would very soon.

## December 23rd

Janet pulled up outside Ruth's house, put on the handbrake, and cut the engine. She paused for a moment before opening the door and watched a young mum with a pram and a toddler struggling against the wind. She thought briefly about her niece then shook her head, climbed out of the car, locked it, and walked up the path to the front door.

"Hello, love." Ruth kissed Janet's cheek. "Come in out of the wind. Awful today isn't it? I've just made some mince pies. Fancy one with a cuppa?"

"Hello Ruth. Freezing out there. I'd love a pie. Don't know how you manage it. I can't remember how long it is since I did any proper cooking."

"Well, if you will have three jobs, what can you expect!"

Janet followed her sister into the kitchen.

"Oh, it so lovely and warm. Shall we have tea in here?"

Ruth hesitated. She preferred to entertain in her living room, but after all, having tea with her sister wasn't exactly entertaining, was it?

"Yes, of course we can. Give me your coat and get comfy. The kettle's on. Won't take long."

Ruth made the tea and the sisters chatted for a while about price rises in the supermarket, local sales and what the neighbours were up to. Ruth began to recount what she'd seen on television the night before, when Janet interrupted her.

"Sorry! I knew there was something I wanted to tell you! Do you remember when I told you about that girl who collapsed outside the shop?"

"The homeless one?"

"We think she was living in a druggie squat, but we didn't know for sure, but yes, that's the one. Well, I called into the shop yesterday afternoon after I finished at the hospital and as I was walking past that scruffy pub down the end of Grover Street, I'm sure I saw her. I was going to say something to her, but she looked scared to death, so I let it go. Weird that, isn't it?"

"You're right there. Didn't you say that the police came to the shop looking for her?"

"Well they came to see if I knew anything about her. I told you she'd left the hospital with the baby not long after he was born and Social Services, and the medics, were worried that she'd do something bad, I think."

"Do you think you should tell them that you saw her?"

"I'm not sure. I only thought it was her and even if it was, she looked clean and tidy. No sign of the baby, though. If she's coping, doesn't seem fair to drop her in it, although I'm not sure if she'd know how to take care of a baby properly. Maybe she's living with someone? Maybe they already found her and the baby's in care?"

"Still, perhaps you should think about letting them know. It's not the same as calling them out to pick her up, is it? It's not as if you know where she's living, just that she's probably still in the area. Better safe than sorry."

"You're right. I'll find the card they left me and give them a ring later. Any more tea?"

\*\*\*

God, I'm so tired. Can't believe how many times Luke woke up in the night. I hope he's not ill. He's been so good 'til now, considering everything. All very well Kay going on about baby jabs and the clinic and all. I bet they're still on the lookout for us, and the doctors will be as well. I wonder how long before it might be safe to risk a check-up. P'raps I could go to another town in a month or so and say I'm visiting someone there. Who knows where I'll be then, anyway. Good job that I went into town yesterday. Didn't expect Slinx and the others to be there. At least I know what to look for at the house now. Maybe I'll try for something tomorrow morning. The only problem with dealing with Slinx is that he might tell Jake that he's seen me and what I'm up to. I'll have to take the risk though. Got no choice, really. I nearly died when I saw that woman from the charity shop. Don't think she recognised me, though. Must be more careful about going into town in the daytime. I need to get some sleep now. Think about it later. I hope Kay doesn't get up too early.

***

Kay lay in bed and watched the patterns that the morning light was making on the walls. Adam was still asleep, and Kay smiled at him. She'd heard Luke crying through the night and guessed that Tia would be asleep now that it was quiet. She propped herself up on her pillows and looked around the room. She felt so lucky to have her own place but worried that was she taking too much of a risk by having Tia stay. She knew they'd have to make some plans after Christmas.

She frowned when she thought about all the things Tia had brought home the day before. That pram must have been expensive when it was new. Still, if it wasn't needed anymore and the people couldn't be bothered to sell it themselves, good luck to her. A fiver, though! Mad. And all those clothes. What did she say she'd paid for those? Another fiver?

Kay began to tot up what Tia must have spent at the sale, as well as on some of other things that she'd bought after her short spell of 'work', plus the money she'd given to Kay for the bills. The problem was that she kept confusing herself over what had been given to, or bought for, Tia by the 'house-clearance' woman and what Tia had bought herself. Still, it certainly seemed that the money had stretched much further than Kay thought it should have.

She jumped out of bed and opened the bottom drawer of her bedside cabinet. She took out some scarves and a pair of gloves and put her hand to the back of the drawer. *Thank God!* She pulled out a large envelope and tipped the contents on the bed. A quick check reassured her that nothing was missing but made her think that a safer hiding place would be a good idea. She hadn't thought about it before, but it wasn't worth risking the loss. She pushed the envelope back into the drawer and covered it over.

After a lazy start to the day, Kay decided to walk to the Co-op to buy the chicken for their Christmas dinner. The butcher's had proved to be too expensive. She'd sorted out what Tia had bought and they only needed a few odds and ends to finish off. She'd thought about asking if Tia wanted to go with her and try out the new pram but then thought better of it. Besides, Tia could take her turn to look after the boys!

When Kay left, Tia flopped on the settee and thought she'd take a nap but Adam started crying. She checked his nappy but he was dry and he'd been fed. She found his dummy and sat on the bed patting his back until he went to sleep. When she stood up, she noticed something sticking out of the bedside cabinet drawer. She hesitated. She'd been on her own in the flat quite a lot but she'd never thought about going through Kay's things. Odd – given her past, but it just hadn't occurred to her.

She listened but the flat was quiet. Kay had only been gone about twenty minutes and Tia knew that she wasn't likely to be back before an hour, unless she'd forgotten something. She leant forward and gently opened the drawer. Just some scarves and gloves. Oh well. She started to close the drawer when it jammed. She opened it again and flattened the pile of scarves. Same again. Jammed. She tutted, opened the drawer as far as she could and pulled out the scarves. She knelt on the floor and could see that there was something bunched up at the back of the drawer. When she pulled out the envelope and opened it, she started to shake. *Sly old Kay!* There must have been a couple of hundred pounds there. Tia's heart was hammering in her chest and her head was pounding. She tipped out the money and began to count it. Five hundred and forty-seven pounds! Where on earth had she managed to get this from? Maybe Adam's dad or the family had paid her off? It might explain why they didn't stay together.

Tia was shaking as she put the money back and replaced the scarves with a bit poking out. Just the way she'd found it. She had a fleeting thought about taking the money and making a run for it, or just taking a few pounds, but thought better of it. Even if she took all of it, how was she going to find somewhere half as decent as Kay's flat to live, especially just before the holidays, and Kay had been good to her when no-one else would have given her the time of day. Tempting as it was, Tia realised that this was the only place where Luke and she would be safe for a while.

In the evening, Kay and Tia made themselves comfortable on the settee.

"Come on then, Kay Jones. You going to finish telling me about Adam's dad or what?"

"Don't suppose you'll give me any peace 'til I do, will you?"

Tia poked out her tongue and Kay laughed. She didn't mind really. It felt good to be able to explain to somebody that wouldn't judge her. At least, she didn't think that Tia would.

"Where did I leave off? Oh yes. Kal left for uni and Jazz started college. I saw him a few times but we didn't really have anywhere to go, so it was just a quick snog and a fumble in the bus shelter. I was doing all right at school at first but just after half term Jazz asked if I'd bunk off school to meet him one day. Said we could go to the cinema. So I did. Well, I bunked off for the afternoon. It was certainly better in the cinema than in the bus shelter but I could tell that Jazz wanted a lot more than he was getting. He asked me if my house was ever empty and if we could go there sometime. Problem was, that my mother didn't work, so she was home most of the time, except if she met my auntie in town or had an appointment somewhere. I told him I'd have a look at the kitchen calendar. She always wrote down stuff like that, as well as any school events or if my dad was going to be away with work."

"Why couldn't he take you to his house?"

"Same thing. Mum at home all day and I think that if we got caught, he'd have preferred it to be by my parents!"

"Cheek!"

"Yeah, well. Couple of weeks later, I knew my mum had a hair appointment in town, then she was meeting my auntie for lunch and then going to do some shopping. She told me on that morning that she probably wouldn't be home until after me, so I felt pretty safe about going back after she'd gone. I pretended to go to school but I just walked around for a bit, then I met Jazz at the park. I told him to wait for ten minutes, then follow me home. It was bloody scary going in the door. I checked everywhere but it was all clear, so I let Jazz in and we went up to my room."

"Ah! The interesting bit." Tia giggled.

"Not really. I was scared but Jazz obviously knew what to do. Can't say I particularly enjoyed it. Bit of a let-down, I suppose. All the stuff before, that was exciting but once we'd done it …"

"What? Did he get out of the house as fast as he could?"

"No, it wasn't that. He stayed for ages and we did it again. It was just me, I think. Don't know what I was expecting but it didn't seem like such a big deal."

"Weren't you scared about getting pregnant?"

"Not really. He'd brought rubbers and he did use them. I asked him if he still wanted to keep seeing me. I'd heard of blokes who chased a girl 'til she gave in then dumped her, but he said he did and could we use my house again. So that's what we did whenever we could."

"But what happened about school? Didn't they let your folks know that you were bunking off?"

"A few times. I got a lecture for it but I just said that I'd gone into town with some of the other girls. My mum never connected the times with when she was out of the house. By Christmas Jazz was pushing all the time to be together. I knew he was skipping college some days, but he still seemed to be able to keep up with the work. Not like me. I was failing fast. When I bumped into Anna - a girl who'd been one of my best friends before she moved out of the area - it made up my mind for me. To get out of school and leave home."

"How come?"

"She said that after her parents had divorced, her mum had bought a place over the other side of Alderbridge – towards Crompton. It was quite big and she was taking lodgers. Anna had quit school and was working in a local hairdressing salon. She said they were looking for more juniors so why didn't I go along, and she'd ask her mother if I could have a room as well, and that's what I did. I waited 'til after Christmas and then I just packed up and left."

"What? You didn't tell your mum and dad what you were doing? Why not? You hadn't had a fight with them or anything, had you? Bit cruel, that."

Kay shrugged. "I know but I wasn't thinking straight. All I wanted to do was to be able to see Jazz whenever I could and staying in school and sneaking around my house was doing my head in. I knew my dad would go ballistic if I said I was leaving school, let alone leaving home. It was just easier to go. I felt sorry for my mother, though. I was just being selfish, I know, but it seemed right at the time."

"But how did you think you could see Jazz any more than when you were at home? The woman wasn't going to let you have him there all the time, was she?"

"No, I knew that. She'd made it very clear that there'd be no 'messing about with boys' but she worked all day and the job at the hairdressers' was only part-time to start with. They said they'd up the hours if they thought I was a quick learner. I could see Jazz on my days off."

"All very convenient! But did you get paid enough? I mean you had to pay rent and everything, didn't you?"

"I got enough to pay the rent and a bit over but Anna's mum, Mrs Connor, said I could eat with them until I was full-time, and she'd knock a bit off the rent – what she normally added to cover bills – so that made it just about manageable. She knew someone who worked in the dole office as well, and she said she'd have a word to see if there might be anything I could claim for. Didn't seem likely 'cos I did have a job, but it was nice of her to do it."

"Did you let your mum know where you were after you'd settled in?"

"No. Not at first. When I did go and see them my dad was a bit shitty, so I never told them where I was living, just that I had a job. Didn't go down well, but he came around after a bit. My mum was harder work. Kept crying, asking what she'd done wrong. Bla bla bla. She was okay later but I didn't see them too often after that."

"How did Jazz take it?"

"Like a pig in muck! Couldn't get enough of it. I swear he must have been keeping the chemist in business."

"What about you? Was it any better for you – having your own place?"

"Sort of. I was still crapping myself that Anna's mum would catch us one day, but I had started to like what we were doing. Well, for a while anyway."

"Why? What happened?"

"Jazz changed. He'd always been louder and more forceful than Kal, but he'd been fine when we were together. Real kind. Thoughtful. We talked about everything. I thought he was pleased that I had a job but then he started questioning me about who I worked with and who I met when I wasn't with him. Did I go out with Anna to pubs or dances? Did blokes try to pick me up. All that sort of rubbish. I'd never put him down as the jealous type. S'pose I was flattered at first. Thought he was showing that I meant something to him.

What a joke. I think it was about six weeks after I'd moved in that he first punched me."

"Bastard! So that's what you meant about us having things in common?"

"Yeah. We'd done it three times and he wanted more but I didn't. Called me all sorts of names. Said I'd probably given too much away the night before and maybe I should start charging for it. He ranted on for ages and when I tried to calm him down, he lashed out at me and punched me on my shoulder. I think it frightened him as much as me 'cos he started crying and kissing me and saying sorry."

"Bet he did. Sorry 'til the next time, eh?"

"Right. Next time came around pretty damn quick. Same pattern but we'd only done it once before he started on me. I was black and blue when he'd finished. Then he had the nerve to ask for it again. Told him to sod off!"

"Did he?"

"No. He just laughed at me then started playing around as if nothing had happened. Kissing me all over the place and then he did it. I didn't fight him. I was too scared. When he'd finished, he told me to clean up the room. That's when I saw what he'd done."

"No rubber?"

"Right. Said it was to teach me a lesson. Guess it did. When he said he'd be back the next week, I told him not to bother but he laughed at me again. I didn't know what he'd do but I had no intention of being at home for him ever again. I took a chance that he wouldn't want his parents finding out about us, so I left a note on the door on the day he said he was coming and made it clear that I'd go to them if he bothered me again. When I got back the note had gone."

"Adam is Jazz's son, then?"

"Ummmm … It's a bit more complicated than that."

"What? But you said that his dad was an identical twin. How? You didn't? Did you?"

Tia had never seen Kay blush before and her mouth dropped open when Kay's face became redder and redder.

"I could murder a drink right now, but we'll have to make

do with coffee." Kay ran into the kitchen and by the time she returned, Tia had almost composed herself.

"Come on then. Spill the beans. How many more skeletons in your cupboard?"

"A few. I didn't know what to do or who to talk to. I knew after a few days that I wasn't up the duff but I still thought I was going crazy. Even after what he'd done, I missed Jazz. I know, mad, but I'd got used to being with him. I don't know what made me think that seeing Kal might help. All I'd had from him was a note that Jazz had passed on just after he started uni. Said he was settling in and had made some new friends. Once the idea came into my head, I couldn't get rid of it. One weekend, I told Anna and her mum that I was going to see my cousin in Carston and I'd probably stay the night. That Friday evening, I set off to find Kal with no idea what I was going to say, or what I'd do if he turned me away."

"No prizes for guessing what happened."

"Guess not, but I didn't go for that reason – honest. I knew that Kal wouldn't be in the student union bar, but I was hoping someone could tell me how to get to his block. Took a while but I found someone who showed me how to find it. It only took a few minutes but I had to wait ages before someone came to open the door. Daft bloke had forgotten to tell me that I needed a code to get in! I didn't know the room number so I wandered around the corridors for a while but I couldn't get through to the room doors. I was going to head back to the bar when a girl came out of her room and saw me. She told me that Kal was on the floor above and she came up and opened the outer door, and said he was in number twenty. His name was next to the number, but I just couldn't knock. I stood there for ages, then he opened the door! Gave me hell of a fright."

"Probably gave him a bigger one."

"You're right. He looked like he'd seen a ghost, but he did ask me in. Nice room. Typical Kal. All neat and tidy. He made me some coffee and we chatted, but he wasn't the same as before. When I asked him what was wrong he said I shouldn't be there and that he knew about me and Jazz. I nearly died. I didn't know where to look, what to say or do. I tried to explain but he didn't want to listen at first. I told him it was over and why, and I showed him some of the bruises that Jazz had given me. Didn't tell him about the rubbers though. Don't know why. He didn't seem shocked, said Jazz had always had a temper and was quick to lash out. He was more surprised it had taken so long for him to lose it with me. More or less said it was my own fault, that I shouldn't have started messing with Jazz in the first place. That hurt. It wasn't like the Kal I used to know, and I cried."

"Not surprising. Thought you said he was the sensitive one."

"He was. Turned out that he really did have a thing for me until Jazz muscled in. Even though he knew he wouldn't have done anything about it, he was still hurt when Jazz bragged to him about how often he was shagging me."

"Nice."

"He said he didn't mean to make me cry and came and sat by me on the bed and well …"

"One thing led to another?"

"Yeah. Have to admit, it was me that led the way. He didn't seem to mind the snogging or exploring in my shirt. Got a bit hot then. I could tell that he was nervous but I kept on pushing him until – well – we did it."

"Did he use anything? Stupid question!"

"I wouldn't have expected Kal to have anything like that around, and I certainly didn't have any. I've tried to convince myself that I didn't go looking for it with him, but I'd be lying if I said I didn't think about it. Didn't take long the first time, but it was so much better than with Jazz. Don't ask me why, 'cos I can't tell you. Just felt right."

"Was he all right afterwards? Didn't get all dramatic about it? Or soppy?"

"He was fine. Said I could stay the night 'cos it was too late for the bus back. We did it a few times more so neither of us got much sleep."

"You must have been barmy! All without any protection? What were you thinking of? More to the point, what was HE thinking of. He's not that stupid, surely."

"After the first time I just didn't care. All I wanted was to be with Kal, but …"

"Not again. He wasn't like Jazz, was he?"

"No, but it was worse, in a way. When he came back from the bathroom in the morning, he told me that he wanted us to be together. Said he'd give up on everything his family wanted for him, if I'd be with him – that we could work out something. He said that Jazz had told him it was me who'd done the chasing, but he didn't believe him. I felt so happy, but the sensible part of me soon kicked in, and I knew I couldn't be responsible for him throwing his life away. I can still see his face when I told him but I had to do it. I left right away. Waited around for ages for a bus and went back to my room. I thought about writing to him to say sorry, but never did."

"God, what a mess. Kal is Adam's dad and he doesn't even know?"

"Yeah. I saw Jazz when I was about six months gone and he jumped to the conclusion that it was his. Looked a bit sheepish. Then he started mouthing off about what he'd do to me if I ever told anyone. I said it wasn't his and that he'd been right, I'd been screwing a bloke that I'd met in a pub. You should have seen the look he gave me! Got rid of him, at least. Listen, Tia, I'm bloody knackered. There's nothing much more to tell you. I went home when I was about three months. Knew I couldn't manage to work, pay rent, and have a kid at Anna's place. Told her mother and she understood. Said if I ever needed help to come to her. Nice lady."

"Did your folks freak out?"

"What do you think? Like World War Three broke out at first. My mum told me afterwards that my dad was disappointed rather than angry. Didn't seem like that to me, 'specially when I wouldn't tell them who'd knocked me up. Still, can't blame him. They set me up in my old room and my mum started fussing about. Dragged me off to the doctor's, the clinic and God knows where else. My head was spinning. I stood it for about two months, but I knew it wasn't going to work, so I legged it again."

"Oh Kay. How could you? You had somewhere safe with people who wanted to take care of you and the baby, and you threw it away? They were your mum and dad!"

"Don't lecture me, Tia. I know it was a shitty thing to do but I did it and I have to live with it. I can't ever go back, 'specially as …" Kay paused and bit her lip.

"As what? What else did you do?"

"I stole a lot of money from my dad. The night I decided to go he'd brought a pile of cash home from the shop. He didn't usually do that, but he'd missed the bank. I heard him telling my mother. That was another decision clinched for me. I waited 'til they were asleep, took what I could carry, plus the money, and left. I went back to Anna's and her mother helped me to sort out benefits and stuff and she pulled some strings with the council and I got offered this flat."

"And what about the money?"

Kay hesitated. "I left it with Anna. She didn't like it but she said she'd hide it for me. I call in to the salon if I'm a bit short anytime."

Tia nodded and looked away.

## December 24th

I hope no one's awake yet. Good job it's still dark. I can't believe how easy it all was. Seems like the cleaner hadn't noticed anything. I just hope the woman doesn't telephone her. Not yet. I need a few more trips. It would have been great to have stayed there today – pretending it was all mine. So quiet. It's strange being in someone else's house. Someone you don't know. Exciting as well. I'm glad I went today. At least I know where most things are now. Reckon what I got today will fetch a fair bit after Christmas. I'll have to hide it. Maybe I can use one of those empty boxes in the storeroom. I can write Kay's name on it and shove it at the back. No reason for her to go poking about and I'll get rid of it in a few days. Slinx'll be chuffed. All small stuff – just like he said. Nothing too showy or different. Next time I'll get something for me. Something to keep. Never had any proper jewellery. Probably lots more I could have if I can keep it hidden. If I use the storeroom for it again, it might be all right. Even if anyone looked, they wouldn't know it's mine.

***

Kay heard the click of the front door and climbed out of bed. Before she could open the bedroom door, Adam began to cry so she picked him up and rocked him back to sleep. When she went into the living room, Tia was in her pyjamas and was sitting on the settee with Luke on her lap.

"Hello. I thought you'd gone out."

"Hi. Why's that?"

"Thought I heard the door closing a few minutes ago."

"Yeah, that was me, but I just borrowed next door's paper for a bit."

"Tia! You'll get us shot. For God's sake put it back. What's so important that you need to see?"

"Nothing. Just wanted to check if they've stopped putting stuff about me in there. I'll have a quick look and put it back."

Kay tutted and went into the kitchen. Tia pretended to flick through the paper.

After breakfast and baby duties, the girls sat at the table and began to plan for next day. Kay had made a list of the things they needed to do, and Tia had begun to pile up the gifts they were going to wrap for the Twinnies.

"Do you have any sticky tape, Kay? Can't find any in the bag of wrapping paper. I thought you bought it at the Co-op?"

"So did I. Don't say I dropped it. Friggin' hell. That means another trip out in the cold. I hoped we could stay in all over Christmas, nice and snug. Mrs W's going to her daughter's this morning. She told me yesterday when I saw her in the corridor. Wanted to know if I'd be all right on my own. Did I want her to ask anyone to check in on me? Like hell! Told her I was going to stay at my auntie's and that I'd only be back the day before her. She seemed happy at that. At least we won't have to worry about her for a few days. None of the others bother much and Mrs Carter next door is as deaf as a post. Right then, who's going out for the tape?"

"I don't mind. I'll just go the paper shop. Too damn cold to walk to the Co-op, and Costcutter's is almost as far. Won't be long. Sure there's nothing else we need? I wouldn't have a clue. You're the chef! Did your mum teach you?"

"Yeah. She was always cooking up something. Best cakes I ever had and her beef pies were something else." Kay's eyes filled up and Tia looked away.

"I'm sure your Christmas dinner's going to be the best as well. Shame the boys aren't old enough to have some. When I think of what I ate last year!"

Tia hurried along the pavement with her hood pulled up and her head down. The wind was gusting through the street and small flakes of snow were whirling in front of it. Her stomach began to churn and she tried to walk even faster. When she reached the newsagent's, she stood in the doorway for a few moments to catch her breath. As she stretched out her hand to open the door, she heard voices coming from around the corner. She couldn't catch everything that they were saying, but there was no mistaking one of them. Jake! What on earth was he doing here? Surely, he'd not found her? She went inside quickly and moved behind the card display-stand so that she could see through the window without being seen herself.

Jake and his companion stopped outside. She recognised the other boy as someone who hung around the pub in town. What were they up to? She hoped that they weren't planning to do the place over. She didn't want to get caught up in something like that. The boy opened the door and went up to the counter. He said something to the girl who was serving but before she'd answered him, the shop owner and his son came out from the storeroom. The boy stiffened, and he left the shop more quickly than he'd come in. Tia saw him talking to Jake then they both jogged away. She bought the tape and a funny card for Kay, then she almost ran back to the safety of the flats.

That evening the girls sat admiring the tree, the decorations, and the pile of presents on the floor. They'd cleaned and prepared all the vegetables for their Christmas dinner and were feeling pleased with themselves. They chatted about how they'd spend their day, whether they'd go out for a walk together if the weather was all right, and how much they'd both love to have a drink. It had been doubly hard to resist buying a bottle or two – or stealing them, in Tia's case.

"Anything you want to watch on TV tonight?"

Tia shook her head. "Not really. I'm bored with *Eastenders. Only Fools and Horses* is on at half seven. Don't mind that."

Kay pulled back the curtains, put on the lamp and switched off the main light.

"Okay. Let's just sit for a bit, then. There. Cosy in here, isn't it? You were right about the snow. Belting down now. Sorry. D'you want me to shut the curtains again?"

"No, it's okay. It'll pass. Gets me for a bit then I'm all right. Might have a few nightmares later but I'll just get up and start on the chocolates!"

"Don't you dare. I'll make you do all the washing up if you do and you know how much there's going to be of that."

They sat watching the snow for a long time. Kay began humming a haunting tune and Tia felt goosebumps rise up along her arms.

"What's that, Kay? It's really sad."

"Can't remember what it's called right now. We used to have a snow globe at home when I was a kid. It wasn't like the ones that you shake and the glittery stuff swirls around; it was bigger and fixed on top of a music box. You had to switch it on, and a blue light flickered through it, then the music would play and the snow would move. That tune was what it played. I was terrified of it."

"Why? It sounds great."

"Inside the globe there was a log or a tree trunk – can't remember which – and it was made to look all icy. Jack Frost was sitting on it and he was made of icicles. When the snow started whirling about it was so spooky. I swore he knew

75

what I was thinking! I used to hide behind the chair and wouldn't come out 'til someone turned it off. I had nightmares about it as well. In the end my mother put it away somewhere. Weird to think of it now. Probably the snow and the streetlights. Dunno. The tune just popped into my head. Didn't even know I'd remembered it."

"Sing it again. I like it, even if it is sad."

## December 25th

"Happy Christmas, Kay!"

Tia handed Kay an envelope and Kay looked puzzled.

"What's this?"

"One way to find out."

Kay ripped open the envelope and pulled out the card that Tia had bought in the newsagents. She laughed at the corny joke, then she noticed that there was something else inside the envelope. She shook it and a small package fell out. She raised her eyebrows and glanced at Tia who was grinning and chewing the skin on the side of her thumb. When Kay tore off the tissue wrapping, a necklace fell into her lap. She held it up and gasped. It was in the shape of a snowflake, with five white stones.

"Tia! What the bleedin' hell have you done? How could you afford this?"

Tia went white. "It's all right, Kay. It's only from the market. I wanted to get you something to say thanks for everything. I thought you'd like it. It's like the one you said you'd seen in the jeweller's down the road."

"Sorry. It's lovely but it gave me a fright. Thought you'd gone back to your bad ways. Only joking! I'll wear it when I'm dressed. Here, this is for you."

Kay handed Tia a small package and a card. Tia's hands shook and she opened the card first. It had been a long time since she'd had one. The front had a picture of two children playing in the snow outside a small cottage. The lights from a Christmas tree were shining through the window.

"It's great. Thanks. This might be us in a few years, eh?

Not a bad start, two cards on the windowsill."

She unwrapped her gift and laughed out loud at the keyring inside. It had a tab with a picture of a baby's feet and handprints on both sides.

"Now you'll never forget the Twinnies, will you? And here's something else you might need." Kay handed Tia a set of keys.

"What …"

"Well, seems daft having to share the one set. If you're going to stay for a while, you might as well have your own. Now you've got the pram you might want to take off when I'm out or something."

Tia grinned at Kay.

"You mean it? Honest?"

"Honest to God. Cross my heart and hope to die! We still have to be careful, though. Can't take risks. Let's just see how it goes. Now, how about breakfast?"

***

The overnight snow had settled and Janet thought that the garden of her sister's house looked like some alien landscape. She was trying to decide what the strange shapes were next to the fence when Ruth tapped her on the shoulder.

"Come on, dreamer. Want to give me a hand? If you could lay the table while I finish off the veg, that'd be great. All right?"

"Of course. Where's Paul?"

"Fiddling with something in the garage. Must be freezing out there but once he gets a bee in his bonnet, nothing will stop him. I'll give him a call soon. I'm so glad you came last night. I don't think you would have made it this morning."

"You're right. My car's not made for this kind of weather. I was supposed to have been helping out at the church hall – you know – the 'soup kitchen' last night, but I had a call to tell me that the mobile unit was going out instead. Just for an hour or so but at least the poor devils would have something warm inside them."

77

Ruth tutted. "I can see why you work at the shop, but I don't understand why you do the night stuff as well. Sounds a bit dodgy to me."

"It's all right. Some of them are a bit rough and ready, and we've had a few that have caused a bit of trouble, but they're not a bad lot, really. Down on their luck, mostly. They get into a mess and can't find a way out. It's hard, not being able to offer them any more than a bite to eat and a few hours' warmth but at least that's something. Come on. I'm starving!"

After they'd eaten, and the dishes cleared away, Ruth refilled their wine glasses and they took them into the living room. She was about to switch on the television when her husband stopped her.

"Wait a minute. Close your eyes, both of you."

Janet and Ruth looked at each other and shrugged, then did as they'd been told. They heard the flick of a switch then the tinkling sounds of *A Winter Lullaby*. It took a moment for them to recognise the tune. Ruth was first to open her eyes and she clamped her hand over her mouth.

"Paul! You fixed it. I didn't think …"

"I know, love. I know. But you're right. No good living in the past or burying things under the carpet. You always loved this and it's not right to hide it away just because it reminds us of Kay. It's yours and if you need to see it every day, that's fine with me."

Janet thought that was probably the most she'd heard Paul say in a long time, and she was happy for her sister. Must be awful to lose a child, and a grandchild. Even if there was the tiniest chance that they'd get back together, Ruth and Paul would still miss some of the best times of the baby's life. Maybe she was better off being single and having no ties. She sighed and watched the snow swirling around inside the globe.

# 1992

## February

The letterbox rattled and Kay went into the hallway to collect the mail. She frowned when she saw the white envelope marked with the council logo. What if someone had reported her for having Tia here? It was a nagging thought that was never far below the surface, yet she had to admit that she was enjoying Tia's company and, as the boys were growing, it was funny to see them laughing and gurgling together. On the other hand, the flat seemed claustrophobic at times, and when either or both the babies had a bad night, it made her so irritable. Money was becoming tighter as well. It was lucky that Tia had found a cleaning job a month ago, but it was only for a couple of hours a week and hardly contributed much. She'd have to take some more out of her dad's money. No other way. Then there were the baby jabs. Tia couldn't just walk into the clinic and ask for them. She wasn't on the doctor's list either. And she hadn't even registered Luke's birth. Kay had gone into the registry office almost as soon as she came home. It was kind of Mrs W to watch Adam for her. She'd said that you had something like six weeks to do it.

Kay counted on her fingers. Bloody hell! Tia had gone over. Kay remembered pushing her about it just after Christmas but had completely forgotten it after that. Something else to worry about even though it wasn't really her problem. She sighed as she opened the council's letter but it was just a circular about some work on the central heating boiler in the storage room.

## April 15th

What a night! Both the kids crying. I can't believe the
neighbour won't know there's more than one baby in here
now. Never knew they could make so much noise. Kay's
going to be sniping again today. Maybe I should get out of
her way. I'd rather to go back to sleep but better not. Looks
cold out there, but at least it's dry. Damn. It's supposed to be
my workday. She'll be even more narked if she's got to have
Luke as well. I'll tell her that I'm taking him with me. Say
the woman's not going to be there so I can get away with it.
If I go up to the park I can cut through into the precinct and
go in the café. They don't mind prams in there, I know.

I'll have to miss out on going to town, but I've got enough
for a while. Can't believe how much I managed to screw out
of Slinx and that other one after Christmas. Still, those
cameras and watches must have cost a bit when they were
new. Shame I only got back to the house twice more but can't
complain about what I got. Never heard anything about them
reporting the stuff stolen. Probably haven't missed most of it.
I wonder if they've changed the lock in the garage. Might be
too risky. Better to find somewhere else. I'm glad I've shifted
most of it too. I nearly died when those council workers
turned up in the storeroom. Good job I was in there when
they came. Can't believe Kay didn't tell me about them.

It'll be good when the weather warms up a bit. Wandering
around for a couple of hours twice a week in the rain's been
hard. I don't think Kay liked it at first when I said I had a job,
but I had to make up some excuse to be out of the flat on my
own, and to explain the money. Couldn't cart Luke into town
with me to get rid of the stuff, either. It's going to get harder
to find anything when the mornings are really light, and I
can't risk going out in the dark. She'd never believe me if I
said I'd just gone for a walk. More thinking!

## April 20th

"I'm off now, Tia. Try to keep Luke quiet if you can. I know that Mrs W's going to be in with Sally next door, and they know I'm going to clinic today."

"Why d'you tell them, then?" Tia pouted.

"Mrs W asked me when I met her at the shops yesterday. Took me by surprise."

"Could have told her clinic was some other time."

"Yeah, just didn't think quickly enough. Anyway, he seems settled now. Should be fine. Probably best if you stay in. Yeah? See you later."

Kay pulled the door shut behind her. Tia flopped onto the settee and glanced at Luke but he was in a deep sleep. She went to the window but pulled back when she saw Kay leaving the flats. Better not give her anything else to moan about. She wandered around the flat, picking things up and putting them down again. She went into Kay's room and looked around. A quick check confirmed that the money had been moved. Oh well, maybe for the best. Although … she shook her head. No good thinking like that. Things had been a bit rough the past few weeks but Tia knew that she couldn't manage on her own. Not yet. Maybe not ever, but they were bound to be found out sometime. She hoped it would only be her that was kicked out, not Kay as well.

Two hours later Kay returned. She carried Adam into the bedroom and put him in his cot.

"Everything okay?"

Tia nodded. "Yeah. No problems. Luke woke up but he wasn't any trouble. I took him into the kitchen so they wouldn't hear him if he did cry. How was the clinic?"

"Busy. I got talking to some of the other mums again. There's one baby, the same age as Adam, who's huge! Don't know what she feeds him on."

Tia huffed. She was sick of hearing about the other babies and their mums.

"The nurse gave me some samples of cereal to try. She said Adam was a good weight and to try a spoonful in the morning before his bottle. You can have some for Luke if you want, although he is quite a bit smaller. What d'you think?"

"Dunno. Maybe wait a bit? He is small, isn't he?"

"Yeah, but he's healthy. He's doing all the same things as Adam. You're not very big, are you?"

"Cheek!"

Tia stood up and stretched as high as she could. Kay smiled and they both relaxed. With the tension eased, the rest of the day passed smoothly and Tia forgot her earlier worries.

## May 15th

The girls were enjoying a few days of freedom from the watchfulness of Mrs Walker, who was visiting a relative. They'd been to the park, to the precinct and even walked to the little boating lake in the next village. On their way home they'd stopped to look in the newsagent's window and Tia spotted a poster for a fete in Crompton Town Hall the next day.

"Look. Why haven't we seen this before. D'you fancy going? Might be a laugh. Mrs W won't be back yet, will she?"

Kay looked at the poster. "She's not back 'til the day after. It's a bit of a trek but we could go in the afternoon for an hour or so if you like? What sort of stuff is going on?"

"Says there's some stalls with second-hand clothes and books. Cake and bread stalls. There's somebody making animals with balloons. Someone doing photographs. We can just have a walk around. Don't have to spend anything, do we?"

"Yeah, that's right. Okay. We'll go."

\*\*\*

"Hello, Ruth. Sorry to call so late but I didn't get away from the hospital until seven. We had two emergencies right before I was supposed to finish."

"That's all right. I was only watching some rubbish on the TV. I can't keep up with you and your jobs! You must have to keep a chart with where you're supposed to be every day. What can I do for you?"

"I did a shift at the soup kitchen last night – don't laugh – and there was a poster up about a fete in Crompton. I'm sure it's the one that Marge from the shop told me about ages ago, but I'd forgotten. She said her sister was running a stall for the local school. Selling all the jumpers that she knits, apparently, and her husband's selling plants and seedlings. I know it's a bit out of the way, but do you fancy going? You might see something for the garden. We could have an early lunch in town then go, or go the fete first and eat later if you want. What do you think?"

## May 16th

Kay and Tia were up early and changed their minds about going the fete in the afternoon.

"It's a nice day. Why don't we go this morning – they open at eleven. If we get there for about twelve, we can have a look around, then we'll have time to take the Twinnies to the park on the way back. We can take some bottles with us and Adam doesn't mind having some of that food in the jar cold. I can make some sarnies, or if we don't spend much at the fete, we can get some chips. What d'you think?"

Tia shrugged. "Suits me. Be nice to be out together all day for a change."

They finished tidying the flat and were soon strolling along the street towards the shops. Outside the butcher's Kay spotted one of the other mums from the clinic and stopped to chat. Tia was bored.

"I'm just popping in the paper shop, Kay. Look after Luke for me, eh?"

Kay's friend raised her eyebrows at the interruption, but Kay just nodded. She was used to Tia by now.

The paper shop was busy. Tia didn't really want anything, but she also didn't want to stand and listen to Kay and that other girl going on and on about weight and teeth and feeding and sleepless nights. She looked around and picked up a tube of mints. They helped a bit when the booze cravings hit. She checked her pocket for change and her knuckles brushed against something hard. She fingered the key and smiled. Her insurance maybe.

As Tia queued to pay, she overheard the woman in front of her chatting to the manager.

"Haven't seen you for ages, Mrs Carter. How are things?"

"Fine thanks. I've kept meaning to call in to apologise for the mix up after Christmas, but the time's just disappeared. I was sure I'd left the money for Helen to bring along but she swore it wasn't there. It was such a rush leaving early like that. Maybe I did forget, but it was even stranger that she said I didn't mention it in my note."

"Yes, I heard about what happened from your neighbour. Much taken? Any luck with the police?"

"No, not really. We didn't notice right away with the smaller stuff. It was the baby's room that gave it away. It was so obvious. Seemed strange what was taken all together."

"Did they make much mess?"

"That's another odd thing. Hardly any mess inside and no signs of any break-in. The police asked about unlocked doors, but we checked as soon as we noticed things were missing. The outside garage door was off the latch but the inside one – into the kitchen – was locked. The police thought we might have left the key in the lock, but we hadn't. I know we sometimes do if we're in a rush, but it was hanging in the usual place. They wanted to know if we had a spare. We said that Helen had one as well as a key for the front door. Tim remembered afterwards that there used to be another one on the passage windowsill, but I hadn't seen that for ages."

"Strange."

"Yes. It made it very awkward because they kept asking Helen about whether she'd noticed anything when she came in. Made her feel like they suspected her. The other thing that I know I wrote on the note was about a bag of food in the fridge. That had gone too, but Helen says she didn't have it and it wasn't on the note, either. Shame that she threw the note away. The police came and questioned her a few times and she was so upset the last time that she quit. Have to start looking for another cleaner now. I might pop back later in the week and put up a card. Unless you know anyone?"

"Not right now, sorry. But put a card up by all means."

"Thanks, I'll try that. I need to get someone started soon. We're going to be away most of August and I want to make sure – well – you know."

"Yes. Quite right. Might be better to cancel for the month. Can't get dirty if you're not there."

"True. Maybe that's what I'll do. Awful, isn't it, when something like this happens. You end up not trusting anyone."

"Too right. Anything else I can get you? No? Well, see you soon. Take care."

The woman moved away, and Tia held out the money for her mints. Interesting what you could pick up just waiting in a queue.

"Thanks love. How are you today?"

Tia smiled. "I'm good. Thanks."

She didn't want to hang around. Although the woman could have no idea that the 'intruder' had been stood behind her, Tia was afraid she'd recognise the pram that was parked just two shops away. Lucky! Kay had moved her pushchair and was standing in front of Luke's pram, still talking to her new friend. The woman had walked the other way towards Maple Avenue.

"There you are Tia. This is Maisie, by the way, and the little one is Holly. I've asked her to come to the fete with us, but she's got something to do right now. She'll come along later. Okay?"

Tia smiled tightly and clenched her fists but Kay didn't notice. Maisie waved goodbye and the girls moved on. Once again, Tia gritted her teeth as Kay repeated everything Maisie had said.

\*\*\*

"Ready to go, Ruth?" Janet picked up the bill from the table.

"Yes, that was lovely, but let me pay."

"No, my turn. I'm glad we decided to have lunch first. My late shift caught up with me and I slept on this morning. Didn't have time for breakfast, but I'm better now and at least I won't be looking at all those cakes on sale! Come on then."

Half an hour later the sisters were at the fete. They planned to look at the inside stalls first, then to do a circuit of the field at the back of the hall where the plants and other garden stalls were. The hall was busy and noisy. Janet looked around and spotted Marge talking to someone who could only be her sister. She nudged Ruth, who was looking at the book stall, and pointed to Marge.

"Be back in a minute. Don't move or I might not find you again."

Ruth bought two books and was putting her change away when she glanced towards the door at the far end of the hall. Two young women were struggling to get through the narrow doorway and Ruth thought that it was madness to bring prams into a place like this. But what was the alternative these days? She remembered her mother telling her how all the mums used to leave babies in prams in their gardens, or outside the shops, without a single worry. She tried to remember whether she'd ever done that with Kay but couldn't.

She looked up at the girls again. Her eyes opened wide and she felt a tremor running down her spine. She tried to move forward but it was as if her feet were glued to the floor. She called out but the sound was swallowed by the din in the hall.

"Whatever's the matter, Ruth? You're as white as a sheet. Come on, let's get you outside and find a seat."

Ruth wanted to tell Janet what she'd seen but all that came out was a garbled whine. Janet helped her sister through the crowd to the main door and looked around for somewhere to sit. At the side of the hall was a bench and she guided Ruth to it.

"Now sit there. Will you be all right if I get you a cup of tea, or do you need to see a doctor? Your pulse is a bit fast but your colour's coming back."

Ruth grabbed Janet's hand and pointed to the car park at the far end of the hall.

"Quick. Down there. Where the other door comes out. I think I saw Kay with a pram. Hurry. You might catch her. She was with someone else. She had a pram as well. Maybe they're going to the field stalls. Hurry. Quick!"

Janet looked puzzled but her sister was so insistent that she almost ran to the other door. She looked into the field but there was no sign of anyone with prams. She ran into the car park and up to the gate onto the road. At the crossroads she spotted two young women waiting for the lights to change. They both had prams and Janet's heart nearly jumped out of her chest. She called out and waved at them, and one of them looked towards her. Definitely wasn't Kay. Much too small, but the other one could be. The woman looked away. Janet couldn't decide whether to try to catch up with them, to get in the car and follow them, or to go back for Ruth and then look for her niece. She decided on the car.

By the time Janet had located the car, opened it up and reversed out onto the path, the women had disappeared. She knew they had crossed the road at the lights but which way after that? She took a guess at the road opposite and turned into it. It was a long street that curled around into a housing estate. If the women had gone in there, then it was unlikely she'd find them. Access from this side was for pedestrians only.

Janet went back to the lights and tried both of the other streets but there was no sign of Kay. She saw someone walking towards the fete pushing a pram and wondered if Kay – if it was her who Ruth had seen – had spotted them and had decided to return. She put her foot down on the accelerator and swung into the car park just as the young woman was coming through the gates. She felt sick. Not Kay.

"Are you all right, Ruth? Sorry I was so long. I did see two girls with prams up the road and I drove around everywhere, but I lost them. I'm so sorry. Are you sure it was Kay?"

"I don't know, Janet. I thought it was, but I see her everywhere, all the time. This time, though … God, what if it really was her and I missed her."

She began to cry and Janet put her arm around her. What had started out as a pleasant day for both of them had turned into a nightmare. She cursed her niece. Even though she loved her, this was too hard to bear.

"Come on, let's get you home. We'll have a think about where she might be and I'll ask around a bit. Marge's sister lives around here and she's got young grandchildren. She might know something. If it was Kay, that is."

\*\*\*

"That was all right, wasn't it? Bit crowded and full of old biddies but makes a change. Don't fancy the stuff in the field. Do you? I'm ready for the park. I hope the chippie is still open."

Kay glanced at her watch and looked along the street.

"Yeah. Me too. I wonder what happened to Maisie. Perhaps Holly's playing her up. Maybe we should wait a bit longer."

Tia had no intention of hanging about for another episode of 'mummy talk' and she turned the pram towards the lights at the crossroads.

"Up to you, but I'm heading off. Luke's waking up and he'll kick off with his screaming if I don't feed him." She screwed up her nose. "Smells like he's done a packet in his nappy as well!"

Kay hesitated for a moment then turned the buggy and followed Tia. As they waited at the lights Tia thought she could hear someone calling. She looked back down the road and could see a woman waving. At them? Maybe. She looked vaguely familiar but Tia couldn't quite place her. She glanced at Kay who was fussing with Adam's cover. Maybe someone she knew. Dodgy. The lights changed and the girls hurried across and into the street opposite. Halfway along the road was a lane that led into a housing estate. They debated whether to buy chips there or push on to the one nearer the park. It was at least another fifteen minutes away but that meant a shorter walk home afterwards. Decision made.

Nappies changed, babies fed, chips eaten. The girls sat on the grass in the park and watched people walking their dogs or playing with their children. Everyday normal things. Tia shook her head. Sometimes she thought she was dreaming. Her, with a kid, living in a flat. Sober. How things had changed. Well, a lot had, but there were some that might take a bit longer. When Kay walked over to the rubbish basket, Tia slipped her hand under Luke's blanket and felt around until she found the purses nestled up against his foot. She glanced at Kay before pulling them out and opening the first. Not much in the coin part. Couple of quid and a key. She flipped it over and looked into the notes section. Lovely! The second one was slimmer but still had more than thirty pounds in it. She pushed the purses back into the pram and smiled. Why were people so careless? Pity they'd left the fete so soon.

"Fancy an ice cream?"

Tia jumped. "Eh? What was that?"

"I asked if you wanted an ice cream. My treat. There's a van over the other side."

"Yeah. If you're sure."

"Any kind?"

Chocolate or mint. I don't mind. Thanks."

Tia watched Kay crossing the grass and shook her head. Something had to work out right. It did.

"Well, if it isn't Princess fuckin' Tia. All dolled up and playing mummy."

Tia jumped, turned around and went white.

"Jake! What the hell are you doing here?"

Jake smirked. "Nice way to greet an old friend. This the sprog then?" He peered into Luke's pram. "Ugly mutt isn't he? Can't be mine."

"Who knows." Tia stood up. "Never thought I'd see you out in the daylight. Why don't you go away? We don't need you. I've got my own life now."

"Yeah. I heard. Slinx said you'd been around so you haven't given up the old life all together, eh? Said he thought you were out this way. Saw Binny as well – "

"Binny wouldn't have told you anything."

"Naw. Well let's say he had a few more bruises after I'd finished talking to him than he did before, but he told me enough. Been coming down here for a while now. Didn't think I saw you at Christmas, did you? Lurking in the paper shop. Knew it was you even with the weird haircut. Gave us the slip, though, didn't you?"

"But why would you want to look for me? After what you and your mates did?"

"What you talking about? What I did? Only a bit of fun. We thought you'd have liked it. You'd been a bit down – we wanted to cheer you up. You're the one who sloped off. Anyway, you owe me, and I want paying."

Tia laughed. "Owe you? Owe you? Are you completely mad? I could have gone to the cops after what you and your mates put me through."

"Yeah, but you didn't, did you? Why's that then, little miss high and mighty? 'Cos they'd have had that kid off you right away, eh? Tart, alkie – great mother you'd have been. How d'you manage it, then?"

"What?"

"Keeping him. Getting clean. The council give you somewhere, did they? That how you met her?" Jake nodded his head towards Kay, who was still waiting to be served. He saw Tia blush and watched as her face grew redder and redder.

"Oh. I get it. Tia the fuckin' blagger strikes again. Wormed your way in, haven't you?"

"Look, Jake," Tia touched his arm. "I don't want any trouble. I'm in a good place now and the kid is all right. We won't bother you and I'm not going to the cops – honest. We're doing okay and I don't want to rock the boat. I haven't got much but you can have it all if you'll leave me alone. Deal?"

Jake looked at Tia and weighed up his options. He didn't really know what he wanted to happen. He hadn't exactly thought anything through. He was just mad that Tia had slipped through his fingers. She'd been a good earner at first. Still, maybe it was better to cut his losses. Not much good to him with a sprog in tow.

"Fair enough, girl. No hard feelings, eh? What you got then?"

Tia took one of the purses from Luke's pram. She hesitated before handing it over to Jake and hoped that there was nothing inside to prove it wasn't hers.

"That's all I have, Jake. Slinx had everything I had to sell and that's the last of what I got from him. It's not easy now. Not many chances 'round here. Take it but promise me you won't come back. There's nothing here for you, I swear."

Jake rifled through the purse and grumbled. "S'only about forty quid here. Won't buy me much. Why don't you come back with me and you can pay me the rest in kind?"

Tia stepped backwards. "Get out of here, Jake. I mean it. I don't care what happens, but I'll call plod, I swear I will. That's all I have and all you'll get."

Jake carried on grumbling but started to walk away. When he reached the path, he turned around.

"If you change your mind, you know where we are. Nice looking girl, your friend. Bet she wouldn't kick me out of bed on a cold night."

Before Tia could say anything, Jake walked quickly out of the park. Tia was still shaking when Kay came back with the ice creams.

"You all right? Who was that bloke you were talking to? Looked a bit rough."

"Oh, thanks. Yeah, I'm fine. Just some scrounger looking for a handout. Sent him packing."

"Good. I thought for a moment it was that bloke Jake that you told me about."

"Why d'you think that? The squat's miles away. Besides, he's like Dracula – can't stand the light!"

Kay laughed and they sat together eating their ice creams.

## Early June

Kay walked along her street and looked forward to reaching the flat. It had been so hot at the clinic and Adam was cranky.

The nurse had said that he was probably teething and given her some advice about what to do. Another thing to pass on to Tia. It would be so much easier if Tia and Luke could go to the clinic with her but unless Tia got her act together and sorted out a place to live and some benefits, that wasn't going to happen. The boys were six months old now and not so much like Twinnies anymore. Adam had gained weight and was trying to sit up. He ate like a horse, but Luke was fussy with his food and hadn't grown at the same rate. Maybe Tia gave up a bit too quickly. He only had to refuse two spoonsful and she'd give him a bottle. Kay sighed. She had to admit that there wasn't a lot of fun in sharing the flat anymore. She felt hemmed in, yet how could she tell Tia to go?

"Hello, Kay. How's the little one today?"

"Oh, Mrs Walker! You made me jump. I was miles away. He's fine, thanks. Just been to the clinic. How are you?"

"I'm all right. Do you have a minute before you go up to the flat? I wanted a quick word. Shall we sit on the wall?"

Kay looked puzzled but she followed her neighbour and sat down.

"What is it? Adam hasn't been keeping you awake again, has he? It's hard to keep him quiet when he's out of sorts, and the walls are a bit thin, aren't they?"

She realised that she was gabbling, but she had a feeling she knew what Mrs Walker wanted to say.

"That's no problem, really. Had enough of it when mine were small to know what it's like. No, dear, there's something else. It's your – well - cousin, if that's what she is. She seems to be here an awful lot, doesn't she? It's not just me that's noticed. Some of the others have been talking and they think that she's living here. It's not for me to judge, but you do know that you're not supposed to have anyone staying more than a few nights, don't you?"

Kay nodded.

"I know it must be hard for you, living here. I mean, the place is full of oldies, like me! I don't know why the council put you here, really. They must have had more suitable places, but whatever the reason, do you want to risk losing the flat just to help out a friend? Can't she get somewhere of her own?"

"No. It's difficult."

"That's as maybe, but you'd better start thinking of something before someone tells the council. Don't worry, it won't be me, for now, but you should know that there's been some talk about her."

"What do you mean?"

"Mostly gossip, I'm sure, but Mrs Carter's son – you know, he lives over in Maple Avenue? – well, they had a break-in last Christmas while they were away."

Kay scratched her head. "But what's that got to do with Tia?"

"There was quite a bit of jewellery stolen but whoever it was took a lot of baby things and an almost new pram as well. Mrs Carter swears that she saw your friend in the park with the pram and that the little boy was wearing her grandson's clothes."

Kay looked shocked. "But that's crazy. How on earth would Tia do that? We're together most of the time. Mrs Carter must be mistaken. I bet there are lots of prams like that around here. Besides, Tia got hers from a charity sale in a church hall, and a lot of the clothes."

"If you say so, but think about what I've said, Kay. Don't put yourself and Adam at risk. You know, if it's younger company you want, have you thought about moving?"

"Moving? How would I do that?"

"Well, two ways. You could ask the council if they've got anything on the Brooks estate behind the park, or the Hollybush, the one a bit further out on the other side of the precinct. Lots of younger families over there. It's mostly houses but there are a couple of blocks of flats like these. They might only put you on a list for transfer, until Adam's too big to share your room, but it's worth asking. The other way might be quicker for you. You just look for someone to swap with you. As long as it's about the same size property, the council don't usually mind."

"I never knew that. So how would I find someone?"

"Just put a card in some of the shop windows and you

could try the post office and the launderette, maybe. That new Blockbuster video shop might be a good place, too. If you want to do that, let me know and I'll help you write it out, if you like. I'll have a word with some of the ladies at bingo, as well. A few of them live out that way."

"Thanks, Mrs Walker. I'll think about that. I know that some of the mums from the clinic live on the estate near the park. And thanks for what you said about Tia. I'll think about that, too."

Kay pushed open the door of the flats and pressed the button for the lift. She wondered if Tia was in or had gone for a walk. She wanted some time to herself to consider what Mrs W had told her. Tia couldn't possibly have broken into that house. She did seem to have an extraordinary amount of luck, though, where money was concerned. Once again, Kay found herself trying to calculate what Tia had spent, or had given her, in relation to the money she said she earned from her cleaning job. By the time the lift reached her floor, she was sure that the figures didn't add up.

## Mid-June

I never realised how hard this would be. Maybe it's because we're all jammed in here, but I feel like I'm going mad. All I seem to do is feed Luke and change him. Every day's mostly the same. I don't think he even likes me. He smiles at Kay more than at me. I don't know what she finds to talk to Adam about but she's always jabbering to him. Seems a bit daft. Probably something Maisie told her about again. She reads too many books, that one. Kay's always coming back with some new-fangled idea. I need to be careful, though. She got really narked last week when I laughed about reading to the kids. I mean. Come on. Time enough for that when they're older. God, it would be great to have my own place. Yeah. Dream on.

I wonder how long she's going to be at the clinic today. Maybe I can risk taking Lulu out and I can meet her on her way back. Trouble is, that Maisie woman will probably be with her. Right know-all about babies, she is. You'd think she had about four not just the one. Don't know what Kay sees in her. And what's with the la di dah voice? Kay's always effing and blinding when she's with me, but I don't think I've heard her cuss once whenever we've met that Maisie. I bet she wouldn't have much fun with her around all the time. I can't believe she asked Kay to her place last week and Kay went on her own! Didn't think that I might like to go. Oh no. Cosy coffee time for the mum-friends. Never mind the lodger. I don't suppose Kay's told her I live here, though. Why would she? Kay's been different the past few weeks as well. Everything I do seems to be wrong, and fancy trying to get another flat without even a word to me. Closer to Maisie, of course. Not sure I believe her that I can go with her, even if it's still a one-bedroom.

It's getting scary now, but I just don't know where to start with finding somewhere for me and Lulu. I'd better think of something soon but my money's almost gone. Maybe Kay would lend me some. I'd better check to see if it's still there – just in case. Sly boots! Under Adam's mattress. Clever, but not clever enough. Four hundred and ninety pounds. She's spent some but there's still a fair bit left. I wonder if she'd miss a few quid.

*** 

Kay hurried along the street. She'd taken Mrs Walker's advice and approached the council about a transfer, but Mrs W had been right, they'd just agreed to put her on a list. Non-urgent, they said. She'd put cards in the shop windows as well, but it was almost impossible to keep things from Tia. She sighed. That hadn't been an easy conversation. She was so clingy. Kay had kicked herself for agreeing to take Tia and Luke with her if she did find someone to make a swap. And what if she got a two-bedroomed flat? It would be much harder to shift her increasingly unwelcome guests then.

There was a group of women chatting on the pavement, just ahead of Kay, and they moved aside for her to pass. She caught sight of Mrs Walker and nodded. Her neighbour left the group and followed Kay towards the flats.

"Hold up a minute, Kay. There's something I need to tell you."

Kay groaned quietly. "Yes? What is it?"

"I've just been to bingo with two of the ladies from the top floor and one of them has a sister who lives on that estate you were interested in. Well, I told them last week about you wanting to exchange and the sister asked around for you. I've just seen her again now and, guess what?"

"You don't mean …"

"I do! Not just one interested, but two of them. Both widows and looking for somewhere a bit quieter. One of them has a two-bedroomed flat, and the other a one-bedroomed. I said I'd let you know and perhaps you can go and see them first. They wrote down their addresses for you and said to call over anytime. You'd better check with the council again, just to make sure they wouldn't mind you having a two-bedder. All right?"

"Thank you, Mrs Walker. That's so kind of you. I'll let you know how I get on."

Kay was grinning when she stepped out of the lift. She decided not to tell Tia right away.

## Late June

Kay had been to see both flats and hoped that at least one of the occupants would like hers enough to swap. She'd arranged for them to come and look around and had been forced to tell Tia what was happening. Tia and Luke had gone out for a walk and Kay had frantically tidied up, pushing things into cupboards and under the bed. By the time Tia returned, Kay had offers from both the ladies.

"So, what are you going to do?" Tia chewed her thumb nail.

"If the council will let me, I'm going to take the two bedroomed of course. Adam can't sleep in my room forever."

Tia pouted. "No, but it'll be a while before you have to give him his own room, won't it?"

"Oh. Yeah, I see. Well – you're right. We'll be able to manage for a while."

"Yeah. A room each, eh? What's the place like, anyway? You never said."

The next morning, before Kay had time to go to the council offices to start the ball rolling, the post brought an unexpected bombshell. Mrs Walker's predictions had proved right. The council told her that there would be an inspection of the premises the following Wednesday. Less than a week! There was no going back now, she had to do something about Tia. This was not going to be a good day.

"But what am I going to do, Kay?" Tia's face was white and she was trembling from head to toe. "Can I go out somewhere until they're gone? I could stash all my stuff in the storeroom as well?"

Kay shook her head. "I think it's time to face facts, Tia. We've had a bleedin' good run and we knew someone would drop us in it sooner or later. You've got to do something for yourself now. Tell you what, I'll go and see Anna's mum. I know where she works. She might have some ideas about what to do. I won't tell her everything – just that you had to leave where you were living, and you came here last week. I'll say I know you from way back. Okay? If you'll look after Adam, I'll go as soon as I'm dressed."

Tia paced the floor. Thankfully the boys were quiet, but it still didn't help her to think clearly. What a mess. Just when she thought things were going to work out with the new flat. Maybe she could find somewhere temporary until Kay moved. That would work but it still left the problem of where to go in the meantime.

"Hello! I'm back. Everything all right?"

"Yeah, they've been great. How did you get on? Did she have any ideas?"

"Well, she wasn't too happy that you've been staying here, even for a week. She'd have friggin' flipped if I told her how long you've really been here. She asked me a few questions, then she telephoned her friend – the one who works for the housing department. She was talking to her for ages."

"Yeah, but what did she say?"

"First thing Monday morning you've got to go to the council offices in Alderbridge. The local offices don't do allocations or emergency stuff. Here's the name of the person you need to see. She said that it's best if you go on your own to see what's what. You have to tell them about Luke of course, but …"

"What?"

"Well, there's a small chance that they might want to put him into temporary care. Just until they can get you somewhere. The Social might have to be told …"

"Bloody hell, no! Not the Social. What if they take him off me for good? I can't risk that. Please Kay, let me stay with you. I'll find somewhere until they've been to check you out and agreed your swap, but don't make me give Lulu up."

"Look, Tia. It's been great having you both here, but why not give it a try? We can still be friends if you have your own place and it might even be close to where I'm going. If you do like Anna's mum said, and go on your own on Monday, they'll tell you what they can do, and you can decide then if you want to let them help. If not, well, I don't know what to suggest but I can't risk losing my home anymore."

Tia grabbed her bag from the chair and ran out of the flat. She slammed the door so hard that the windows rattled. Kay sighed and shook her head. The next few days were going to be a nightmare. She suddenly panicked that Tia had bolted and left Luke behind but convinced herself that wasn't possible.

## Monday July 1st

"How did you get on? Come and have a cup of coffee. You look shattered."

Kay put two cups on the table and the girls sat down.

"They were quite nice, really. I told them the story, like you said, about knowing you from when we were kids. Said I'd been living with my auntie down south but that she'd kicked me out 'cos of the noise and mess with Lulu, so I'd come back up this way and bumped into you in town."

"Are they going to help? And what about Luke?"

Tia huffed. "They were really nosey about him. Asked all sorts of stuff. Told them I'd left his birth certificate at my auntie's house and I'd have to write to her. Said they'd have to inform the Social 'cos I was 'technically homeless with a small child'."

"Yeah, but can they help you now? Have they got anywhere for you?"

"Not like this place. I can have a room in some hostel for a while but that's all."

"At least it's a start. I'm sure they'll find you something as soon as they can, considering Luke and everything. What are you going to do?"

"Said I'd go and look at it tomorrow morning. If I take it, I can move in with Lulu in the afternoon. It's over the other side of Crompton. A bit far, but we can still meet up, maybe?"

"Of course, we will."

Kay picked up the cups and carried them into the kitchen. She didn't see the venom in Tia's look, the whiteness of her clenched knuckles, or the flush of pink across her face.

*** 

That's it then. Out on my ear. She can't wait to get rid of us now, I can see it. Not a flicker when I said that we'd be in some poxy dosshouse. And she never even asked about money. How was I going to manage? Were they sorting out benefits for me? Nothing. Must remember to check the storeroom before I go. I think I cleared everything, but best to be on the safe side.

## Tuesday July 2nd

Kay looked at Adam in his cot. He was watching the shadows on the ceiling and trying to stick his foot in his mouth. Kay chuckled. Soon it would be just the two of them in the flat and, with a bit of luck, Adam could have his own room if they moved. She began to plan how she'd arrange her furniture and wondered whether she should buy some more. It was going to be so good to be able to please herself when and what she ate, when she went out, came in, and went to bed. No more sneaking around. No more walk rotas, and no more interrogations after every clinic visit.

Seven o'clock, but no sounds from the living room. Kay slipped out of bed and opened the curtains. The sun was bright and it looked as though it was going to be a beautiful day. Beautiful in all sorts of ways.

"Morning. I thought you were still asleep."

Tia yawned. "No. I've been awake for ages."

"Coffee?"

"Yeah. Thanks."

Kay had agreed to look after Luke again while Tia went to view the hostel room she'd been allocated. She didn't mind having him. He was a quiet child and rarely complained whether he was being bathed, having his hair washed or having his nappy changed. After she'd dressed him she propped him up against the pillow on the settee while she dressed Adam. She chatted to both of them all the time. Adam gurgled and cooed back, but Luke just watched everything she did without making a sound.

"Well, that's that then." Tia closed the front door and threw her bag onto the settee. "I'll have a quick bite to eat, then start packing. Not sure if I'll manage it all in one go."

Kay looked up. She thought this might be yet another delaying tactic but realised that Tia did seem to have accumulated quite a collection while she'd been in the flat.

"You've taken it then? What's it like? It won't be for long, I'm sure. Do you want me to come with you? I could carry some of your stuff."

"No thanks. The place is all right but isn't very big and it's quite a long walk. Even one way will be a trek. I'll have to take all of Lulu's stuff, but I can chuck some of mine if I need to. Can't leave it, can I, in case the council see it tomorrow."

Kay's stomach began to knot. She glanced at the clock and

wished that she could close her eyes and wake up when it was night.

"Okay. Look, why don't you take what you can, then put the rest in the storage room. They might look in there, but I can say it's my winter coat and things. Perhaps I can meet you half-way next week and bring it to you. What do you think?"

"Yeah. Thanks. I'll do that."

Tia pushed what she could into Luke's pram and onto the basket underneath. Then she filled four large carrier bags.

"Right. I think I can manage two of these bags, but I'll just run down to the storeroom with the others. I'll put them near the door, so you'll be able to find them easily next week."

"I'll come down with you when you go. I can leave the flat door on the latch. Adam will be all right for five minutes."

The girls stood inside the main door of the flats while Tia adjusted the bags and packages around Luke. Her face was bright red and Kay was afraid that she was going to make a scene. Kay looked at Luke and wondered if she'd see him again. She would miss him a lot. She bent over to kiss him and started rocking the pram.

"Damn! I've left my bag on the settee. Hang on a minute."

Before Kay could say a word, Tia had rushed towards the lift. Kay shrugged. Just a few more minutes. When Tia returned, she was still flushed and Kay could see how tense she was.

"I'm really sorry, Tia, but …"

"It's okay. I only asked for a few days when I turned up on your doorstep and I've been here more than six months. I don't know what I would have done without you. You've been great, but you're right, I have to sort my life out now. Lulu's getting easier to manage and I can find a clinic near the hostel or wherever else they give me, and I can sort him out as well. Sorry I nearly messed things up with the flat. When will you know about the swap?"

"I'm going to see the housing people as soon as the other

101

lot have been here tomorrow. If they say it's all right for me have the two-bed place, Mrs Jenkins and me'll have to go in together to sign some forms. They'll tell us when we can move then."

"How will I know where you are? There's a phone at the hostel, but I forgot to get the number. I left the address on the table upstairs – just in case. You could write to me?"

Kay nodded. "Of course. If we meet in the precinct next week like we said, I can give you the address of the new flat and I should know when I can move in. We'll work something out."

"Kay? Just in case they say that they can't offer me anything for ages, would you … "

"Look, Tia. Let's wait and see, eh? If things are really, really bad for you, well, maybe … but no promises. Take care of yourself, and Luke. Here, I know you can't have much left and it'll be a while until you get your benefits sorted."

Kay handed Tia some folded notes and Tia went a deeper shade of red.

"No, it's not right. It's yours. I can't… "

Kay pushed the money into Tia's hand, kissed her cheek, then ran back to the lift. She was just stepping out when she realised that Tia hadn't given the keys back.

Tia stood still for a moment then began to walk slowly down the street. She was on her own now. Time to grow up and make a life for herself and Luke. She knew that Kay wouldn't take her back in and she couldn't blame her.


The precinct was quiet when Tia arrived. She was hot and tired as she crossed the square to the benches under the trees. Two women were sitting on the bench next to Tia's, deep in conversation. Tia closed her eyes, but her ears were fully open.

"What happened, then? I thought you were going for four weeks."

"We were. Well, I was going with Toby for the first two weeks, then Mark was going to take his two weeks holiday and come and join us. He took us over on Saturday, we settled in, had a nice weekend and he came home Sunday night. Then I had message from the site office on Monday morning telling me my mum had had a fall and might have had a stroke. Mark came for us last night. No idea if we'll be able to get back there. If we hadn't paid up-front it wouldn't be quite so bad."

"Maybe they'd give you something back if you explained? They're friends of your mum aren't they?"

"Yeah, they are. But they let us have the van for next to nothing. They don't usually let it in the summer 'cos they stay there themselves, but one of their kids in Canada is having a baby and they've gone to stay for a couple of months. They said if I wanted to stay on through August as well, I could. We've only had to pay what the site charges for any electric and water. They pay forty quid a month, every three months in advance, so we agreed to pay them for July and then if we do use it in August, we'll pay them that when they get back. We weren't going to have a holiday this year, with money being tight – that's why they offered. They said we could have it for free, but Mark wasn't having that. You know what he's like."

"Nice. Maybe you can do that if your mum is better by then. Perhaps she could go with you. Could Mark change his holiday dates with work?"

"Maybe. The baby's not due 'til mid-September, but we thought that going now would give me a break while I can still get about and manage Toby as well, then I'd be home when I got bigger. Depends on how mum is. We'll see, but I don't think she's coming out of hospital soon. Anyway, the caravan wouldn't be big enough for all of us."

"What are you going to do then?"

"Not much I can do. They told me to hand in the key to the office whenever we left 'cos they'll go straight there when they get back. I didn't leave it yesterday, though, just in case we can go later. If we can't, I might put a card in the post office. Maybe someone would take it for a few weeks."

"What's it like there? I know it's not far, but I've never been."

"Nice. The site's only a field away from the lake and there's a little village about ten minutes' walk away. Couple of shops, pub and a doctor's surgery twice a week. There's only a small shop on the site but it's all right if you run out of anything. Bit pricey, though."

The two women stood up to leave and Tia opened her eyes. She did a quick calculation on her fingers and cleared her throat.

"Excuse me. I'm sorry, but I couldn't help overhearing you just now. I think we might be able to help each other, if you've got a moment?"

The women looked at each other, then back at Tia.

"I'm listening." The pregnant woman sat down, and her friend moved away a little.

"I'm in a bit of a fix." Tia shrugged. "I've just moved back to the area and the council are giving me a flat, but I can't move in 'til the first of September. They've put me in a temporary place – that's where I'm going now – but it's not very nice. One room, shared bathroom and kitchen. I'm afraid that the baby will suffer more than me. If you'd let me take the caravan, I'll pay you double what you've spent. That way you'll get your money back and have some more to put towards a holiday when you can go. I'll pay you for August as well, if you want. What do you think?"

"I'm not sure. I mean, the owners are friends of my mother's. If anything happened …"

"I promise I'll look after it. You can come and check anytime you want. I can get the money now. Only take me ten minutes to pop in the bank. What do you say?"

"Well, all right, but here's what we'll do. You can have it for July for definite. We'll come down on the last weekend and if we want it, you'll have to move out. If we don't want it, you can stay, but only 'til the end of August. You have to get out before they come back. We can come down and help you bring your stuff back if you like. Mark's got the work's van. You can pay for the two months, but I'll give you something back if you only have July. Fair enough?"

Tia clapped her hands. "Thank you so much. Wait here, I

won't be long. The bank's just over there. Oh – where is the site? Is it easy to get there? I don't have a car or anything."

"It's out at Appleton Lake. You can get the train from Crompton station and it only takes about half an hour. Costs a couple of quid for a single, I think. Cheaper on the bus but you'd never manage with the pram and all that stuff."

Tia crossed the road and went into the foyer of the bank. She waited behind the doors for five minutes, then she crossed the square and handed over one hundred and sixty pounds to the pregnant woman in exchange for a key and a piece of paper with the address of the caravan site and how to get there.

"Try to keep out of the way of the site manager if you can. The owners told him I was coming with Toby, but he wasn't around at the weekend, so he wouldn't know what I look like. If you do bump into him, remember that your name is Mandy. Husband's Mark and he's a fitter, and the little boy is Toby. The owners are Mr and Mrs Castle. Any problems, ring this number and one of us will try to help. If you do decide to leave early, put the key in an envelope with the owner's name on it and push it into the site office when it's quiet. Please keep the place clean and tidy. Promise?"

"Yeah, of course I will. You've saved my life. Do the trains run often?"

"Every two hours, I think. Just follow the main road up to the library and the station's around the back. The ticket bloke can tell you the timetable and they'll help you with the pram as well. Good luck, and we'll see you in a couple of weeks."

\*\*\*

Well wasn't that the best bit of real luck ever. Even Kay would be impressed. Almost eight whole weeks if I'm lucky but at least four. I can work something out if I have a bit of peace and quiet. I know I can. I hope I can get there without too much hassle. It's hard work with this pram so loaded up. Shouldn't need to feed Lulu for a few hours anyway. He'll just have to have a cold bottle if he starts squawking. It's made a bit of a dent in the money, but I'll just have to watch what I'm spending when I'm there. Shouldn't think there'll be many opportunities to top up the cash either. Never mind. I've got a roof over our heads and no one will know where we are. Suits me for now.

## July 9th

Kay let herself into the flat, put Adam in his cot, and flopped down on the settee. She was hot, tired, and cross. After all the fuss that Tia had made about keeping in touch and swapping addresses and the like, and then she hadn't turned up where they'd arranged to meet. Kay had thought about not going herself but felt mean. She'd collected Tia's bags from the storeroom and strolled down to the precinct and sat on one of the benches. She waited for half an hour, but Tia didn't show. Kay had started walking back home but turned around, crossed the road and headed for the address that Tia had scribbled on the piece of paper she'd left on the table the previous week.

Southerby Road was quiet when Kay reached it and she'd walked slowly, looking for number forty-six. The house at the top of the street was number one hundred and four. When she reached the houses in the sixties, she sat on a wall for a few minutes. Tia had been right. This was a long trek.

Number forty-six turned out to be a big, detached house in its own grounds, and Kay had wondered why Tia said it wasn't very nice. After a brief chat with the lady who'd opened the door, Kay left without seeing Tia. All the way home she'd worried at her memory. Had she misunderstood what Tia had said? But it was Tia who'd written down the address.

Kay poured herself a cold drink and sat at the table. The lady at the house had told her that there wasn't, and never had been, council accommodation there, so what on earth had Tia been on about? Kay slammed down her glass. She had enough to think about with the move. She hugged herself. Only two weeks and she'd be in her new flat. Just her and

Adam and a bedroom each. She was so glad that Maisie's husband had said he'd help with moving her stuff. She had to pay for the hire van, but he'd drive it and get a mate to help with the shifting for a few quid.

Kay jumped out of her chair so quickly that it tipped over. She ran into the bedroom, took Adam out of his cot, dumped him onto the bed, and she was shaking as she removed his mattress. The envelope was still there but when Kay tipped out the money, there was just fifty pounds left. *Friggin', friggin' bitch*!

## July 16th

Ruth was in the kitchen reading the newspaper when she heard the post clatter onto the floor in the hallway. She carried the pile of envelopes and circulars back to the table and began sorting through them. A few bills, two letters for Paul, some holiday brochures and a brown envelope addressed to her. She frowned, then ripped it open. A photograph fell out and Ruth's hand shook when she turned it over and looked at it. She could feel her heart hammering and the prickling behind her eyes increased. She put the photograph down and looked inside the envelope. There was a single sheet of paper. She scanned it, then picked up the telephone.

"Hello, Janet? I'm glad I caught you. Are you working today?"

"Hello Ruth. No. We had the rota changed at the hospital. What can I do for you?"

"I wondered if you'd have time to come over? I've had a really strange letter today with a photo as well."

"Not from Kay?"

"No, but the photo is of her and the girl she went to stay with. The note is from the girl's mother, Mrs Connor. Says she'd like to meet to talk about Kay. It's thrown me a bit."

"That's a bolt of the blue. Not surprised you're shaken. Look, I've got to call in the bank and then I'll head over to you. Anything you need me to pick up?"

"No thanks. Just come when you can."

The sisters sat in the garden and passed the letter and photograph back and fore between them. It was clear that the picture had been taken after Kay had left home for the second time, as her baby bump was obvious. Janet stared at the face of the friend then shook her head.

"Nope. Don't recognise her at all. Any idea where this was taken?"

Ruth shook her head and pointed to the letter.

"No, this woman just says that it was in her garden. Said she'd been with them for a while, but it looks like the woman managed to pull some strings with the council and get Kay her own flat."

"But why's she writing to you now? And how did she know where you lived? I can't believe that Kay would have given her your address. She didn't want you to know where she was, did she? Can I see it again?"

Ruth handed over the letter and sighed. She shook her head and rubbed the back of her neck. "Doesn't give much away, does she? She must know about the baby, but she doesn't mention it. I can't think of any reason why she'd do this just to upset us. What would be the point? And like you said, why now? You don't think that Kay's in some kind of trouble, do you? I know she probably wouldn't come to us but maybe she's still in touch with this woman and she can't or won't help. What d'you think?"

"I think we should meet her. No need to tell Paul unless you have to. Don't get your hopes up, though, will you? I mean, there's all sorts of weird people out there. If she's got an agenda, we don't know it yet."

"You're right, love. It's been almost a year now. Since Paul fixed the snow globe at Christmas, he's talked about her much more. Never mentions the baby, though. This would send him through the roof again, I think. He likes things clear cut. If she's sorry for what she did and wants to patch things up, he'd want her to say it herself, not pussyfoot around going through someone else. It's not like her, either. Kay never had a problem standing up for herself. Just like you, and Dad!"

"True, but no good second-guessing things. It's up to you in the end, but if you want to meet her, I'll gladly go with you. Might be better for us both to go, just in case it is a scam. She's put a phone number. Do you want to call now, while I'm here? I can tell you when I'm not working then."

"Would you ring her, Jan? Whatever you agree is fine by me. Just make sure that Paul's not going to be at home when we go."

## July 22nd

Janet and Ruth arranged to meet Anna's mother in a café in Alderbridge. Ruth was resentful that Kay had found the woman's home and company preferable to what she and Paul had provided, but Janet reminded her that if she wanted to have any chance of a reconciliation with Kay, Mrs Connor was her only link.

After a difficult few minutes, Janet found herself liking the woman and was glad that Kay had someone who had been prepared to help her. Mrs Connor told them about Kay's flat and also about the baby. Ruth couldn't help crying when she learned his name. It had been what both her father and her grandfather were called.

"The thing is, Mrs Jones, I'm a bit worried about someone that Kay's become friendly with." Mrs Connor fiddled with the spoon in her saucer.

"Oh? Why should that bother you?"

Janet nudged her sister's arm and Ruth blushed.

"Sorry."

Mrs Connor shrugged. "That's all right. It's a strange situation, I know. It's just that Kay came to see me a few weeks ago asking if I could help out a friend of hers who needed to find somewhere to live. She said the girl and her baby had been staying with her for a week, but I heard from a friend it had been a lot longer than that, and that some of the people who lived in the block of flats where Kay was had suspicions that the girl had been stealing. Someone told the council and Kay said they were planning an inspection, so the girl had to get out. A friend of mine arranged an appointment for her with the emergency housing people, but she never showed up. I'm afraid that she's still with Kay. It would be a shame if Kay lost her flat because she's trying to help this girl but I don't think she'd listen to me. Besides, she hasn't been in touch since that visit and I think she might be avoiding me."

"What makes you think she'd listen to me? She probably wouldn't even see me, and she'd know that it was you who told me, wouldn't she?" Ruth pushed her cup away so suddenly that the tea splashed over the table.

"Maybe, but it would be worth it. If she does get evicted, she'll have nowhere to go. I can't have her back with me, not with the baby as well, and with her not working. But if you don't want to try, that's your decision. Look, I'll give you her address and you think it over. There's no phone, but you'd probably be better off just turning up at her door."

Mrs Connor pulled out a sheet of paper from her bag and pushed it across the table. Ruth stared at it but made no attempt to pick it up. Janet slid it towards herself and glanced at the address.

"Crompton. It probably was her we saw at that fete, and the one with her was probably this girl who's been staying with her. Thanks, Mrs Connor. Shall we let you know what we decide, or do you want to leave it here?"

"Whatever you think is best, but it would be good to know how things work out. Good luck."

## July 23rd

Kay closed the door of her new flat and looked around. She picked up Adam and walked from room to room, chatting to him all the time. Another new start, but this time it would be just the two of them. No more hard-luck stories, no more soft touches. She remembered an old saying of her mother's. *Once bitten, twice shy.* Well, she'd been well and truly bitten. It was still hard for her to believe Tia would have done that to her. Even more of a slap in the face was the fifty pounds that she'd given Tia as a parting gift. So much for friendship. She'd be much more careful in future.

Kay laid Adam in his cot and stroked his head. He was such a happy baby.

"Here we are then little man. This is your new bedroom. All for you. We'll get some more furniture for you soon, and when you're bigger you can have your own little bed. Mummy'll have to save for that, but we'll get by. I promise."

She knew life was going to be a lot more difficult than she'd thought now that her money was almost all gone, but she was determined that Adam wouldn't suffer for that. Mrs Jenkins had left a wardrobe and a few other things behind as she wouldn't have room for them in Kay's old flat, so that helped, but there was still more that Kay needed to buy. She sighed. Time enough to worry about that. She looked around again and smiled. Free.

***

This the best ever. I can't believe how lucky I was. Nobody asking me where I'm going or what I'm doing. Not having to creep around like a criminal, either. Shame about Kay's new flat. That would have been good. Damn nosey neighbours. Another few weeks and we could have got away with it. I'm not sure about Kay, though. Got a feeling she might have chucked me out anyway. Too cosy with that Maisie woman, I think. Thank God I found the money. It was a bit awkward when she gave me the fifty quid but at least I didn't wipe her out completely. Good job she'd taken it out before I swiped the rest. That would have been hard to explain! I don't know what would have happened if she hadn't taken us in, but at least she's got some real family. There's always somewhere she could go if she was desperate. Not like us. Not too long before Mandy comes here. I'd better clean up a bit. Can't believe how much mess a kid creates. Still, he seems to like it here. Another month would be great. I'm sure it'll be okay.

# July 24th

"There's a space at the end of the road. I'll park there. All right?"

Janet turned to look at her sister. Ruth nodded. Her lips were drawn tight and she was clutching the strap of her handbag. They'd argued over whether Kay's dad should be told, but Ruth had won, and Paul was left in the dark. They'd agreed that they wouldn't contact Kay before they visited, in case she tried to avoid them.

They hesitated at the outer door of the flats but when one of the residents came out and held the door open, they slipped inside. All the better. Even less notice for Kay. The lift doors whined as they opened, and Ruth caught her breath. She grasped Janet's arm as they walked along the corridor.

"This is the right thing to do, isn't it, Janet? But what if she won't talk to me, or shuts the door in my face? I don't think I could bear it."

"Come on, Ruth. We've got this far. No point worrying about stuff like that now. You said this was how you wanted to do it, so let's get it over with. We'll deal with one thing at a time. Ready?"

Janet knocked on the flat door. She knocked again. There was a sinking feeling in her stomach as she glanced towards Ruth, who was white faced and trembling.

"She's not here, is she?"

Janet screwed up her nose. "Mmm. Why don't we ask one of the neighbours? Maybe it's clinic day or something."

She rang Mrs Carter's bell, but it was sometime before the elderly lady opened the door. It soon became apparent that Mrs Carter was severely hard of hearing and their conversation wouldn't have looked out of place in one of the local amateur dramatic productions. What they did learn was that Kay had moved out the day before and that Mrs Carter had no idea of the new address. As the sisters left the building, they passed Mrs Walker, but Ruth was too upset to do more than nod at the smiling woman who held the door.

# July 30th

Tia yawned and stretched out on the bed. Luke was awake and watching her. He was a funny kid. Didn't cry much anymore, just looked at everything around him with his eyes wide. Tia shrugged. It was time to start cleaning the caravan before Mandy and her husband arrived. If she had to move out today, she needed to be ready, although she hadn't quite worked out where she would go. She remembered the overheard conversation in the newsagents and considered going back to Maple Avenue but had enough sense to realise that she wouldn't be able to keep hidden for long, and certainly not for a month. The time had slipped by so quickly. She prayed that Mandy wouldn't be able to use the van after all.

The scrunch of tyres on gravel made Tia jump. She glanced around the caravan and nodded.

"Hello. Everything all right?" Mandy waved to Tia and climbed the van steps. She dropped onto the seating unit and flapped her hands in front of her face. "God, it's hot, and I've got so big in the last month. Feels like I'm having twins!"

Tia smiled. "Yeah, you have grown quite a bit. Are you feeling okay though?"

"I'm fine. Just a bit tired, what with looking after my mum and all. She's doing all right but still needs a lot of help, so we can't stay long. Do you still want to stay for August as well?"

Tia caught her breath. Another four weeks!

"That would be great. I'm sure the council will have my flat ready by the end of the month. If you're sure it's okay? I've kept the place tidy and haven't seen much of the site manager or his wife. Just waved a few times."

"It'll be fine. We'll come back on the last Saturday. If I can't make it, Mark will come on his own, but he's said that he'll take you and your stuff back to Crompton, if that's what you want? Save messing about with the train. If you want to go any earlier, just leave the key like we said before, but you'll have to get the train then."

"No, I'll stay here, thanks. And Crompton or Alderbridge

will be fine. See you in a couple of weeks then. Unless you go in early. Good luck if you do."

Mandy patted her stomach. "With the size of this one, I wouldn't mind being early! Bye."

That evening Tia put Luke in his pram and walked as far as the village. She bought some bread and milk and was just about to pay when she spotted the special offer on the cans of cider. One wouldn't hurt, would it? It had been so long since she'd had any, and it was so hot in the caravan. She dropped four cans into her basket and moved to the counter.

## August 7th

Oh God, my head's banging and my eyes feel like someone's trying to poke them out.

"Shut up your whining, Lulu. I'll see to you in a minute. Here, have your dummy. Lulu? Luke?"

Shit. Where's the bloody kid now? I'm sure I put him in bed with me last night. I remember undressing him … Hell! How did he get there? He's starkers and look at the shit all over the place. Poor little bugger's freezing.

"I'm sorry, baby. I'll get you cleaned up and you can have a nice big bottle. All right? Don't cry now. Mummy's sorry. I won't do it again, I promise."

I've got to get myself sorted out. Buying that cider last week was the first mistake but I could have managed. The vodka was the killer. What's the matter with me? I've got to start thinking of a way out. Just a few weeks and we're back on the street again. Think!

## August 15th

Where the hell am I? This isn't my caravan. Whose place is it? And where's Lulu? I know I fed him and put him into bed about seven. I only had two vodkas, I know, 'cos that's all that was left.

Oh! The shop – walking back. Dark. Barbeque by the lake.

Blokes. No! I couldn't have. Not again. God, I emptied that whole bottle. No wonder I feel so rough. And what about Lulu? I left him on his own in the caravan. I've really blown it now. Someone's bound to have heard him crying. Shit! It's nearly one o'clock. By the time I get back it'll be almost eighteen hours since I left. Idiot. Moron. I've got to get out of here.

I can't believe how stupid I've been. After all we've been through – the luck we've had – and I almost blew it all. I didn't think that nosey cow next door completely believed me about Luke having colic and crying all night but at least I don't think she's done anything about it. Thank God I locked the caravan door. She couldn't have seen me coming back 'cos she was out herself. God, he was in a mess again. I just hope the bruises have gone by the time I have to leave. Why can't I get my act together and make some proper plans? If I knew where Kay was I'd beg her to take me back. Perhaps I could hang around the clinic. I'm sure she goes to the same one 'cos that Maisie came from one of the estates where the new flat is. Trouble is I've lost track of the clinic rota and anyway, that bloody know-all would most likely be with her. Maybe I could check out the park. One last shot – but then what?

## August 17th

Janet pulled into the station car park and switched off the engine. She had about five minutes until Ruth and Paul's train was due. She was pleased that Ruth had agreed to go on the surprise holiday Paul had organised, but it had taken some persuading. Ruth had been devastated at missing Kay by one day and despite their best efforts, they'd been unable to trace her. Mrs Connor couldn't, or wouldn't, help anymore and Ruth had become more and more withdrawn. It was made even harder because she'd insisted that Paul should be kept in the dark. Janet didn't agree but she knew better than to argue with Ruth when she was in one of her rare, stubborn moods. Hopefully, ten days in the sun had done her good, and it meant Janet had had a little more time to herself. The past month had been draining.

"Ruth! Over here. It's so good to see you, and you too, Paul. You both look great. Come on, let's get you home and you can tell me all about it over a cup of tea. I bought some milk and a few basics, so you don't have to go shopping right away."

"Good idea, Jan. Tea's the thing I've missed the most!"

As Paul was putting the cases in the boot, Ruth whispered, "I told him everything about Kay and the flat. We had a long talk about her, and we've sorted things out. I'll tell you later, when we're on our own."

That evening Janet and Ruth sat in the garden enjoying the sounds and smells of the August night. Ruth ran her hand through a lavender bush and inhaled deeply.

"Beautiful. The cruise was lovely and the places we stopped at were so interesting, but I couldn't wait to come home. I'm glad we went, though. It gave us chance to wind down and to talk. Paul's always so tired in the evenings. He works so hard. That's one of the things we've agreed – that he'll take on some more help. We talked about moving somewhere smaller, but I'm still not sure about that."

"Because of Kay?"

"Mmm. That's the main reason, but I really like this house and the area. Paul thinks it would help us to move on, but wherever I am, I know I'll never stop thinking about her, or looking, either. I don't suppose there's been any news?"

"Not really. I went back to her old flat to see if the person who lives there now could tell me anything, but she clammed up. I tried the council offices but they said they couldn't give me that kind of information either."

Ruth brushed a tear from her cheek. "Paul's right. We have to let her come to us, if she wants to."

## August 21st

Kay was hot and she felt lazy. Adam was playing with his feet as he lay next to her on the settee and Kay smiled as she

116

watched him. He looked more and more like Kal as he grew and she had a sudden pang of fear that someone might see the likeness one day. She yawned. Time enough to worry about that later. For now, she wanted to concentrate on making a better life for them both. Who knew? Maybe they'd be able to move somewhere else. Somewhere nobody knew them – or the Khatri twins.

Kay put Adam in his pushchair and looked out of the window. The sun was bright, so she went back into the bedroom for his hat. She laughed when he tried to snatch it off his head and he grinned at her, showing his two new teeth. It was amazing how much he'd developed in the six weeks since they'd moved. Kay loved her flat and loved having it all to herself. She often thought about Tia, and worried about Luke, but she consoled herself with the knowledge that she'd done her best to help them. Tia's betrayal had been a punch in the face but not entirely unexpected. She shrugged and left the flat to meet Maisie in the park. They'd become good friends and spent a lot of time together. Maisie had asked her to think about doing an evening class in September, but Kay wasn't sure, even though Maisie's husband said he'd watch the children for them. Still, it wouldn't hurt to look at the brochures.

The park was busy and Kay looked around for somewhere shady to sit. In the far corner, near the gates, there was an empty seat and Kay hurried to claim it. She pulled out her book but she found it hard to concentrate.

"Hi, Kay. All right?" Kay woke from her daydream and waved at Maisie.

"Sorry, I was miles away. Thinking about that evening class. Anything you fancy? I don't think I'd want to do one that would mean a lot of homework, but I quite like the idea of a practical one. Something like hairdressing? I did a bit of salon work before I had Adam, but that was mostly sweeping floors and shampooing! If I could work towards a qualification, I could get a better job when he's older."

Maisie smiled. "Good idea. I was looking at the beauty courses. Especially the manicure and facial ones. Who knows

– in a few years' time we could set up in business together!"

"Look." Kay pointed at the sky. "Pigs!"

The girls laughed and chatted while the babies kicked and gurgled on a rug on the grass. Adam was already well on the way to being able to crawl, so Kay had her work cut out keeping an eye on him. She had just retrieved him for the fourth time when Maisie tapped her on the shoulder.

"Kay. There's something I want to tell you."

"Well, spit it out, then. Nothing bad, I hope."

Maisie puffed out her cheeks. "Not really but I think you might be interested. We took Holly out for a run to Appleton Lake last weekend."

Kay looked puzzled. "And?"

"I saw Tia, I'm sure of it. She didn't see me but what was she doing there?"

"Who knows? I really did try to help her and Luke but sometimes there are people you just can't help. I worry about the little one, though. How did he look?"

"He wasn't with her."

"She must have found somewhere to stay and someone to help with him, perhaps. I really hope so, but I don't want to go down that road again. Is that awful of me?"

Maisie shook her head. Kay had told her all about Tia and she'd been horrified.

"Look, Kay, you did far more than a lot of others would have. You put yourself at risk to help her, and then for her to turn her back on you and lie like she did – well, I couldn't forgive her, that's for sure. She's made her choices and you need to move on."

Kay and Maisie sat on the grass next to the sleeping babies so that a group of elderly women could use the seat. Maisie sat up suddenly.

"Talk of the devil. Look. Isn't that Tia over there, heading this way?"

Kay shielded eyes. "It certainly looks like her. You don't think she's come looking for me, do you?"

"Damn cheek if she has. Duck your head down and she might not see us behind these old dears. Quick!"

Kay held her breath as Tia came closer. Despite everything that Tia had done, Kay still felt sorry for her. She would have loved to see Luke again, but she couldn't take the risk. Tia was trouble. No matter how much help she was given, it never seemed to be enough. Kay wiped away a tear and shook her head. Tia had to stand on her own two feet from now on. Kay's priority was Adam, and her own future.

Tia circled the park. It had taken days to pluck up the courage to try to find Kay, but desperation had won. She spotted Kay right away and her stomach flipped, but then she saw Maisie, and she hurried by as quickly as she could.

## August 27th

Kay opened her front door and let Maisie in.

"Hello. How's tricks? Fancy a coffee?"

"Great. Thanks. Jeff's looking after Holly for a while so I thought I'd let you know about the night classes. I think I know what I'm going to do but we can have another look through these leaflets to see if there's anything you fancy. I'm going to the college next week to have a look around and have a chat to the people there. I rang up yesterday to ask about help with the fees and things. They were really nice. You can come as well, if you like?"

"Maybe. Let's have a look at the courses first. I still think hairdressing is my best choice, but can I do that at evening class?"

Maisie nodded. "Yes. I checked and it's the same set-up as the course I want – the manicure and facials one, and on the same night. You have to do a foundation course first and then, if you do all right with that, you can do the proper course - full time or part time – but that's only in the day."

"Oh. Well that's not going to work, is it? Even if I could pay the fees, or get some help with them, I couldn't afford to pay someone to look after Adam. How would you manage? I know Jeff said he'd cover the evening class but with him working you'd be in the same boat as me, wouldn't you?"

"Ah. Well now, there might a solution to that!" Maisie grinned. "The woman on the phone said that there was a nursery at the college and if you qualified for help with fees, you could get free childcare as well. She said that it takes a bit of time to get things sorted so if we decided to do the foundation course, we should make it clear on the application forms that we'd also need financial assistance if we progressed to the next level. Apparently whoever decides on it doesn't take long to let you know. We have to show some proof of what kind of benefits we get, or whatever you might be earning, but there's something about that in the envelope at the back of the pack. You'll probably qualify for more help than me because Jeff's working, but I think we'll be able to manage. Anyway, I've got an idea."

Kay's jaw dropped and she put her hands up to her face. Maybe, just maybe, this could be the start of something good. Maisie went on. "I got talking to some girls when I picked up the leaflets and they're just starting their second year. They said that if you get through the foundation part and go on, you have to have your own basic kit. For the course I want it's an overall and a box with manicure, nail painting and facial stuff in it. They weren't sure about the hairdressing, but they thought it was similar – scissors, combs and things. It's a bit pricey but you can get a grant to spread it. I was thinking that if we could get to that part, maybe we could do some work here, on the estate. There are lots of the older ones who can't get out as much as they'd like to, and mums who aren't working. If we kept it low key and cash-in-hand, we wouldn't have to declare anything. What do you think?"

"Oh yes! Good idea. If anyone did check up on us, we could always say we were just doing some homework – you know – practising for the course. How long is the foundation part?"

"It's only a term. Just so you learn the basics before they let you loose on real people! That's why there's the evening class option. We can find out more next week. We'll be all right for that because Jeff will have the kids. It's only a couple of hours and he knows how much I want to do this."

"That's brilliant. He's so good. You're lucky to have him. I might be changing my mind about being better off on my own!"

Ten o'clock. Mark will be here soon. I can't believe it's been two months since I moved in. If only I could stay a bit longer, but no good wishing for things like that. It's not going to happen. My best bet is to get back into town and find somewhere for Lulu and me to stay. I might be able to afford a B & B for a couple of nights, but then what? Shit! What a mess and my head is thumping. I should never have bought another bottle of vodka. Who was I kidding that I'd be able to keep it unopened, or just have a small glass now and then? Think. Think.

"Hi, Mark. How's Mandy? Okay? Thanks ever so much for giving me a lift. Everything's ready to go."

"Hello. Mandy's all right. Nearly there. Where do you want me to drop you off? Flat ready yet?"

"I've got to pick up the keys first so I guess somewhere near the High Street in Alderbridge would be great, if you don't mind?"

"You sure you can manage with all this stuff and the little one? I can wait in the van outside the council offices if you want. Where's the flat?"

"Oh, well, I don't know how long I'll be. The woman told me I'd have to fill in a load of forms. I don't think you can park there for long. Anyway, I'll be fine. Once I get there, I can leave some of this stuff behind the desk 'til I get the keys, and perhaps they'll keep it for me 'til I've seen the flat. It's in that new block they built over near the library."

"Fair enough. Come on then. I'll just drop off the keys and we'll be away."

Bloody hell, that was close! He seems like a nice bloke, but I still have to be careful. He's right, though. I have got a ton of stuff. Poor Lulu. He's going to have a lot of it in the pram with him. Still, I'll find us somewhere and we'll be fine. It can't be that hard.

"Thanks, Mark. Hope it all goes well with the baby, and with Mandy's mum. Thanks again for the caravan – saved my bacon!"

Well, that's it. Thank God it's not raining. I need to find a B & B. I can't cart all this around the town for long, though. That paper shop on the corner of Nelson Road used to have loads of ads in the window and there's a phone box outside. A couple of nights should be fine if it's not too pricey. Maybe I should have got Mark to drop me in Crompton. I've still got Kay's keys and perhaps I could use the storeroom until I find somewhere. It's a long walk, but Plan B perhaps.

"Just me, and my little boy. Oh, he's nine months. Right."

That's it, then. Bloody five of them, all the same. It's not as if I was asking for the moon. Three bloody nights, that's all. Wouldn't have killed them. Anyway, Lulu's quiet. Probably quieter than me. Poor little sod. Better get something to eat and change him. He stinks!

"Want a pasty, Lulu? Don't stare at me like that. You really freak me out, sometimes. Come on, let's find somewhere to sit down and you can have a jar of chocolate pud. All right? Then we'll sort out where we're going to stay tonight."


The precinct's busy today. All the mum's rushing around for school stuff for the new term. Wonder if I'll ever get to that stage. I can't see it somehow, especially if I can't find somewhere to live, and that's looking too likely right now. Even if I do, what am I going to live on? I can't take Lulu with me when I'm nicking stuff. The begging scam works all right but it's too risky with a kid – can't get away quick enough if the cops are around. Maybe all this baby thing was a mistake. I mean, I love him and all that, but it's getting too hard. If I'd been as lucky as Kay it might have worked but ...

"Tia, love. What you doin' 'ere? 'aven't seen you for a bit. This your nipper, then?"

"Hello, Binny. How you doing? Yeh, this is Luke. We've been staying out at Appleton Lake all summer. Friend's place."

"Nice. So why're you 'ere now with all this stuff? Not on the street again, love?"

"Looks like it. Friend needed the van back for a couple of months and the caravan park shuts for the winter, anyway. The mate I was staying with last Christmas has moved and

I've lost her new address."

"Bummer. What're you gonna do?"

"B & Bs won't take us. I was wondering if you had any ideas? Any chance of a space where you doss down?"

"No offence, like, but tha's not a good idea. 'ave to be real quiet. Some o' the porters knows abou' me, but as long as I cleans up and don' make any noise, they turns a blind eye. But with a nipper? Naw, wouldn't work. Sorry."

"That's okay. Worth asking. I'm desperate, Binny. I've got to get somewhere."

"Look, I'll ask around. Meet me back 'ere tomorra at the same time."

"But what about tonight? I can't stay here. Come on, Binny. You've been around here for ages. You must know somewhere that's safe. Please."

"Gawd! A'right, a'right. Stop snivellin'. There's the Mission. You might get a bed on account o' the kid, but they wanna know a lot, and you 'ave to pay. Yer best bet is the train station. Get a platform ticket and 'ead for platform four. Check no-one's abou' then make for the waitin' room. There's a door next to it. S'posed to be a cleaner's store or summat. 'ardly ever locked. Plenty of room for yer stuff but you betta not take it all when you get yer ticket. Stash it near the lifts if you can. If they ask, say yer meetin' someone off the train."

"What if the door's locked?"

"Takes yer chances, love. Dunno what time they lock the waitin' room, if they do. If you gets kicked out, go 'round the back, down the lane to the car park. There's some big bins in the corner. Get in the space at the back. Be a'right for one night."

"Thanks, Binny. See you here same time tomorrow."

## August 26th

"Come on, Lulu. Stop crying, now. I know it's cold but the sun will be out soon and then we can go walkies. Here, have your dummy and snuggle up. I'm sorry, baby."

What a night. Good job Binny told me about the car park.

He can't have been to the station for a while. Bloody porters! God, I could do with a drink. I hope Binny's found somewhere for us 'cos I don't think I can do the outdoors stuff again. Just a few hours more. I've got to make some decisions about Lulu, poor little sod. It's not right – him living like this. If we can't get a place in the next few days, I'll have to find somewhere to take him – just for a while – 'til I get myself straight.

"Well, well, well. Lookee what we got here, boys. The bloody sleeping princess and her little frog."

Tia jumped. She was aching all over and totally disorientated. Two coats on a concrete floor didn't make the best mattress. It took a moment for her to realise that she hadn't been dreaming.

"Jake! What's going on? Why are you here? What have you done with my pram?"

"Ooh! Get her with 'my pram'. Never mind 'my baby'. Got your priorities right again, eh?"

Tia looked down at the little nest that she'd made next to her for Luke. He'd been so cross in the pram. Empty. She screamed at Jake.

"You bastard. Where is he? What do you want with us. Give him back to me and clear off and leave us alone."

"He's all right. Look over there. He's having fun with Bones and Loco."

Tia clasped her hands over her mouth. The two young men were throwing Luke to each other as if he was a rugby ball. As he screamed, she felt her knees buckle.

"Stop it, Jake, please. Why d'you want to hurt him? He's done nothing to you."

"Oh, please, is it now? I don't care about the sprog, it's you I was looking for. We ran into a mate of yours last night. Binny. Remember him? Scruffy bloke, rotten teeth? Heard he was asking around for a place for you and the kid to stay. Don't know why he didn't want to tell us where you were after I offered to let you come to ours. Took a bit of persuading, I can tell you, but he saw sense in the end."

"You didn't hurt him, did you? He was only trying to help."

"Hurt him? Us? Let's just say he's got a few less teeth to worry about now, and he's probably a lot cleaner after his bath in the river. Now, you and me have some talking to do, but first of all you'd better put me in a good mood."

Jake grabbed Tia's hair with one hand and slapped her hard across the side of her head with the other. As she stumbled, he kicked her legs and she fell forward onto her knees. He shuffled backwards and dragged her with him until his back was against one of the bins. She struggled and tried to pull his hand away from her hair. She knew only too well what would happen next.

"No, Jake, no. Not this. Please. I've got some money. You can have it all, just let us go."

"Money!" Jake laughed. "That's a bonus, darling. Should have kept your mouth shut. On second thoughts, I think I prefer it when it's open."

Tia screamed again as Jake tightened his hold on her hair. He opened the zip of his jeans and forced Tia's head down, but she clamped her teeth together. When his knee shot up under her chin she almost passed out.

"Bitch! Whore! Come on, it's not like it's new to you. Or have you got a taste for something sweeter now? Be a good girl and it won't take long. Or maybe you'd prefer the sprog to do it for you? Never tried that before. I hope he hasn't got any teeth yet. Wouldn't take much to yank them out though, would it? Changed your mind, eh? Good."

When Jake was finished, Tia threw up on the floor. Her scalp was burning, and her knees were cut and bleeding. She used Luke's blanket to wipe away the blood, and the tears, snot and Jake's 'gift' from her face. For good measure, Jake kicked her in the back.

"Get up. Pack all this shit into the pram and get moving."

"Where are you taking me? What about Lulu? Don't let them hurt him."

"Lulu? That's a bleedin' dog's name! Better off without you, if you ask me."

"No! No! Please let me have him back. I'll do whatever you want, but don't take him away from me. Not now."

"Stop your whinging, you stupid bitch and shift your arse. Nice Jake is going to take you home with him. The sprog can come for the time being but any nonsense out of you and I'll let the boys have him for target practice. Now, where's the money?"

***

Janet swung the car into a parking bay at the back of the station and switched off the engine. She was so pleased to have found a space near the entrance. She glanced at her watch. Twelve o'clock. Ruth's train wasn't due in for another half an hour. Plenty of time for a coffee and a browse in the book shop. She found some change in her purse and headed towards the ticket machine. As she took her parking ticket, she noticed something brightly coloured on the ground next to some large garbage bins. She crossed the path and bent forward to get a better look. It was baby's blanket. Janet picked it up and was just about to lay it on the wall, in case the owner came back for it, when she saw that the underneath was stained with what looked like blood and something slimy. Yuk! She grimaced, dropped it back to the floor and returned to her car. She put the ticket on the dashboard and opened the glove compartment where she always kept a pack of handwipes.

Five minutes later she was in the station coffee shop. Ruth's train was due in on time so Janet decided against the coffee and headed for the bookstore.

***

Kay and Maisie giggled together as they looked through the papers they'd just been given at the college.

"Flipping heck, Maisie! It'll take hours to fill in all these. Do you want to come back to my place and we can do some of it together?"

"Okay." Maisie checked the time. "It's ten past twelve

126

now. We've missed the bus, but if we get the train we can call in at the bookshop at the station – I've got to get a present for Jeff's mum – then I can come straight back with you."

The girls turned into the lane that led to the main concourse. The bookshop was next to the entrance, so Kay waited outside with both pushchairs while Maisie made her choice. She didn't notice Maisie talking to a woman at the till.

## September 7th

Poor Lulu. He hasn't stopped crying since we got here. Good job Jake and his crew have been out a lot, or I think they would have done something to him. I don't know what else to do. If I had a kettle it would help. At least I could warm some food for him. There's not much left now but Jake's never going to let me go out for any. Maybe he's left the door unlocked. No. Just as I thought. Trapped. I've got to think of some way out of here. It's a better place than the last one but I can't stay here with Lulu. If last night was a taster of what's coming, then I need to get as far away as possible. Jake's made it quite clear what the price of staying here is – even if I don't want to stay! But what's the alternative? One night sleeping rough was enough, and even if I could find some kind of shelter, what next? I should have tried harder to stay with Kay. If I can get out, I'll have another go at finding her. When she knows about Jake and what's happened, she'll be certain to help. Soft, she is, but in a good way. If I can't find her, then I'll have to find somewhere safe for Lulu. Oh God, Jake's back.

"Is that bloody kid still whining? For fuck's sake shut him up and get in the bathroom. You both smell like you've had a week in the sewers. Hurry up, then come downstairs. We got something to talk about."

\*\*\*

Tia grabbed Luke and ran for the bathroom. Despite the good weather, it was damp and a bit mouldy but at least there was running water, even it was mostly cold. She filled the sink, stripped off Luke's clothes and nappy, and washed him gently. The shock of the cold water stopped him crying and Tia smiled. She dried him as best she could on a piece of old sheet, put on a clean nappy, dressed him and laid him on the floor. She refilled the sink, stripped off, and began to wash herself. She winced when she touched the livid bruises along her arms and shoulders, and she cried out loud when she washed between her legs. There was a cracked mirror above the sink, but Tia avoided looking at her reflection. She didn't need any mirror to tell her what her face looked like.

Back in the bedroom, Tia found a jar of strained carrots and wondered if she could sneak into the kitchen to warm it up for Luke. He'd only had some cold baby porridge in the morning, and that had been made with water from the jug that Jake had left for her the day before. She crept down the stairs. The living room door was open but Jake was asleep in the armchair. For one moment Tia thought about making a dash for the front door but for once, common sense pulled her up. She had no shoes, no coat, and Luke was in the same state. She had no money and nowhere to go. She buried her face in his hair, whispered 'sorry' and slipped into the kitchen.

Fifteen minutes later Tia quietly cleared away the evidence of Luke's meal, swallowed the last crumbs of a piece of bread that she'd found on a plate next to the sink, and emptied her cup of tea. There'd been no milk, of course, but it was better than stale water, and it had been hot. She wondered how Jake had managed to get this place, and how he had electricity. It didn't seem like some of the squats his mates had had in town when she was with him. Come to think of it, he'd opened the front door with a key the other night. There was no way he had a legal job to pay for all of this. What was he up to?

"Here you are. Hope you haven't pinched any of my food. You're gonna have to start earning now, you know, for you and the kid. Can't stay here for nothing. Don't look at me like that. I know we didn't get off to a good start this time, but I've been thinking…"

*That's dangerous!*

"What if I found you some work to do? No, I don't mean

whoring, although you can earn some extra with that if you want to. I mean something different."

"Like what?"

"I've got a couple of mates who are doing all right for themselves. Fair bit of cash in their pockets and plenty more coming in regular. This is their place but since I started working for them, they let me have it. Bones and Loco and a few of the others stay here sometimes, but they don't live here. If you're up for the work, you and the kid can stay. 'course, you'll be my woman – know what I mean? But I'll look after you this time."

"And what about the tart who's your woman now? Don't think I haven't heard what's been going on."

"Silly cow." Jake smirked. "Just something to pass the time. She's out of here if you say so. Not jealous, are you? I knew you'd come 'round in the end."

"Not so fast, Jake. You haven't told me what the 'work' is. What about Lulu? Will I be able to take him with me? And do I get anything for myself, or is staying here all it is?"

"Cheeky bitch! ALL? It's a bloody good place. Better than anything your mate, Binny, could have found you. And how did you expect to pay for anything then? Fine mess you'd have been in before long. Once you prove you can handle the job and that we can trust you, you can keep a share of the earnings for whatever you want, but don't go getting any ideas about trying to run off. The guys I work for don't stand for anyone pissing them about or ripping them off. They wouldn't think twice about gutting the sprog as well as you. 'til then, you get a bed, food and whatever you need for the kid – within reason. When we need you to go out, I'll get one of the girls to look after him."

Tia thought for a moment then nodded. She followed Jake into the living room, and he told her exactly how her time was to be spent.

***

When Kay woke she could hear birds calling to each other, and muffled strains of *Abide With Me* from the flat next door.

She lay in bed staring at the ceiling and thinking about the day to come. Tonight was the start of the evening classes Maisie and she had signed up for, and Kay's stomach was somersaulting. Not that she was worried about being able to cope with the lessons, but a little bit scared about being a single mum and also about leaving Adam, even for a few hours. Since he'd been born, she'd spent hardly any time away from him, but she knew that the course was a solid opportunity to move their lives forward, and it would do Adam good to mix with other people a little more.

She sighed and an image of her mum and dad floated across her mind. They'd have been delighted to help out with Adam, but she'd burned her bridges for sure. There was no way that she could go back after what she'd done. Even now, the thought of her dad's pain when he found the money missing made her face redden and her stomach twist into knots. What had made her do it? Desperation? Stubbornness? She knew she'd never have dreamed of doing something like that before she became involved with Jazz. But was it completely fair to blame him? He hadn't exactly forced her to do anything, and certainly not to take the money. She considered whether there was something bad in her that had just lain dormant until the circumstances were right for it to emerge. Her mum and dad had given her the world. They'd had rules, but on the whole she hadn't minded. At least her life had had structure and boundaries. Security. Not like Tia's.

Kay wondered what had become of her friend. Despite everything Tia had done, Kay still thought of her in that way. Was Tia a bad person? Was her stealing of the money from Kay any worse than what Kay herself had done? If Tia's story had been true, and Kay did question some of it, then her upbringing had been totally different from Kay's. Not knowing who, or what, her parents were; being abandoned into care; a series of not-so-successful fosterings; years of what sounded like an ideal placement; back into care, and then living in a squat with some really dodgy characters, must have completely screwed with her head. Was it possible for people to change after such experiences? Kay wasn't sure. She hoped, for Tia and Luke's sake, that it was and yet she couldn't envisage how Tia would be able to work herself out of the mess she was obviously in. And to expose Luke to probably the same kind of existence? Kay knew she could never do that to Adam.

She sat up, swung her legs onto the floor and padded into the corridor and across to Adam's room. He was still sleeping with his thumb in his mouth. Kay leant over his cot and gently stroked his hair.

"I promise you that if can't give you everything you need, and protect you from everything bad, then I'll swallow my pride and ask Gran and Grandpa for help. As soon as I can I'm going to start saving so that I can pay Grandpa back some day. It'll take a while, but I must try. Unless I'm desperate I can't go back to them empty-handed. Just know that you'll come first in everything that I do. It's another new start for us today and it's going to be fine."

## December 1st

Tia groaned. It seemed as though she'd only been asleep for an hour or two. She felt a tug at her hair and turned over. Luke was standing at the side of the bed staring at her.

"God, Lulu, you made me jump. Shhh! Don't make any noise. We don't want to wake up Uncle Jake, do we?"

Tia slid out of bed, picked up the little boy and carried him back into his own room. It was little more than a cupboard really, but big enough for a camp bed and small chest of drawers. Tia shivered and looked around for something to cover herself and Luke.

"Come on then. Under the blanket with Mum. Better? Do you know what today is? It's your birthday. You're one year old. What do think of that?"

Luke didn't make a sound. He just stared at Tia's face. He did it so often that Tia had begun to wonder if he was deaf, or if there was something else wrong with him. He hardly ever tried to form words or make any kind of noise at all.

"Look at the window, Lulu. Can you see what's out there?

Look, it's snowing. Brrr! Cold, isn't it. Mummy doesn't like the snow."

Luke turned his head and looked out of the window. So, he could hear, and he did understand some things, but he still didn't make a sound. Tia ran her hands along his spine. God, he was so thin. But then, she wasn't very big either. At least they had shelter and food now, even if it wasn't the most suitable. Tia thought about the past few months and how different they might have been if she hadn't become ensnared by Jake again. To be fair to him, he had taken care of them, after a fashion, although the price was high by any standards. She raised her arm towards the pale light filtering through the raggedy curtains and looked at the bruises. Some were livid blacks and blues, while others were fading and showed up yellow, or pale blue. Even though Jake was free from the drugs – a condition of his friends with the money – he still could shift his booze, and his temper had not improved in the least.

Tia shivered. The work that Jake had pushed her into was certainly easier than what he'd had her do before, but it carried far greater risks. She hated leaving Luke with any of the girls Jake brought to the house, but there was no other way.

"One day, Lulu, I'll get us out of here. We have to stay for a while but when the summer comes again, I'll look for a place of our own. We'll have to go far away, 'cos they'll never just let us go. You be a good boy and I promise to get us out somehow. I've got a present for you, but we'll wait until Uncle Jake's gone out. All right?"

\*\*\*

"Happy birthday, Adam!"

Adam clapped his hands together and gurgled along as Maisie and Kay sang to him. His eyes widened when he saw the lighted candle on his cake, and he stretched out for it. Holly was in Maisie's arms and was trying to sing as well.

"God, Kay. He's one! Just look at him – he's so lovely. That smile, and those eyes. He's going to be a real lady-killer. Aren't you, my lad?"

Kay laughed and looked at her son. Maisie was right. He was lovely, and she felt a surge of pride that she'd managed a whole year with him on her own. Adam had thrived. He was happy, healthy and well-advanced for his age. He was just about walking, and he could manage quite a few words. What the rest of the burbling that he constantly made meant, Kay could only guess!

"Holly's turn next. Only a few days to go, and then we need to think about Christmas."

Maisie groaned.

## December 14th

"Well, that's it, Maisie. Last class of the course. I can't believe how quickly the time's gone. It's been great, though, hasn't it?"

"Yeah! My head's buzzing with everything. Did you get told tonight about next year? You know, if you can go on? I did all right in the assessments. I think there were only about three or four who failed. Mostly because they messed about too much, and one hardly turned up at all."

"Same with us. Thank heavens I'm okay as well. Will we be in on the same days? I've got a free nursery place for Adam if I need it but if you're on different days, I could help out with Holly if you can't afford a place for her."

"Would you? That would be magic. Jeff's mum said she'd help as well, and I think we could afford one day at a push. Let's check on the notice board on our way out."

"Okay. If we get a wriggle on, we should just catch the nine o'clock bus. Do you fancy getting off a stop early and picking up some chips? We could get some for Jeff as well."

"Too right!"

The girls checked the notice board then hurried towards the bus station. They could see that the Crompton bus was waiting so they ran along the walkway as fast as they could. If they'd had time, they might have noticed the person sitting alone in the next shelter. There again, even if they had seen her, it's unlikely that they would have recognised her with her badly cut hair and the even worse dirty blonde colouring. She was also a lot thinner than when they'd known her, and she'd been tiny then.

But Tia recognised them. There was no mistaking Kay's loud laugh and Maisie's high-pitched voice. She shrank back against the shelter wall and lowered her head until the Crompton bus pulled out. When she looked up, she could see Kay and Maisie through the window, leaning towards each other and laughing. For one moment Tia wanted to run after the bus and shout for it to stop. Then she remembered Luke and pulled herself up short. Time enough to think about Crompton or further afield next year. For now, she had a job to do and she had to focus on that. There was no room for mistakes. One slip and she could end up in goal and Luke in care, or worse. Besides, Jake had told her his friends were pleased with what she'd done and that after Christmas she'd start getting some money of her own. Whether Jake would hand it over remained to be seen, but why would he bother telling her if he meant to keep it for himself?

A gentle cough drew Tia's attention and she moved into the shadowed part of the shelter. She sat down and put the rucksack she'd been carrying onto the floor next to her feet. A tall man sat down next to her. Tia didn't look at him. Her rucksack slid away and was replaced with an identical one. She still didn't look as the tall man quietly and quickly left the shelter and crossed the walkway to the road, where a dark-coloured car was waiting for him.

Tia took the next bus that came along and rode the full circuit back to the station. Even though she'd been on the bus for over an hour, she still looked around nervously before taking another bus back to the house.

## December 16th

"Look, Lulu. Mummy's got you a lovely new pushchair. Like it? See, it's got a cover and a hood, so you won't get wet. Look at the teddies on this blanket, and there's a lovely soft pillow as well, so you can sleep whenever you want. Aren't you a lucky boy?"

Lucky mummy, too! Never seen so many people in the precinct and the arcade. God, people are so careless with things. Maybe if they didn't have it so easy, they'd look after their stuff more. It'll be much easier to take Lulu out now. That's if Jake loosens the reins a bit. Once I start getting my own money after Christmas, I'll have to figure out some way of getting free of him again. Got to be careful, though. Especially after the vodka. I didn't think it would be so hard to stay off it. S'pose it was easier when I was with Kay, and with Lulu being so small, and having almost no money. But with Jake having it around most of the time – well.

"Come on, Lulu. Stop whining now. I know your arm hurts, but it'll be better tomorrow, I promise. Mummy didn't mean it. It was an accident. Here, have some sugar on your dummy. Nice?"

***

Adam was sleeping on the settee and Kay curled up next to him and read through the information about the following year's hairdressing course. She'd really enjoyed the foundation stage and looked forward to moving on to more advanced work. She agreed with Maisie that by the half term break they should be competent enough to try to find some work in the flats where Kay lived and in the small street where Maisie lived. Kay wondered how Adam would enjoy the nursery. She didn't have any fears about him, even though it would be for three days a week. He was a happy and sociable lad. Maisie would be in college on the same days, so her mother-in-law had agreed to look after Holly for two days and she was paying for one at the nursery. Kay was glad, as it meant that they'd still be able to meet up for lunch breaks and travel together. They'd also be able to meet up on their days off.

The letterbox rattled and Kay went into the hallway. No Christmas cards, but it was a faint hope anyway. Just some more adverts for toys and festive food. She was so grateful to

Maisie and her husband for inviting Adam and her to their place for Christmas day. It would have been so lonely on their own. Kay thought back to the previous Christmas and sighed. Despite the constant fear of being found out, it had been a magical time with Tia and Luke. She wondered how they'd be spending the day this year.

# 1993

## February 13th

"Wake up, sleepyhead. Mummy's got work to do today."

Kay lifted Adam from his cot and wrapped a blanket around him. She carried him into the living room and sat him in his highchair. He rubbed his eyes and yawned. Kay laughed at him and ruffled his hair. It was nine o'clock and she'd agreed that Maisie would call in around ten. They were going to make plans about the work they were hoping to do. Maisie had already lined up a few clients for manicures and nail-painting and she said that one or two were interested in having their hair done as well. Kay wasn't sure if she felt confident enough to do any cutting just yet, but she was quite happy with washing and styling. She knew she needed a lot more practice with blow drying but she guessed that most of the women in the flats would prefer her to use curlers, and she was fine with that. It was exciting to plan for the future, and she was so pleased Maisie had become her friend. They supported each other with their coursework and with the babies, and it was good to have someone to share Adam's milestones with. Kay was beginning to feel proud of what she'd achieved since Adam was born, but there was always the underlying guilt about her family. She thought about calling them but convinced herself it would be better to wait a little longer. She switched on the radio just as Whitney Houston began to sing *I Will Always Love You*, and Kal's face formed on the windowpane. She shook her head and blinked. Where had that come from?

Ruth gazed out of the window as she waited for Janet to pick up the phone. Perhaps she was working. Ruth could never keep up with Janet's schedule, no matter how hard she tried. Even if she wrote it down it could change suddenly if there was an emergency at the hospital, or the shifts were altered. She smiled. Janet had always been the one with more energy!

"Hello? Jan? Good. I'm glad I've caught you. My appointment with the specialist has come through and I wondered if you'd be able to come with me?"

"Hi, Ruth. As long as it doesn't clash with one of my hospital shifts, it should be fine. A week Thursday? That's the 25th? Eleven thirty, yes, that's fine. I'll pick you up about ten forty-five. Should give us plenty of time. Are you feeling all right?"

"Not too bad. The pills seem to be working. No more dizzy spells. It'll be good to have things checked out, though, to make sure it's nothing more serious than high blood pressure. It scared me the last time I had a funny turn."

"I'm sure it'll be fine. Let's see what the consultant has to say. I don't think I know anyone in that hospital. Shame you couldn't have been referred to my place. How is Paul by the way? Has he got over that chest infection yet?"

"Much better, thanks. I told him he shouldn't have gone back to work so soon, but you know what he's like! At least he's been coming home a bit earlier the past week."

"Good. I probably won't be able to get over to see you, but I'll speak to you before the 25th."

"Lovely. See you soon. Bye."

Thank God the snow's gone. Hanging about in bus shelters and train stations and the like is no fun. I thought I was going to freeze to death last night. Wonder what made them so late picking up. I'm sure there was someone watching me. Still, better to be nicked with the money than the other stuff. Jake was in a right mood when I got back. Don't know what he thinks I'm going to do. He knows damn well I wouldn't leave Luke behind. I'm not happy about the girls he brings here, though. None of them look as if they know anything about kids. They're more like kids themselves. He's probably shagging them as well, when I'm out. That one last night looked so sheepish when I came in and I could tell that Luke hadn't been fed or washed. Jake said she's new to the game. Huh!

Fancy his mates running a couple of houses as well as the drugs. Seventeen girls must bring in a fair bit of cash. Jake seems to have got in with a right crowd since he left the squat. Earns a fair bit though and apart from the drink, he's cleaned up, too. Pity he doesn't spend a bit more on the heating!

I'd better get up, I suppose. Luke's awfully quiet, but then he always is. It's funny that he doesn't try to talk. I hope there's nothing wrong with him. I've been lucky that he hasn't had much more than a couple of colds since he was born. I feel bad about his jabs and stuff but I can't risk it. Not yet. Maybe if we can get away later in the year and I can find somewhere for us to live, then I can put things right. There's not much to save out of the money I get paid for the drop offs though, especially since Jake makes me pay for my booze. I know there's loads of cash in the rucksack every week, but it's more than my life's worth to touch that, even if I could open the padlock. That reminds me. I need to find somewhere safe to stash the bit of savings I do have. I don't think Jake would take it, unless he got wind of my plans to leave, but I don't trust any of those girls.

## July 16th

Kay and Maisie strolled through the town centre towards the bus station. It was four o'clock and still as hot as it had been at twelve. Kay stopped to give Adam a drink while Maisie went into the newspaper shop. Across the road, Tia was coming out of a small grocery store carrying a bag that clinked every time she moved. She stopped to wedge her purse between the bottles, then she glanced up. She spotted Kay right away and almost called out to her but drew back into the doorway of the shop. She was amazed at how much Adam had grown. Luke was only about half his size! Kay looked good. She'd obviously had her hair cut professionally and she was wearing smart blue trousers and a white blouse. All right for some! Tia looked down at the faded shorts she was wearing and pouted.

Kay frowned as she caught sight of the familiar-looking figure in a shop doorway. She shaded her eyes with her hand, but she still couldn't see clearly. By the time she'd found her sunglasses, the woman had gone.

"Ready?" Maisie tapped Kay on the shoulder.

"What? Oh yes. Sorry, I was miles away. I just saw someone that reminded me of Tia. Funny thing is, I haven't thought about her for ages. I've been so busy with the course and everything and looking after Adam and the flat."

"Best to forget her altogether, if you can. I know you felt sorry for her, but she wasn't much of a friend, was she?"

"You're right. It's just every now and then something brings her to mind. I suppose I'm more concerned about Luke. I'm not convinced that she'd have been able to cope with him on her own. There again, knowing Tia, she'll probably have found someone else to latch onto."

"For sure. Now, what are we going to do to celebrate the end of term and being such ace students? Too hot for fish and chips. What about one of those fancy ice creams in that new place near the station? They put a leaflet through the door the other day. Did you get one?"

"Yes. Looks like a great place. Have you got time, though?"

"I'm fine. Jeff's mum said she'd take Holly out for the day and she'd be back about six. Come on. We can have a chat about next term. I'm not sure if we'll have the same days again but I hope so. I picked up the pack with all the details about options. Did you get yours?"

"God, Maisie, you're relentless. We've only just finished this term!" Kay laughed loudly and prodded Maisie in the arm.

"Someone's got to keep us on the straight and narrow."

Maisie laughed as well.

Tia was following a short distance behind them and heard their laughter. She scowled. She'd never liked Maisie but now she hated her. It should be her walking along with Kay, laughing and joking, not bloody Maisie. When they went into the ice cream parlour, Tia stopped across the road. She could see where they were sitting, and they were still laughing. She wanted to join them so badly but didn't want to risk another rejection from Kay. Besides, there was still the small matter of the money to overcome. She shifted her bag to her other hand and the bottles clinked together. Maybe the ice cream could wait.

Kay and Maisie sat in the garden and Adam slept on a rug next to their chairs. The girls chatted about the future and made plans for the private work they hoped to do. Kay stretched and yawned. It was a beautiful day and as she looked at Maisie's washing gently swaying on the line, and the flower borders bursting with colour, she sighed.

"It's really lovely here. You're lucky to have a garden like this. How were you and Jeff given a house, not a flat?"

"It was his gran's. When he left school, he got a place on the engineering course at the college in Alderbridge, but it would have taken him almost an hour and half each way on the bus, so he moved in with her. The first course was two years, then he got an apprenticeship with day release, so he stayed here. He used to come home at weekends. He was friends with my brother, so I'd known him most of my life but when I was sixteen, we just kind of connected. We were engaged when I was eighteen and planned to get married when he finished his apprenticeship but when I found out I was expecting Holly, we brought everything forward and I moved in here as well. Jeff's gran had already told the council that he was living here and let them know about me and the baby as well. She asked if they could transfer the tenancy to Jeff, and they agreed. When Holly was born Jeff's mum asked his gran to go and live with her."

"Wow. There was never anyone else?"

"No, nothing serious. Jeff was the same. It just worked for us. Still is! What about you?"

"Same really, except for the ending. I knew Adam's dad for quite a long time, but we didn't do anything about it until … well … you know."

"Oh. No chance of getting back together?"

"No. Can't ever see that happening. Right now, I'm happy with just Adam and me on our own. Maybe when he's a bit older I'll think about dating again, but where am I going to meet someone suitable? Got any single blokes in the cupboard?"

"You never know, there could be someone around the corner just waiting for a ready-made family like yours."

Kay pointed at the sky. "There go those pigs again!"

## September 5th

Kay stretched out in her bed and glanced at the clock. Lovely Sunday! There was no sound from Adam's room, so she knew that he was still asleep. It was almost impossible for him to be awake without chattering or laughing. She felt very lucky that he was such a happy child. Everyone commented on his beautiful smile and his little dimpled cheeks. He'd adapted so well to the college nursery and had developed his speech and other skills very quickly. Kay knew the next year was going to be hard for her, but she was looking forward to it. The second year of the course offered lots of opportunities to specialise and now that she was comfortable with Adam's arrangements and he was a little easier to manage, she was sure she'd be able to cope. She was glad that Maisie's course was running on the same days again. It made the journeys more bearable, especially in the winter, and it was good to have someone around to talk things over.

It hadn't been a brilliant summer, weather wise, but Maisie and Kay had taken some day trips and had continued to build on their budding business on the estate. Kay's confidence had grown and so had her client base. Sometimes they came to her place, sometimes she went to theirs. Occasionally, Maisie had someone who wanted the full works, so Kay went to her house and they worked together. They were careful not to charge too much and it seemed to be paying off. Kay worried a little about not declaring the money to the tax and the benefit offices but promised herself that she'd stop when she found a job in a salon. She had to admit that the extra money was useful, and she'd been able to keep the promise she'd made about saving to pay back her father. It would take some time but the box where she hid the money was slowly filling up. She tried to picture what it would be like to see her mum and dad again. To show them their grandson. To put a pile of banknotes on the table. But she worried that they might turn her away, that it was too late. Adam would probably be about five before she'd saved enough, and she would have robbed her parents of all those years with him. She started to cry but then shook herself. She had made her decisions and she wanted to stick by them. No more wallowing in self-pity. She had a good life and so did Adam, despite not having a dad around. When the time came, if her parents didn't want to know her, then so be it.

***

Another summer nearly over. Still here. Still working for Jake's mates. Still dreaming about a place of my own. It's like wading through a sewer. Shit. All shit! What's the matter with me? When I was with Kay I thought I could make a go of things. It's all her fault, really. If she'd let me move with her, we'd be all right. Lulu would be talking and not be so bloody skinny and miserable, and I'd probably have a proper job in a shop or something. That Maisie's got a lot to answer for, as well. I bet it was her that talked Kay into throwing me out. Always looking down her nose at me. She's nothing special, is she? An hour with some of Jake's old mates might sort her out. Soon wipe the smile off her face. If he's in a good mood one of these days, he might do me a favour and arrange a little party for her. Not Kay, though.

I wonder what she's doing now. She has no idea how many times I've seen her since that time in town. Seen her; followed her; watched her. I know where she lives, and that Maisie as well. Very nice, thank you very much. Would have been plenty big enough for me and Lulu as well. She's not likely to welcome me back now that she's got herself all cosy.

"You gettin' up today, you lazy cow? That kid's whining for food or something and he stinks. Too much bloody booze again last night. You know you can't take it. Maybe you havin' your own money's not such a good idea if you're gonna spend it all on vodka."

Bloody Jake. Always moaning about something. Lulu's fine. He never eats much anyway. My head's thumping. I'm sure Jake put something in my drink last night. Better get moving before he comes back. At least he leaves my face alone now. Can't stay unnoticed around town with a face all colours of the rainbow. I just hope he doesn't think one of the other girls can do the drop offs. I'll have to make sure I'm dead sober on those days. Good job there's a set plan for the drops even if the place and time changes. Every eight days. Let's see, the last one was Friday night, so the next will be Saturday. Fine. I'll lay off on Friday night and Saturday 'til I get back. And anyway, it's my money, I can spend it however I want. If he wasn't so mean with his stash of booze I wouldn't have to buy my own and I could be saving for a place for me and Lulu.

"What's the matter, Lulu? Stop whingeing, will you. Mummy's got a headache. Not that you care. Come here. Bloody hell, Uncle Jake's right – you do stink! Upstairs, QUICK. You need a good scrub. Why can't you learn to use the toilet? You must be old enough now. You can't go on wearing nappies forever, you know. Stop wriggling. I know the water's cold but that's not my fault. Look, Mummy's got some cream for your bum. All right, no need to cry. It'll get better soon. Yes, and your leg as well. See, the nasty old bruise has nearly gone. Want some breakfast? Toast?"

## December 1st

"Happy birthday, Adam!" Kay lifted Adam out of his bed and kissed him. He laughed at her and wriggled to be put on the floor. "Come on, mister. No nonsense this morning. We have to get ready for playschool. You like that, don't you? You're such a good boy. We'll have a party on Saturday for you. Holly's coming and Sam and Tom from nursery. Come and see your present from Mummy."

She watched as Adam ripped the paper and laughed when she saw the expression on his face. She'd managed to find a wooden fire engine and he chuckled as he pushed it along the floor. He was fascinated with the sirens of the big, red trucks that sometimes passed them on the streets. She was so happy that one of the mums on her course mentioned she was clearing out lots of her son's toys, as he'd outgrown them, and that one of them was the fire engine.

Kay found it hard to believe that her 'baby' was now two years old. As usual, whenever she thought of his birthday, she thought of Tia and Luke, and she was sad about the way things had turned out. Maybe if Tia had tried to get some help before Luke had been born, or even thrown herself on the mercy of Social Services, it might have been better all round. She wondered if Tia had been able to shake herself and make a decent life for her and Luke, but there was still that nagging doubt; that niggling feeling all had not gone well for Tia.

She huffed. No good going down that road. What was done was done. She had to stay strong for Adam's sake, and things were going well. She was loving the second part of her college course and was excelling at it. It was a bit of a struggle trying to manage the three days of college but having Adam's place in the nursery was a great help. Just another two terms and she'd be able to look for a proper job and she could continue her training in a salon. Some of the local salons worked with the college and offered not only placement opportunities but also the prospect of employment after the course. Maisie wasn't sure what she wanted to do yet. She was still thinking about setting up her own little business, but Kay didn't think that would be secure enough for her. Maybe if she didn't find a job in a salon, she might consider it. At least it was another option and Maisie had worked hard at gathering a regular group of customers.

Kay checked the flat, strapped Adam in his pushchair, pulled his mittens over his chubby hands, and opened the front door. She was surprised to find an envelope on the mat. The post usually arrived much later. It was rather dirty, and she could barely make out what was written on the front. Adam. Must be a card from someone in the block. She pushed it into her bag.

It was lunchtime before Kay remembered the card and she pulled the grubby envelope from her bag.

"What's that?" Maisie leaned over and pointed to the card.

"Not sure. It's addressed to Adam, so I guess it's a birthday card, but I don't know who sent it. It didn't come with the post, so someone must have pushed it through the letterbox after I came home last night. I suppose I could have walked over it, but I don't think so."

Kay ripped open the envelope and slid out the card. She thought that it wasn't particularly appropriate for a two-year-old, with its picture of a lake and fishing boats, and she wondered again who could have sent it. When she flipped it open, the blood drained from her face, her mouth went dry and she felt a cold shiver run the length of her spine. Tiny beads of sweat prickled her forehead and her hands started to shake.

"Blimey Kay, whatever's the matter?" Maisie put her hand on Kay's shoulder. "You look like you've seen a ghost."

"It might well be one. Look." Kay passed the card to Maisie and she gasped.

"Oh no, not her again. I thought she'd gone for good."

Kay shook her head slowly. The card was inscribed, '*To Twinnie, love Tia and Lulu.*' There was nothing else. No note, no contact details. But one thing was clear. Tia had found out where they lived, and she had been outside their door the night before.

"What am I going to do, Maisie? I can't go through that again. Not after I've worked so hard. But I know if I see her, and especially Luke, and if they're in a bad way, I'll feel guilty if I don't help."

"Listen Kay. You did her a massive favour when she came to you before. You didn't have to. You didn't even know her.

She dumped herself and the baby on you and put everything you had at risk. She didn't have much to lose if you ask me. Seems as though it might have been better all-round if the little boy had been taken into care. From what you've told me, and what I saw of her, she wasn't going to win any mother-of-the-year awards, was she?"

"I know," Kay shook her head, "but she'd had such a rough time and the poor baby hadn't done anyone any harm."

"Okay, that's enough. Tell me to mind my own business if you want, but you need to toughen up about her. What's more important, you and Adam, or bailing out some so-called friend who did nothing but take from you? Come on, Kay. Don't risk everything you've worked for."

"You're right, but what if she comes to my flat again? I don't want to feel like a prisoner in there, but she can be so persuasive that I know if I let her in and she spins me a sob story …"

"Then don't let in her look, I'll ask Jeff if he can fit you one of those spy-hole things in your front door. You know, where you can see who's outside, but they don't know you're there? You just need to check before you open the door. If it's her, or you think it is, you don't open it. Even if she guesses, or knows, that you're inside, she won't be able to talk to you directly, so she can't con you again. Perhaps she'll finally get the message that you don't want anything to do with her anymore. What do you think?"

"That would be a help, although I'll still feel bad about it. There's still a risk she could catch me on my way in or out."

"Then you'll have to deal with her. Tell her straight. Try not to even look at the boy. If you seriously think he's in danger in any way, then you'll have to report her, but if you don't know where she's living, it'll make it hard for the Social to catch up with her. Come on, Kay, don't let her spoil things now. We've got plans, remember?"

Kay smiled at her friend and pushed the card back into her bag, but she was afraid that she'd never be free from Tia and her problems.

Luke sat on the floor in the living room. He was shivering and there was a livid weal on his arm. His hair was filthy and stuck together in clumps. He was too tired to cry anymore and desperately wanted a drink. He pulled himself up against a chair and tottered into the kitchen, but there was nothing within reach for him to eat or drink. He tried to pull a chair over to the sink, but it was too heavy. One of the cupboard doors wasn't fastened and he managed to open it fully. He pulled out a bottle that had no top on it and tried to lift it to his mouth. There wasn't much liquid inside and Luke eventually manoeuvred it into position. He took several big gulps before the taste hit him and he dropped the bottle to the floor, where the remains of the vodka spilled onto the mat. He crawled back into the living room, threw up on the carpet, and began to cry again. He had no idea it was his second birthday.

"What the hell have you been doing, Lulu? Look at the state on you. And what about the carpet? Uncle Jake'll be hopping mad, you know. Come on, lie on the sofa for a minute and I'll get a towel."

Tia lifted the little boy onto the settee and went into the kitchen. When she saw the empty bottle on the floor she cursed and quickly pushed it into the rubbish sack next to the back door.

"Stupid kid. Now I'll have to put my bottle in there, won't I? And it's the last one." She shook Luke until he opened his eyes. "What's the matter with you, eh? Why can't you leave things alone? It's only eleven o'clock. You can't be that thirsty. You had plenty of milk last night, didn't you?" In truth, Tia couldn't remember what her son had drunk, or eaten, or when.

Luke stared at her. His brown eyes looked huge in his little, pinched face. He moaned and threw up again. Tia grabbed him and ran into the kitchen. She turned on the cold water tap and pushed his head under the flow. He struggled and kicked out, but she held him tightly. When he went limp, she turned off the tap, rubbed him roughly with a towel, and put him on the floor. Then she used the same towel to scrub at the vomit on the settee and the carpet in the living room, before mopping up the last of the spilt vodka in the kitchen. She threw the towel into the garbage sack, then made herself a cup of coffee. Luke still had not moved so she nudged him with her foot, and he coughed. Tia sighed, lifted him onto a chair and put a beaker of milk in front of him.

"There. Get that down you. I'll do some toast in a minute." She looked at Luke's arm and frowned. Had that been Jake's handiwork, or hers? Didn't look too bad. Probably be gone in a day or two. For the first time that morning she noticed how much the little boy was shivering and how cold his whole body felt. She grumbled under her breath, went upstairs and came back with an old jumper of Jake's.

"Let's get this on you, Lulu. See. Bit warmer now? You need some socks, as well, don't you? All right, I'll get them after I've had some toast. You want some? No? Well, drink your milk then you can go back to bed. That'll warm you up, won't it?"

This morning, and despite risking a visit to Kay's flat the night before to leave a card for Adam, Tia had forgotten that it was also her own son's second birthday.

## December 25th

Kay slammed the flat door, pressed the button for the lift and checked that she had the bag of gifts she'd packed the night before. It was to be the second Christmas she and Adam had spent at Maisie's, and Kay felt happy she had people to share the holiday with. She'd agonised over whether to ring her mum but had decided against it. That was for another time. For now, she knew she had to keep working towards a better life, a better future for herself and her son.

"Hi Kay. Hello Adam. Merry Christmas! Come in out of the cold." Maisie took Kay's coat and helped her to unwrap Adam from his layers of coat, leggings, scarf, hat and gloves. "Good grief! He's done up like pass-the-parcel."

"Well, it's cold out there." Kay laughed and Adam joined in as well. "Something smells good. Turkey cooking already?"

"Yes. Jeff's mum and grandma did all the vegetables and things last night, and then his mum put the meat in early this morning. She's been ever so kind. I was only going to get a big chicken, like last year, but she said if we paid for the veg, she'd get the turkey."

"Lucky you. Thanks again for asking us. I don't think I'd have done much on my own. Adam's not really old enough to understand just yet, although he loves the tree and the decorations."

"You're welcome. Come on, I'm sure Holly wants to show Adam her presents!"

\*\*\*

"Top up, Jan?" Paul waggled a wine bottle and Janet jumped.

"Sorry, miles away. Yes, please. This is really good. How's Ruth getting on? She banished me from the kitchen half an hour ago!"

Paul laughed. "Me too! Apparently, I was getting in the way. I wanted to ask you, is it all right for her to have a drink? You know, with the pills she's taking?"

"She'll be fine, Paul. A couple of glasses won't hurt. It's not as if she drinks much the rest of the time. Her blood pressure's under control and she's had no more funny turns, so relax. And thanks for having me to stay again this year. It's always so cosy here. Good thing I didn't have to work, although I don't mind the wards at Christmas, especially the children's."

"Don't know how you do it, Jan. I know Ruth's glad to have me here. Probably gets fed up with just my company! Oh, I almost forgot."

Paul crossed the room and bent down to flick a switch on the wall. A soft blue light came on and Janet heard the haunting sound of the *Winter Lullaby*.

"That's perfect on a day like today. I think we might have snow later. It's funny how ..." Janet faltered and was conscious that her cheeks were reddening. "Funny how Jack Frost seems almost alive when the lights flicker, and the snow is swirling."

Paul smiled. "It's all right, you know. We do still talk about her, just not as much as we used to. And yes, it is funny that Kay was scared of the globe, although who knows what goes through a child's mind! I know we decided not to chase after her, and not to keep torturing ourselves about where she might be or what she's doing, but she's still our daughter. When she's ready, she'll come back, and we'll welcome her. That's the only thing I wish, that she actually knew that. I've seen her in town a few times."

"What?" Janet almost spilled her wine. "What do you mean? Spoken to her? Does Ruth know?"

"No, and please don't tell her. I haven't met with her, but I've seen her and the baby – well, little boy now, a few times over the past two years. She didn't know I was watching, and it was quite by accident. Hardest thing I've ever done – not chasing after her."

"How did she look? And what about the little one?"

"Fine. She was with another girl and her child. They all seemed happy, especially the boy. Chubby little thing. Big smile."

Janet could see how hard it was for Paul, so she tried to change the subject, but he interrupted her. "I think I know who the father is now. I guess that Ruth told you about those twins that Kay used to hang around with? Well, if I was a betting man, I'd lay my money on one of them."

Ruth opened the living room door. "Come on you two. Time to eat."


As Janet was drifting off to sleep that night, she thought about her conversation with Paul. It was ironic that it had been him who'd managed to catch a glimpse of Kay as he was rarely in the town centre. She sighed. Despite her work at the hospital, the charity shop and the 'soup kitchen', she still felt there was something missing from her life. She sometimes regretted turning down a proposal of marriage when she was in her early twenties, but she had wanted more than being tied down to a home and children. Then. Now she wasn't so sure, but it was too late. Being involved with Kay's child might have helped, but even that had been snatched away.

\*\*\*

I can't believe those bastards want me to do a drop off tonight. There'll be no buses and a taxi's so damn obvious. It'll take me ages and that rucksack's friggin' heavy. I don't see why they can't wait a day or two. Jake's not exactly sympathetic, either. And if he's going off to have a skinfull with his mates, what am I supposed to do about Lulu? I'll have to lock him in his room before I go. He's getting too used to roaming about the house. Jake made it quite clear there'll be no girls free today or tonight. Too busy partying. I don't get to have a Christmas, I suppose. Oh no, Tia doesn't count for anything. Just the lackey; the mule. Serve him right if I did a bunk with the money. I could easily get something to break the padlock. Come to think of it, if I wait until he's gone, I could grab Lulu and make a run for it. Trouble is, I probably wouldn't get far, especially with Lu in tow. Too easy to spot, and I don't know who any of 'them' are. God, I'm getting sick of all this, but I can't see a way out right now. I've got to get my act together next year.

Nothing much in the fridge, so I guess there's no Christmas dinner for anyone. Lulu wouldn't eat it anyway. Kid seems to pick at everything I give him. I can't even have a drink if I have to go out later. Jake would knock seven bells out of me if I messed things up. No, can't risk it. I'll have something when I get back. I'm not messing about with a detour tonight. Straight home. I should only be a couple of hours and Lulu'll be asleep, most likely. I'm sure I got him a present, but I can't remember where I hid it. Never mind, he wouldn't know if it was Christmas or not. Same with his birthday. I can't believe I forgot it but what with keeping Jake happy and working for his mates, well, things are bound to slip my mind. I'll make up for it next year.

I need to check the time and place for tonight, too. I always seem to get it wrong in my head. Jake told me not to write anything down but after I messed up that time, and after the beating he gave me, I knew I couldn't rely on my memory. He'd kill me if he knew what I'd done, but who's going to suspect a bunch of drawings on a kid's bedroom wall.

"Come on, Lulu. Let's go upstairs and we'll have a look at your nice pictures, eh? You like Mummy's drawings, don't you? Up we go!"

Bloody hell, he's so bony. Got to get him eating a bit more.

"Look, Lu. See the big, red bus? What number is it? It's number nine, isn't? And what about the train? What platform is it on? Number seven. What else can we see? A bridge, over a river with five swans? A big shop with three cars outside? And what's this? A park with eight swings. And what's on the last one? It's a library. That's a place with lots of books. I'll take you there one day. Can you count the books in the picture? Four!"

Okay. It was the precinct last time, so it's the park tonight at eight o'clock. Damn. Pity it wasn't one of the earlier ones. It's probably the first time I've pulled the wool over Jake's eyes. I'll have to be careful, though. If he got wind of my code, he'd make me pay for it as well as burning the pictures, and I'll never remember the order and times. I'll have to think of a backup, just in case.

"Right, now let's put some socks on you and then you can get into bed for a while. Okay?"

He's going to shock me one day and say something back. Trouble is, there's no one to ask about when he should be talking and all the other things. Thank goodness he's out of nappies now, although it would be better if he used the toilet all the time, and not the corner of his room.

"Tia! Tia, where are you? Come on you silly bitch, stop messing about." Jake ran up the stairs and banged open the bedroom door. Tia was sitting on the edge of the bed just staring out of the window. "Right. It's half past six. I'm going soon and I most likely won't be back 'til tomorrow. You sure you know where you're going tonight? Don't screw this one up or we'll all be out on the streets. Big pack tonight. I don't like going out before you but any funny business and you and the kid'll suffer. Get me? The rucksack's ready in the cupboard under the stairs. Make sure you leave early enough. It's icy out there so it might take you longer to walk. They might chance driving right up to the park gates, seeing as it's Christmas, but whatever happens, don't get in the car with them if they offer you a lift. Understand?"

Tia looked up and frowned. Jake was concerned for her? Well, there's a novelty. "What do you mean? Why would they offer me a lift? If they're going to do that, they might as well pick up the money from here in the first place."

"Don't be stupid. They wouldn't be giving you a lift home. Get it?"

"Oh. Right. But what if they don't give me a choice?"

"Then you take your chances. Keep your mouth shut and get away as soon as you can. They probably won't risk it – we don't have anyone else to do the carrying, but they're unpredictable bastards. What're you doing about the kid? You can't take him with you."

"I know. I'll lock him in his room. Jake?"

"Yeah?"

"Happy Christmas."

Jake huffed and slammed the door behind him. Tia shivered. She wondered if Jake had put money in the meter for the heating. The trouble was that it ran out quickly and they were often left in the dark and cold, and with no hot water. Tia checked her bag and coat pockets for pound coins. Then she looked through Jake's things and continued the search downstairs. Altogether she had fifteen coins. She put five in the meter and left the rest on the kitchen table.

Tia found Luke on his bed, looking at some old magazines.

"There now. You be a good boy and I'll be back soon. I'll leave the light on for you and there's some water on your

154

table. If there's anywhere open, I'll get some chips. You'd like that, wouldn't you?"

Luke nodded slowly. He looked at the old electric heater next to the door.

"I know it's cold, but I can't put it on if I'm not here. Get into bed and you'll be warmer."

Almost an hour later, Tia slid through the park gates to the first bench on the path. It was bitterly cold, and she started to shiver as soon as she sat down. The tips of her fingers were burning and her feet felt as though they were wrapped in ice cream. The rucksack was heavier than usual, and the paths had been icy. She'd stopped once or twice to catch her breath and had looked into some of the houses where the curtains were open. Her eyes had begun to prickle as she thought back to two Christmases earlier. She'd been so full of hope then, and determination to carve out a life for Luke and herself, far away from the existence she'd had before he was born. And look at them now. Granted it was a lot better than the time in the squat, but not exactly what she had imagined. If only she could have stayed with Kay.

She felt a hand on her knee and jumped.

"S'okay. Only me. Swap?"

For the first time, Tia looked at the man who was exchanging the rucksacks. He wasn't bad looking but something about the way he carried himself, something about the curve of his mouth, made Tia very afraid. She looked away quickly, grabbed the rucksack and stood up.

"Not so fast." Tia froze. "Wait 'til I've left. Unless you want to have a bit of fun, of course?"

Tia shook her head and sat down quickly. The man put his hand back on her leg and leaned towards her, but just as he was about to kiss her, a car turned in the road and its headlights illuminated the bench. The man swore and ran for the gate. Tia held her breath, waited a moment, then left the park. She kept her head down and walked as fast as she could. The first flakes of snow started to fall, and the familiar feeling of dread washed over her. She picked up her pace and began to sing to try to lift her spirits. She found herself humming a tune that she couldn't quite place. The snow globe tune! She stopped suddenly and wrapped her arms around herself. A searing pain hit her again and again and she had to hold on to a lamppost. *Oh Kay. Where are you now? Why can't you help me, like before?*

Tia wiped away the tears running down her cheeks and decided to take a short detour through the lanes into the road that ran along the back of the house, as she hoped that one of the little shops or take-aways might be open. She was in luck. The new curry house that had only set up business a few weeks earlier had its lights blazing. She smiled. She didn't think they'd have many customers tonight, but there again, who knew how many others were on their own this Christmas. She pushed open the door and dug into her pockets for her last ten-pound note. Good thing she'd already bought the vodka.


"Hey, Lulu. Guess what I've got. Chips."

Tia unlocked Luke's door and grimaced. He was standing in front of the cold heater, half naked. His trousers, pants and socks were on the floor and his legs were streaked with diarrhoea, as was the rug next to his bed. Tia was just about to scream and slap him when he looked up at her and her words caught in her throat.

"Oh Lulu. Poor little bugger. Just look at you. Come on. A quick wash in the bathroom then we can have something to eat. I'll clean you up properly later, and your room as well. You can sleep in with Mummy tonight. Uncle Jake's away."

Luke sat in front of the fire in the living room, wrapped in a towel. Tia had put more money in the meter and had switched on the water heater, as well as the fire in her bedroom. She knew that the old heaters weren't particularly safe, but it was so cold that it was worth the risk for a few hours. She sat down next to Luke and helped him to eat some chips and she broke up a small portion of chicken. He was wary at first. It wasn't what he was used to, but after a few tentative bites, he began to eat steadily.

"Better? Want some water? No? Have some milk later. If you're a good boy, I'll put it in your bottle for you. Yes?"

Tia thought about opening the vodka that she'd hidden under her bed but decided to wait just a little longer. She was beginning to feel warmer and the fear of the encounter in the park had subsided. She was curious about the contents of the rucksack she'd brought back, but knew better than to question Jake about it, or to tamper with the lock. Drugs. That's all she knew; all she wanted to know, really. She was so thankful that they held no real attraction for her. Dealing with the booze was hard enough.

"Right, little man. Mummy's got a treat for you. Come on."

She sat Luke on her bed in front of the fire and went into the bathroom. The wall heater wasn't very effective but at least it took the chill off the room. She put the plug in the bath and turned on the hot water tap. There were no baths salts or anything to put in the water, so she ran downstairs and filled a cup with washing-up liquid.

"Come on Lulu. See the bubbles? Want to play with them?"

Luke's eyes opened wide and he stretched out his hands.

"Bub …"

Tia's jaw dropped. So he could talk – after a fashion.

"That's right, bubbles. Don't be afraid. It's nice and warm for you. Sit down. You won't fall, I'll hold you. Look, Mummy'll come in, too. Better?"

Tia watched while Luke prodded the bubbles with his little fingers. He looked happy and for the first time in a long while, he smiled. Tia's stomach contracted so sharply that she thought she might be sick. She washed Luke's hair very gently and rinsed it off with cold water, which made him shout. Then she washed his skinny, little body and bit her lip when she felt the sharpness of his shoulder blades. She was a crap mother; she just knew it, but next year it was going to be different.

When they were both dry and in clean clothes, Tia put Luke in her bed and went downstairs to warm some milk for

157

him. She'd taken his bottle away some weeks ago after Jake had made some crass comment, but tonight she filled it and carried it back upstairs. Luke could hardly keep his eyes open, but he held out his hands for the bottle and snuggled down. Tia routed through a bag on the floor until she found a few disposable nappies.

"Better safe than sorry, eh Lulu? Just for tonight. Keep you clean and the bed dry. Now, off to sleep. I won't be long."

She took the bottle of vodka from under the bed and went downstairs. An hour later, the bottle was unopened and Tia sat on the settee with tears streaming down her face.

*Stupid, stupid, bitch. After all I promised him. After all I promised myself, and Kay. And look at me. Drugs mule living with a loser. What a mess. No wonder she pretends to be out whenever I go there.*

# 1994

## March 18th

I can't believe it's drop night again. All I seem to do is lurch from one week to the next. My head's banging as well. All that talk about staying sober didn't work, did it? If Jake didn't like the stuff so much, maybe I could keep off it a bit more, but when he's pouring it down his neck … He was in a right mood last night. It's no good asking him direct questions, though. He rolls up like a hedgehog.

I wonder which of the girls will be coming over for Lu. It's the library today, at four, so she should be here soon. I hope it's not that Shelley. Narky cow. Last time she was here she had the cheek to tell me I should be making sure Lulu was eating the right food for a kid his age. And she bathed him and washed his hair and put clean clothes on him. Bloody cheek. Don't know who she thinks she is. Slut. You wouldn't guess what she really does just by looking at her. Most of the others look like tarts, but she looks like butter wouldn't melt in her mouth. Trouble is, if I complain to Jake, he'll bring her here even more and I know if he's home at the same time, he'll shag her. Never mind. I'll be out of here next year, for sure.

\*\*\*

"Well that's it, girl. Another term over and just one to go. I suppose I'd better start thinking about a job. I'd like to have the summer with Adam if I can, but I'll have to take what comes along. What about you?"

Maisie shrugged. She'd been unusually quiet all the way home. "Not sure. I think I'd like to keep the private stuff going for a while longer. What will you do about Adam if you get a job?"

"I haven't really thought it through. Childcare's expensive and I know my wages won't be brilliant to start with. The problem is, if I get a full-time job, I'll lose most, if not all, of my benefits. Maybe you're right about the local work for a while, at least until Adam goes to school."

"You could always see if there's any part-time work around in any of the salons, like you did before. You said that you could work some hours and still get benefits, didn't you?"

"Yeah. I'll have to check it out properly. Maybe I'll go into the benefit office over the holidays. Have you got any work lined up?"

"A bit, and I think one or two want their hair done as well, if you're free next week? They're going to let me know tonight. It'll be at my place. Why not come over for coffee tomorrow? There's something else I want to talk you about, but I don't have time now. Okay?"

The next morning Kay and Maisie were sitting at the table when Maisie made a sudden dash for the door. Kay heard her coughing and then the toilet flushed. When Maisie came back into the living room, Kay could see that she was unwell.

"Bloody hell! Oops, sorry, but whatever's the matter? You look like death warmed up!"

Maisie grimaced. "Thanks, and it'll get worse before it gets better."

"What do you mean? Oh!" Kay clamped her hand over her mouth. "Really? Are you sure?"

Maisie nodded. "Looks very much like it. About nine weeks."

"And you never said anything!" Kay counted on her fingers. "Good Christmas then!"

Maisie blushed. "Well, I wanted to be sure. I only told Jeff a few days ago. He's like a big kid. Going around with a goofy smile all the time. It's going to be a bit of a struggle – that's why I can't look for a job right away – but we're pleased, really. At least I'll be able to finish the course, although I was hoping to do the advanced one in September. There's a business training element to it."

"I know. They told us about it as well. Only trouble is there's limited financial help, and no free childcare."

"That's what I wanted to talk to you about. See, Jeff's mum has come into some money and she wants to help me set up my own business – like we talked about before. What with the baby coming, I can't do the advanced course …"

"And?"

"Well, I was thinking, if you did the course, I could have Adam for you, and help with the fees if you have to pay anything. It's only one full day and one evening for three terms. You pick things up more quickly than I do, so if you could talk me through the business part of it, at least I'd have a basic understanding and I could maybe do the course the following year. You could still do the private work, or anything else, but you'd be much better qualified afterwards. If you wanted, you could set up the business with me and handle the books and stuff as well. We could work out a deal about wages, so you didn't lose your benefits. What do you think?"

"Wow. That's a lot to take in. Let me think it over and I'll let you know next week. All right?"

As Kay walked back to her flat, her head was buzzing. The advanced course was a real opportunity for her to secure a better paid job, but she'd given up the idea when she found out about the costs. Maybe another door was opening for her after all.

## September 6th

The eight-fifteen bus to Alderbridge was crowded and Kay was glad that she would only have to make this journey once a week. Thankfully, the evening bus was never full. After her decision to take up Maisie's offer, the final term of her course, and then the summer break, had seemed to fly by.

Adam was a delight and the college nursery had advanced his development considerably. He was talking quite a lot and loved to make up games to play with his toys. When she took him to clients' flats or houses, he was no trouble at all. She hoped the transition to being cared for by Maisie wouldn't affect him adversely, but it was necessary if their plans were to work out. Maisie only had just over a month to go before the baby came but then her mother and Jeff's would help.

Kay was excited. Although it felt strange to be travelling on her own to the college, she was looking forward to this new challenge. She knew that some of the girls who had been in her class the year before would also be taking the advanced course, so she would know a few people. The business element didn't bother her. She'd never had any problem absorbing knowledge while she'd been at school. Her downfall had been the distraction of the Khatri twins and her own stubbornness. She wondered what the coming year would bring and again, she felt proud of what she had achieved. Her savings were growing and maybe, just maybe, she'd be in a position to contact her parents before too long.

*** 

Ruth pushed open the café door and looked inside. She spotted Janet at a table at the back and waved.

"Hello, love. Sorry I'm a bit late. Paul gave me a lift in, and he needed to stop for petrol."

"That's all right. I've only been here five minutes myself. How come Paul was home?"

"He has a doctor's appointment. He can't seem to shift that cough he picked up on holiday. It's probably nothing but it's wearing him out."

"Best to have it checked out. Any other news?"

"Well, I took your advice and I sent for the college evening class brochure. I'm not sure if I'll do anything yet, but I quite like some of the craft courses. There's one for making cards, and another for quilting. I've always fancied doing that. What do you think?"

"They both sound good. Are they on different nights? If they are, you could do them both. What does Paul think?"

"He's all for it. Says it would do me good to get out of the house a bit more and meet some new people. The card one's on a Tuesday, starting next week. The quilting is on a Thursday. They're both six until eight. I wasn't sure about the winter nights though, but Paul says he'll pick me up. I don't mind going in on the bus."

"Good for you. If I'm around at the right time, I can always bring you home instead."

***

"For crying out loud, Lulu. Can't you shut up for five minutes? I haven't got anything to eat. You'll have to wait until I come back. I'll get some bread and milk in the shop. JUST SHUT UP!"

Luke stopped crying but continued to sob quietly. His whole body shook, and his bottom lip quivered with each breath that he took. He glanced at his mother's face, then looked away quickly. He knew that look. He knew that it would be better for him if he wasn't in the same space as her, so he tottered to the door and climbed the stairs to his room. It was a bleak scene. The curtains were little more than mouldy rags and the walls were a dirty yellow. He was still sleeping on the camp bed and his soiled bedding was thin and smelled like a public urinal. The rug that had been next to his bed had been thrown out after some feeble attempts to clean off the vomit and the excrement that had coated it. Tia, or one of the girls, sometimes cleaned up the mess in the corner of the room, but the little boy still used it as a toilet when he was too scared to use the bathroom, or at the times when he was locked in. He could hear Tia crashing about downstairs and arguing with Jake, so he crawled under his bed and curled up in a ball.

"What's all the bleedin' noise about now? You're the one who wanted to drag the kid into this, not me. I'd have soon as left him at the station when were there, but Lady bloody Tia wanted to play at being Mummy, didn't she? Not too late to change your mind. I can always get one of the boys to dump him in the park or somewhere. What do you say?"

"Shut up, Jake. He just got on my nerves, that's all. There's nothing here to eat and I haven't got time to go to the shop now. The drop's in less than hour."

Tia felt Jake's hand across the back of her head, then he punched her arm and her shoulder.

"Watch your mouth, bitch. Whose fault is it anyway there's no food? You're supposed to be in charge of that. If you didn't spend the shopping money I give you on booze, we might have a decent meal once in a while. P'raps I'd better get one of the girls to live in and let her run the place. With a bit of training she could do the drops as well. You're getting to be a bloody liability. I know for a fact that you haven't been doing the detours on the way back. If the boys get to know, I wouldn't give you very good odds on being around here for long. And if you're no good to them, you're no good to me."

Tia's face reddened. He was right. She had been slipping but she was so tired lately. Still, she knew that Jake's threats were rarely idle.

"Sorry. I'll make sure I don't come straight back anymore. And you're right about the food. I'll do some proper shopping tomorrow. All right?"

Jake grunted.

"Shall I get a Chinese on the way back? Will you be here?"

"Probably. Make sure you get some chips as well."

"Of course. Will you look after Lulu, or shall I lock him in?"

Jake shrugged. "Don't care. Shelley's coming over anyway, just in case I need to go out."

Tia turned away so that Jake couldn't see her face. She'd really come to hate Shelley and her interfering. She knew the girl had ideas about replacing her in Jake's house, and his bed, on a more permanent basis but Tia wasn't going to let that happen without a fight. She knew Jake didn't like clingy women, or ones who made too many demands and even though Shelley was young, this wouldn't necessarily be in her favour.

"That's good. Perhaps she could nip around the launderette. There's a bag in the kitchen. Then we'll have a nice clean bed tonight." She winked at him and waggled her hips.

"Daft bitch. Get out of here or you'll be late. It's nearly half eight now. And don't forget the chips."

Luke heard the front door slam and he wriggled out from under his bed. He opened his door and quietly crossed the landing into Tia's room. The curtains were open and it was still light. He stood on tiptoes and looked down the street. He could see Tia, with the rucksack, hurrying towards the bus stop. As soon as the bus pulled away, he spotted Shelley coming out of the lane at the side of the house. He heard the click of the front door and muffled voices from the hallway. He moved to the top of the stairs and lay down. His stomach growled and he rubbed it. Maybe Shelley would have something for him. She often did. He liked Shelley.

Ten minutes later Luke slid down the stairs, step by step. He waited at the bottom for a minute, then pushed open the living room door. He couldn't see Shelley or Jake, just their feet over the arm of the settee. They were making funny noises and Luke crept closer to see what game they were playing. Jake spotted him first.

"Fuckin' hell, kid! Clear off. Go on, get out of here. NOW."

Luke stumbled back to the hallway and sat on the stairs. Jake's shouting didn't bother him so much these days, but he knew full well how Jake's hands or boots felt. He went into the kitchen and looked around but there was nothing edible in sight. He sat on the floor, suddenly dizzy and exhausted. Shelley found him there half an hour later.

"Never mind, little one. Look here. I've got some chocolate for you. Maybe you ought to have some proper food first, though. Let's see what we can find."

She opened the fridge. Nothing. She looked in the

cupboards and all she could find was a small tin of baked beans.

"Not much choice then, kiddo. No bread, either. Come on, try to sit up to the table. I'll warm these up for you and then you'll feel better, eh? God, I've never known a kid so quiet. Thirsty, are you? Have some water. Doesn't look like you've seen much water on your body since I last cleaned you up, does it? And look at your hair. I wouldn't be surprised if there's something living in there."

Shelley helped Luke to eat a few spoons of beans and then gave him the chocolate. His little face lit up when the rush of sweetness hit his taste buds and he opened his mouth for more. Shelley laughed.

"You look like a little bird."

"Bird."

"What did you say? You said 'bird'. Good for you. Funny little thing. It's not right keeping you caged up in this place day and night. Let's see if there's any hot water, shall we? There must be some scissors around here some place, as well. I'll cut your hair, then we'll see if we can get it a bit cleaner."

After Shelley had cut Luke's hair, given him a tepid bath and washed his hair, she searched for clean pyjamas. After a few minutes it was obvious that he had none and that most of his clothes were too small for him. She tiptoed into Tia's room and looked around. She found some socks, a tee shirt and some of Jake's underpants and she looked for some way to keep them on Luke's tiny body. In the bathroom, she found a safety pin and knew that would have to do.

When he was dressed, Shelley laughed at him. "You look like a little scarecrow now, don't you? Are you tired? Let's see if we can make your bed a bit cleaner, shall we?"

She gagged when she lifted the sheets from Luke's bed. They were stiff with dried urine and other bodily outputs. She threw them in the corner along with the ragged blanket and the soiled pillow. On the landing there was a cupboard and Shelley hoped she might find something useful in there. She glanced at her watch. Tia wouldn't be back for a while, and she could hear Jake's snores shaking the walls.

166

A quick search produced a yellowed, but clean, pillow plus a few large towels that would serve as sheets. On the top shelf there was a bag full of old curtains. Shelley pulled them out and selected a few to use as blankets. They'd be a lot warmer than the rubbish he'd been sleeping under. Ten minutes later, the little boy was tucked up in bed and sleeping. Shelley ran her hand over his still-damp hair and shook her head. She was never going to bring a child into the awful world that she now found herself.

Shelley pushed Luke's dirty bedding into a black bag and took it into the kitchen where she put it into Tia's bag of washing. Jake had already asked her to go to the launderette and she knew she'd have to hurry to get it done before Tia came back. She grabbed the money from the table. Maybe she could get away with a quick wash, although Luke's stuff really needed to be boiled. On an impulse, she took out the bag of soiled bedding and stuffed it into the rubbish bin. The next time she came, she'd bring sheets from her own room.

As Tia closed the front door and stowed the rucksack under the stairs, Shelley came through the back door.

"Oh. Haven't you gone yet? I've got Chinese, but there's only enough for two. I didn't think you'd still be here."

"Sorry. I had to wait for the dryer. Doesn't matter about the food. I'll get something from the chippy when I get back to the house. Do you want me to put these out anywhere?" She held up the laundry bag.

"Naw. I'll see to it later. Is it properly dry? Only Jake and me don't want to be in a damp bed, tonight, do we? Although we'd soon warm it up, I'm sure."

Shelley turned away and smiled. She couldn't believe how stupid, or gullible, Tia seemed. Maybe she was just one of life's losers; a doormat. She didn't understand why Jake still kept her around. She was looking pretty rough at the moment.

"Bye. See you."

"Yeah. Whatever. Hello Jake. Grub's up. Chips as you wanted. Like a drink as well? Maybe we can have an early night. I'll put the sheets on when we've eaten."

Jake just grunted. He hadn't really woken up from his post coital nap and the thought of bedding Tia after chop suey and chips made his toes curl. Of course, Tia drank so much vodka that she passed out on the floor and Jake slept on top of the bare mattress. She had completely forgotten that she hadn't fed Luke.

It was two days before Tia recovered from the heavy drinking bout. Jake had fed Luke, after a fashion, with bread and milk that he'd been forced to go out and buy himself. When Tia went into Luke's room, she convinced herself that it had been her who'd cleaned up the bed, but she couldn't remember it at all, and as for cutting his hair and dressing him in her tee shirt, well that was buried so far in her memory that she didn't even bother trying to recall it. She didn't particularly find it strange that Jake's wet underpants were on the bathroom floor, although why they had a safety pin in them was a mystery.

## October 15th

Kay tapped at Maisie's front door. Jeff's mother opened it and beckoned her in.

"Hello love. How are things? The Health Visitor's in with Maisie so we'll have a cuppa in the kitchen. She won't be long."

"Is everything all right?"

"Yes, fine. Routine call, that's all."

Kay had just finished her tea when the front door slammed and Jeff's mum pointed to the ceiling.

"Go on up. I know you're dying to see him! You can leave the little one with me."

Kay opened the bedroom door and peeped around at Maisie who was sat in bed nursing her son. For a moment Kay felt an intense pang of envy but quickly suppressed it.

"Hello Maisie. Congratulations! How are you?"

Maisie looked up at her friend and grinned. She pointed to the chair next to the bed.

"Kay! It's lovely to see you. Come and sit here. He took us a bit by surprise but we're fine. Jeff's a bit shell-shocked. He didn't think we were going to make it to the hospital. I kept winding him up, telling him he'd have to deliver it in the van. I was only in about forty minutes before he was born. Much better than with Holly."

"Can I see him?" Maisie held the baby towards Kay, and she stroked his cheek. "He's beautiful. Have you decided on a name?"

"Yes. We're thinking of naming him after my dad and Jeff's granddad. Callum Paul."

Kay gulped. It would be hard having contact with a baby whose names would draw up painful memories every time she saw him.

"Lovely."

"I'll be up and about properly in a few days. Perhaps you can come over and we can go through some of the coursework? Mum's coming to stay for a week, then she'll come over in the daytime only, until things settle down. It'll give Jeff's mum a bit of a break, too."

"As long as you feel up to it, that's fine by me. I'm really enjoying the course. It seems more real now – you know – the idea of us working together."

Later that evening, Kay put Adam into his bed, read him a story then tiptoed out of his room. She thought about Maisie's new baby which led her mind to Kal. She wondered what he was doing and whether he ever thought about her. He had no idea about Adam, but it must surely have crossed his mind that they'd been very foolish. She sighed. She knew that it was no use travelling down that path, and besides, she had homework to do.

## December 1st

"Happy birthday, lovely boy. Who's a big lad, now? Three years old. Not too big to give your mum a kiss, are you?"

Adam looked up at Kay and grinned. He held out his arms

and she swung him up from his bed, hugged him tightly and kissed him all over his face. He giggled and buried his head in her neck.

"Phew. You are getting to be a lump. I can hardly lift you anymore. Come on, breakfast first, then you can open your presents. You've got two from Holly and Callum, and some from your friends from nursery last year. There might even be one or two from me!"

An hour later, Adam was sitting on the living room floor surrounded with ripped wrapping paper and an assortment of gifts. Kay watched him playing and she smiled. He was getting easier to manage as each month went by and she began to believe that the plans she and Maisie had put together might work. The first term of the advanced course had gone well, and she'd enjoyed the challenge of the business element. She had thought about skipping class because of Adam's birthday, but when she'd learned there was to be an assessment, she knew she had to go. Besides, it was going to be a shorter session, finishing at eight instead of eight thirty. That meant she could catch the earlier bus home.

***

Ruth glanced at her watch. Ten minutes to eight. Time to pack up if she didn't want to keep Paul waiting. She looked around the classroom and smiled. This had been a brilliant idea of Janet's, and although she'd been hesitant at first, Ruth had really enjoyed the two classes, although she found the quilting a bit more difficult. The travelling arrangements had worked out well. She caught the five fifteen bus from the stop in her road, and Paul or Janet met her at eight. It meant that she didn't have much chance to hang around and chat, like most of the others, but she didn't mind that. Especially on a night like tonight. The weather forecast had said it was likely to snow but it had held off so far. As long as they could reach home safely, Ruth would be happy. She knew that Janet had a hospital shift and hoped she'd take the bus or a taxi instead of driving, but there again, Janet always did her own thing. *Just like Kay*. The unexpected thought caught her unawares, and she drew her breath in sharply. *No. Not down that road again. Not now.*

Paul parked a short distance away from the college under a streetlamp. It was busy with cars and he hoped Ruth would be able to see him. He decided to walk to the entrance to meet her.

"Hello, love. Why are you out in the cold?"

"Had to park down the road and I didn't want you to panic if you couldn't see me."

"Cheek!" They walked slowly towards the car and Ruth glanced up at the sky.

"Look, Paul, it's starting to snow. I'm glad it's held off until now. We'll be home before it gets too bad."


Kay checked over her paper, made one or two small amendments, then put down her pen. Done. She'd found the paper relatively easy but worried that she might have misunderstood some of the questions. Only time would tell. The results wouldn't be given until after Christmas, and even if she had done badly, there was one chance to resit.

The lecturer began to gather in the papers and Kay glanced out of the window. Against the light of the streetlamp, she could see the snowflakes falling and she smiled. Adam would love to see it in the morning. He'd probably be too sleepy to notice when she picked him up from Maisie's. She was just about to turn away from the window when a couple walking along the pavement caught her eye. She stared hard. There was something familiar about the way the woman walked.

Without thinking, Kay threw her things into her bag, grabbed her coat and ran from the classroom. She hurried down the corridor and out into the street. The couple were in their car and the lights were on. She ran as fast as she could, shouting out for them to stop, but the car pulled away slowly. Paul glanced in the mirror as he manoeuvred out from the kerb, but he barely registered his own daughter frantically waving at him.

Kay stopped suddenly and dropped down onto a low wall.

She was out of breath and her heart was racing. She had been so close to them, and despite her assurances to herself that she'd wait a while longer before contacting her parents, she knew that if they'd stopped tonight, she'd have run to them. She wondered what they were doing there and whether they came every week. She knew that some of the evening classes finished at eight. Perhaps that was it. On her way to the bus station, Kay decided she would slip out early from her class next week and wait in the hallway. Just in case.

***

Tia lay on the bathroom floor. An empty vodka bottle was propped against the side of the bath and another, half full, was stood next to it. She had been sick several times and not always in the toilet. The floor was spattered with vomit and urine and the rancid smell seeped under the door and permeated the whole of the upstairs. Jake was in a slightly better condition, but still almost comatose on the bed. He opened one eye and glanced at the clock. He could barely see it. Seven thirty. In the evening? He groaned, rolled out of bed, and staggered to the bathroom, holding onto the walls for support. He wasn't really surprised to find Tia passed out on the floor. It wasn't an unusual occurrence, although perhaps happening a little too often these days. Jake knew he'd have to do something about her soon. She was becoming careless and there had been talk that she was being watched by the law. Maybe time for a change, although in a perverse way, he did like having her around. She was easier to manage than most of the other girls, for one thing.

Jake stepped over Tia and relieved himself in the toilet, missing the bowl only a few times. On his way out he prodded her with his foot, then kicked her a bit harder. She grunted.

"Oi, get up woman. You stink like a bloody sewer again. Get up and make some coffee."

Tia rolled over and squinted at him. Everything was hazy and she felt sick again. Just as she was about to answer Jake, she heaved and threw up on the floor.

"You're disgusting. Clean this mess up. NOW."

Jake stumbled down the stairs and into the kitchen. It was freezing. He looked around for a clean mug but stopped when he heard a strange noise coming from the living room. He pushed open the door and saw that Luke had climbed onto the armchair next to the window and was watching the snowflakes. He was chattering away to himself and pointing at the sky. It was the first time Jake had ever heard him make a sound, except for crying.

Jake stood in the doorway and watched the little boy. It was strange to think that the child could be his. Not that it was likely, of course, but he could be. Still, kids had never been on Jake's agenda and weren't going to be. Luke had been just another means to control Tia, although it looked as though the novelty of being mummy had worn off.

Luke caught sight of Jake and dropped down onto the chair. Jake could see that the child was, yet again, wearing one of Tia's tee shirts, and little else. He had managed to wrap himself in an old coat that had been left in the hallway, and it was clear he'd been foraging among the chip shop wrapping paper for scraps. Jake frowned and scratched his head.

"Bloody hell, mate. When was the last time your mother fed you? Stay there, and I'll see what's in the kitchen."

Ten minutes later Jake returned with a plate of toast and two cups. Luke was still on the chair and he watched every movement that Jake made, ready to escape if he saw the tell-tale look of annoyance or anger come over Jake's face.

"It's all right, kid. Come on. Have some of this."

They sat opposite each other and Luke tentatively reached out for a piece of toast. He took a little bite and the saltiness of the butter made him shudder. It wasn't a taste he was familiar with, but he liked it. A second small bite, then he pushed the food into his mouth as fast as he could.

"Whoa, slow down, kid. You'll choke yourself. Here, have a drink of milk. Good? Okay, now you can have some more toast. Have mine as well. I'll get some more."

173

As Jake stood in the kitchen, he felt a wave of something wash over him. The look of happiness on Luke's face, just because of a piece of toast, had unnerved him. Something deep inside Jake stirred but he didn't want to allow it air. He'd walked a few paths in his life, and he'd chosen the one he was on now, but there was no room in it for sentimentality over a scrawny, filthy kid who might, or might not, be his son. He trudged upstairs and found an old sweater in the cupboard and some socks, as well. They would have to do.

Jake dressed Luke with difficulty, but the child certainly looked a little better afterwards. He stared at Jake with his tiny head tilted to one side. Uncle Jake had never really done anything nice for him before. He was feeling sleepy and a bit sick after the food, so he lay his head on the arm of the chair and soon fell asleep. Jake hunted around for some coins, fed the electric meter and switched on the fire. Unknowingly, he'd given Luke his one and only third birthday present.

## December 2nd

The snow fell steadily all night and drifted in the high winds. By five o'clock it eased but the occasional flurry swirled around the corner of the house. Luke had been awake for hours and found his way back to the armchair next to the window. He pulled back the curtain and stared out at the snow, glistening and crackling under the light of the streetlamp. Nothing was moving. No traffic, no dog walkers, no buses. Everything was completely still and silent. He toddled into the kitchen and found a half-eaten pie on the table. He could only just reach it, but as soon as his fingers grasped the plate, he pulled hard and the pie rolled to the floor. He sat down and ate as fast as he could. He didn't really like the slimy onions or the congealed gravy but at least it went a small way to satisfying the gnawing in his stomach. He couldn't open the fridge or reach the water tap, so he went in search of his mother.

Tia was sound asleep next to Jake. She was on her side facing the door and Luke stood and stared at her. He touched her face gently, but she just swatted his hand away without even opening her eyes. He sat on the floor and continued to stare at her. Tia was in a deep sleep. She hadn't really recovered from the bender two nights earlier and could easily have repeated the process the night before if Jake hadn't reminded her, with a slap, about the next drop.

Luke sneezed and Tia stirred. She opened one eye and shut it again, quickly. Her head was still thumping, and her stomach was doing summersaults. After a few minutes, she risked opening her eyes again.

"Go back to bed, Lulu. It's too early to be up. Go on, now. Mummy's tired. Don't whine."

Luke screwed up his face and his bottom lip quivered. He was shivering so hard that he could barely get to his feet. When he tried to crawl under the cover next to Tia, she kicked out at him and he landed on his back with a sickening thump. He screamed and she jumped out of bed, grabbed him by the arm and dragged him back to his own room.

"What did I tell you, you stupid little bugger? I said back to bed, didn't I? DIDN'T I?" She screamed at him and threw him onto his bed. "If you move from there before I get up, I'll wring your skinny little neck. Now shut up." She slapped his legs, but he didn't make a sound. She intended to lock the door, but the key was missing, so she slammed it shut. Jake grumbled when she crawled back into bed, but within five minutes all was quiet again.

At half past six, Luke was back at the window. The street was still deserted, although there were now some houses that had lights switched on. The windowpane was coated with snow and icy patterns and Luke put out his hand to touch them. He didn't understand that they were on the outside and he struggled to grasp them. He found that if he stood on the arm of the chair, the pretty shapes were much closer to his hand and he grabbed at them again and again until he slipped and pitched towards the window. His foot caught in the fabric of the chair which pulled his body back a little, but his hands made contact with the glass. There was a loud crack. His left

175

arm went through the window and when he fell back, a jagged edge razored down his forearm. It was over in a few seconds.

Jake opened his eyes. It was still dark, but he knew there must have been a lot of snow in the night as it was never this quiet in the mornings, no matter how early. What had woken him? He listed as the sound came again. Screams. Someone was screaming and it was close by. There it was again. The kid!

"Tia! Get up, Tia. Can't you hear that. Something's wrong."

Jake grabbed his trousers and a sweater and ran downstairs into the living room. When he put on the light it took a few moments to comprehend what he was seeing. Luke, sitting on the floor with blood pouring out of his arm. He had stopped screaming and his eyes were glazing over. Jake glanced at the broken window and at the reddened snow on the sill, and the streaks of blood running down the wall. He dashed into the hall, pulled on some boots and ran back upstairs, where he caught Tia by the hair and dragged her out of bed.

"I warned you, didn't I, you stupid little bitch. I told you what would happen, having that kid here. Well now he's screwed it up good and bloody proper. There's no fuckin' way we can explain this one. Get downstairs and do what you can. I need to find something to wrap him in."

*Drama queen!* Tia yawned, pulled a blanket off the bed, wrapped it around her shoulders and stumbled down the stairs. She could hear quiet moans but nothing else. Couldn't be that bad. The sight of Luke on the floor turned her stomach, but it was the blood on the snow that really freaked her out. She was transfixed by the patterns of red on white and stood shaking until Jake slapped her face.

"MOVE! Stupid idiot. Look after the kid, can't you? Find a towel or something and wrap his arm up. Oh, for shit's sake." He pushed her out of the way and ran into the kitchen. The towel was filthy but there was nothing else to use. He wound it around Luke's forearm as tightly as he could, wrapped the boy in a larger towel, then put one of Tia's coats around him. He shrugged on his own overcoat, grabbed his

176

house keys, then lifted Luke as carefully as he could.

"Where are you taking him?" Tia had finally found her voice. She was white and shaking.

"No good calling an ambulance. It'll take me ten minutes to get around to the call box and they might not even be able to get through. I'll go up the lane into Archer Street – if there's any traffic running, it'll be there. I might be able to get someone to take us to the hospital. If not, the phone box is only at the end of the street. We'll have to take our chances from there."

"NO. Jake you can't. I'll never get him back. Can't we find a chemist that's open?"

Jake pushed her back. "Don't be stupid. You saw the state of his arm. Bloody chemist! The kid'll bleed to death if we don't get a move on. Now stay here, get dressed and wait for me to get back. There's supposed to be a drop today so check out the time and place. I'll see if I can make contact to find out if it's going ahead, but be ready, just in case. Shake yourself. There's nothing more you can do for him now."

She closed the front door behind him, sat on the stairs and sobbed. Lulu. Poor Lulu. She hadn't meant to shout at him earlier. She was just so tired.

Jake struggled along the lane at the side of the house. The snow wasn't quite so deep there, but it was very slippery. At the junction of the lane and Bow Street, he paused, shifted Luke's weight and moved on. It was even harder going as the snow was piled in deep drifts and Jake stumbled a few times. He could feel the sweat running down his back and his heart was pounding. When a light went on in the porch of one the houses, he began to panic, but no one came out. Luke moaned and whimpered.

"Sorry, mate. Won't be long." Jake pulled Luke's face closer to his chest and plodded on until they came to the cut-through into Archer Street. In the distance the gritting lorries were out and there was some traffic moving, albeit slowly. At the corner of the street there was a newspaper shop and a small bakery next door. Both shops were lit up and Jake could see customers inside. He hesitated for a moment, looked up and down the street, then quickly laid Luke's trembling body in the doorway of the newsagents.

"You'll be better off, kid. Honest. They'll find you in a minute and get you to hospital. Sorry."

He walked as fast as he could to the cut-through and hid behind a cluster of garbage bins. Then he heard a woman scream and a lot of commotion. Despite the cold and the depth of the snow he pressed his back to the wall and waited for the wails of the siren. Surprisingly, considering the state of the roads, the ambulance arrived within ten minutes. He knew the nearest hospital wasn't far away, and hoped it wouldn't be too late to save Luke. There it was again: that foreign sensation in his stomach. He waited until the ambulance left then walked into Archer Street to the bus stop. If the ambulance could get through, it was likely that the buses were running. He knew he couldn't go back to the house. Tia would know he hadn't gone to the hospital, and he was well aware what she was like when she really kicked off. He needed time to think and make some plans.

Jake let himself into the house and called out for Tia. No answer. He hoped she hadn't done something stupid, like trying to get to the hospital. She wasn't really in the best state for that. He called again. The living room was freezing. Cold air was streaming in through the broken windowpane and it was obvious that she had not made any attempt to clean up. He swore under his breath and ran up the stairs into the bedroom. Tia was fast asleep, and Jake felt the bile rise in his throat. His breath shortened as he tore the blankets off the bed.

"You selfish heartless cow! What the hell are you playing at? Your bloody kid's at death's door and I'm the one who's had to turn out in the snow to try and save him, while soddin' Lady Muck Tia, the grieving mummy, goes back to bed. Are you out of your mind? And I told you to clean up that mess downstairs, didn't I?"

Tia put her hand over her eyes and sat up. "Stop shouting,

178

Jake. I couldn't face the blood down there and I didn't know what else to do. I didn't mean to go to sleep but I was tired."

"Tired, my ass. Still bloody hungover. Now, get up, get dressed, and pack up your stuff –"

"No, please, Jake. Don't throw me out. I'm sorry. I'll do whatever you want."

"Shut up and listen. I'm not throwing you out, but we've got to split. It's too risky now. If the cops start looking into the kid's background, someone might drop us in it. You never know who might have seen him. Even one of the girls might say something if she thought it was a way out for herself. I've spoken to the boss about the drop and things have changed. The law's been getting a bit too close so there's going to be a whole new system. We need to meet the lads somewhere later and they'll find a place for us for a few days until they can arrange something better. They're bloody mad at you, though. They were never happy with the kid being here in the first place, but I talked them around. Now we need to shift. Pack whatever you can carry and any money or sellable stuff. There's a bag in the cupboard you can use. Won't take me long to do mine. Then you check the kitchen for anything handy and I'll sort out the crap in the front room."

"What about Lulu's things. Shall I pack those?"

"He's been wearing your tee shirts for months, so what's the bleedin' point? We can sort out new stuff later."

He couldn't believe that Tia hadn't even asked what happened to Luke, or how he was, yet she was worried about some stinking rags.

Jake threw some water over the windowsill and the wall, then taped a large plastic bag over the broken pane. He opened up some wire coat hangers and wedged them into the window frame. That would do until it could be fixed properly. Tia stood in the hallway with a couple of bags.

"Jake, what about Lulu? What's going to happen?"

"I left him at the hospital. Gave a false name and address. They wanted me to wait but I said my wife was very sick at home and that I'd come back as soon as I'd found someone to look after her. They told me to ring tonight. I don't know how we'll get him back. We'll have to work something out. Maybe wait until he's better then sneak him out at visiting time."

Jake's brain was churning. He hoped he could pull off the next part of his plan without freaking Tia out too much. Only one way to find out, and if she didn't want to play ball – well, tough. He grabbed the rucksack from under the stairs, picked up his bag of clothes and turned out the light.

"Right. Come on, let's get out of here."

## December 3rd

"Get up, Tia. NOW!"

Not again. He's always yelling at me. My head's banging and that's without a drink.

"What? What's the matter? What's going on?"

"We're moving again soon. The boss decided that you're a liability in this area right now. You can't do the drops any more ..."

"NO! You can't put me out on the streets. Please Jake. Please. Please. I'll do anything."

"Belt up and listen, will you? Nobody's putting you out anywhere, as long as you keep your mouth shut. Just making different arrangements. Maybe for a short while, maybe longer. Depends on how much heat the kid's accident stirs up."

"Did you ring the hospital? How's Lulu? Can I see him?"

"He's in a bad way. No visitors yet. Don't start blubbing again – we haven't got time for it. You know about the houses, don't you?"

"Huh. Not what I'd call them, but yes."

"The boss has the three here, but he's got others all over the place. The one we had is going to be rented out, so that if anyone comes sniffing around, no one there will know anything about us. He's moving someone new in to one of the working ones for the time being to manage the girls. He's sending me to one of his other houses in Myrefall to build up the business. If, and when, he thinks it's safe, he'll sort out a new place for me back here."

"Myrefall? Where the hell is that?"

"Near the border with Wales, but you don't need to know any more."

"But that's miles away. And what about me? Can I stay with you, Jake?"

"He's okay about you moving as well, but you won't be doing any drops for a while. He's got other plans for you. He'll let Bones know where the house is, and someone will come for us tomorrow."

"What? How will I manage about Lulu? And what will I be doing? You don't mean…"

"Listen, you'll do whatever they tell you to do. You look like a bloody toothpick so unless the locals wherever he sends us are desperate, I don't think he'll want you for whoring. And forget about the kid. He's not in a bad way. He didn't make it."

My ears are ringing. I can't hear Jake anymore, or maybe I don't want to. Lulu's dead? No, that can't be right. Jake's lying, he must be, but even if he is, there's no way for me to get Lu back now. He's probably better off, either way.

I've lost him.

## December 5th

Ruth opened the front door and held out her arms to hug Janet.

"Hello there. Come on in. I didn't know if you'd make it."

"Thanks." Janet pulled off her boots and left them in the porch. She followed Ruth into the kitchen. "Oooh! It's so warm in here. The roads are much clearer now but it's still a bit icy in places. Are you and Paul all right?"

"I'm fine, but Paul's cough has come back. Try and persuade him to see the doctor again, if you can, eh? He's so stubborn! And what about you? You look worn out."

"Thanks!"

"Sorry, that sounded a bit rude, but you do look tired.

Have you been overdoing it, with all your jobs?"

"No, not really, but I have done a few extra shifts at the hospital because of the snow. There was a real panic in A & E the other day. A little boy was rushed in, covered in blood and almost frozen to death."

"No? What had happened?"

"No one seems to know. Apparently, he was dumped in a shop doorway and left for dead. Real bad cut up his arm. Poor child was only wearing a threadbare, baggy jumper and a woman's tee shirt, and wrapped in a grubby towel. He was so thin you could see every single rib, and his little shoulder blades were like coat hangers. That was bad enough, but he was absolutely filthy. Almost all his body was crusted with grime, or worse. His nails were so long they were starting to curl over, and his hair – well, I've seen cleaner pigsty floors!"

Ruth drew in her breath and covered her ears with her hands. "Oh Jan, don't. That's awful. Do they know who he is, or where he came from?"

"No. Little thing was completely unresponsive. Probably too young to know where he lived, anyway. Looked about two or maybe three? I think they had to almost sterilize him before they could tackle his arm. He'd lost a lot of blood. They've put him in isolation for the time being and the police and social services are dealing with it. I think they're trying to keep it low key. There's been nothing on the news or in the papers. I peeped in yesterday, but he was still out of it."

"How could anyone leave him like that? Do you think someone hurt him deliberately?"

"It's possible. Why dump him if it was an accident? I'm not on duty for a few days now, but I hope he makes it, poor little mite. Time for a cuppa?"

## December 8th

Kay checked her watch. Ten to eight. She'd already told her tutor she wanted to leave early, so she packed away her books and slipped out of the room. She decided to wait inside the front doors of the college as she wanted to speak to her mother first. She was hoping it was just her mum doing a course, and not her dad as well. She didn't think she could handle seeing them together, but if that's how it turned out, so be it. She bit at her lip, wound her hair around her fingers, and tried to settle the spasms in her stomach.

By eight thirty, Kay knew that she wasn't going to have her much anticipated reunion that night. As she hurried towards the bus station, she felt strangely calm, despite the tears streaming down her face. If this is how it was meant to be, she'd have to accept it and make a decision about the future. Just not now. Maybe next term might be better.

*** 

Ruth jumped when the telephone rang. She'd been standing at the kitchen window and daydreaming. About Kay, and her baby. She'd learned to keep her feelings buried most of the time but there were moments when it was all too much for her and she took a perverse kind of pleasure in imagining how it would be to have Kay back home, and the kind of things they'd do with the child.

"Ruth, is that you? I thought I'd check with Paul if he wanted me to pick you up tonight, but obviously you haven't gone to class. Everything all right?"

"Yes, fine thanks. I just didn't feel like going. It's the last session before Christmas and I think it was going to be more of a social get together. I brought my quilting stuff home last week."

"Going back next term?"

"I'm definitely going to carry on with the card course, but I'm not sure about the quilting. I liked it but I'm finding the two nights a bit much. Anyway, how are you? Any news on that little boy?"

Janet smiled. She guessed that Ruth would have been thinking about him. It was such a shame they hadn't been able to locate Kay. Ruth would be a fantastic grandmother, and Janet quite liked the idea of being a great-aunt, as well as a great aunt!

"Not a lot. They gave him a transfusion and antibiotics and fed him through a tube at first. One of the other nurses told me he'd woken up but that he hadn't made a sound. They know he can hear but they're not sure whether he's able to talk. Hasn't even cried. Just looks terrified all the time."

"Poor lamb. What's going to happen?"

"No idea. It's going to be a while before he's even fit enough to leave the ward. Probably go into care then."

"You don't think there's any chance …"

"Of what? Ruth?"

There was a long pause before Ruth opened up about her fears. "Is it possible that he's Kay's child?"

"Oh Ruth. You can't think like that. It's highly unlikely. I can't for one minute believe Kay would have let a child end up like that. She had her own place and money coming in – Mrs Connor told us. No, I can't see it at all."

The sisters chatted for a while longer, then hung up. Ruth pottered about in the kitchen but she couldn't stop thinking about the little abandoned boy.

*** 

Luke opened his eyes and looked around the hospital room. Everything was alien to him, and he was too afraid to move. He listened to the noises coming from the corridor, but nothing made any sense. He put his hand out and touched the bedding that was tucked all around him. It felt soft and warm. He buried his face in his pillow but he didn't recognise the smell of cleanliness. He knew there was something different about the way he was feeling but was unable to formulate the thought that he was no longer hungry. There was a sudden clattering outside and he rolled off the bed onto the floor. When a nurse came in to check on him, he was fast asleep behind a chair in the corner of the room.

# 1995

## April 7th

Luke had been transferred to a specialist care unit once the doctors had declared him medically fit to be moved. In all the time he was in the hospital, he had not uttered one word, but he had become less afraid of everything and everyone, and had even managed to smile a little, especially when the food trolley appeared. He was also clean, dry and warm all of the time, and had even put on some weight. What was worrying the staff who were caring for him was his mental health. No matter what they tried, he couldn't, or wouldn't, talk.

The police had finally decided to go public with his story but apart from one anonymous phone call from a young woman telling them where he might have been living, there had been no response, and no clues or information at the address when they checked it out. In the absence of any kind of identification, it was decided to call him after the first of the ambulance crew on the scene, and his surname was derived from the road where he was found. That's how Jack Archer came into being. The doctors estimated him to be around three years of age, so he was given a birthday of the day he was found. December the second.

\*\*\*

I don't know how much longer I can stand this place. Must be all of four months since they brought us here. Back of beyond. Why on earth boss man has houses in this neck of the woods beats me. Must pay, though. The girls are a bit dull

185

but pretty enough, I guess. They certainly get plenty of business and no street walking for them, either. I thought I was going to have to go back to servicing dodgy blokes, but all I have to do is make sure the houses are clean and properly stocked. It's not a bad life, really. No shortage of food, or money, but not much booze, Jake makes sure of that. It's so boring. I miss Lulu as well. I still think Jake was lying about him, but there's nothing I can do about it now. He's promised to let me go with him when they find him another place to live in Alderbridge, but I'm not sure I believe him. Probably prefer that Shelley in his bed all the time. If I thought I could get away with it, I'd leg it from here, but they have too many connections. I'll have to ride it out for now.

\*\*\*

Kay had completed the second term on the advanced course the previous evening. She couldn't believe how the months had flown. Adam had settled into the new routine and loved spending time at Maisie's with Holly and Callum. Despite her misgivings about the baby's name, Kay enjoyed seeing how the little boy was growing and developing. She sometimes felt a pang of longing for another child of her own but quickly pushed it aside. Maisie had forged ahead with the business and had a regular stream of clients for herself and for Kay. Most of the work now took place in Maisie's front room and kitchen, but they planned to do more in the clients' homes once Kay was qualified. She checked the time. She had an hour before her first appointment.

\*\*\*

Kay put away her scissors, combs and other bits and pieces, swept up the fallen hair clippings, and was about to pick up the newspapers from the floor when an announcement caught her eye. She straightened up and read it through carefully. She felt her scalp tingling, her legs shaking, then she sat down with a thump.

*Acknowledgements: Mrs Ruth Jones of Fieldslea would like*

*to thank family and friends for their condolences, cards and flowers following the sudden passing of her husband Paul on March 14th. Particular thanks to sister, Janet, for all her help making the arrangements and to ....*

"Kay! What's wrong? Are you ill?" Maisie put her hand on Kay's shoulder. Kay pushed the paper towards her and pointed.

"That's my dad. He's gone. My poor mother, she'll be lost without him. What have I done, Maisie? She'll never forgive me, and it's too late for me to say sorry to him."

"I'm sure she'd be more than happy to see you, and Adam. Why not give her the chance?"

"I don't know. It's all a bit of shock right now."

That evening Kay sat at the table and tried to write to her mother. After several attempts, she decided to keep it simple.

*Dear Mum,*

*I understand if your first reaction is to rip up this letter, or burn it, but please, read it all first, then do as you wish.*

*I am SO sorry for all the hurt and pain that my thoughtless behaviour must have caused you and Dad, and now it's too late to make amends with him. I only learned the news today. Please believe me that if I could put the clock back, I would do things very differently. While I have a beautiful son and I am making a life for us, I know how much richer our lives would have been with both of you in them.*

*What I did was very wrong, but it wasn't planned, or designed to hurt you. You always told me that I was too stubborn for my own good, and now I understand what you meant. I got myself into a mess and it was you I should have turned to, but I thought I could manage on my own. Ironically, most of the money that I took from Dad was stolen from me by someone that I considered a friend. It's been hard, but I've managed to save quite a bit and I was intending to pay him back in time. Now he'll never know.*

*I'm sorry that you've missed Adam's early years and I've*

*thought long and hard about what to do next. I hope you don't blame me for what's happened to Dad, but right now I can't face the possibility that you do, so I think it's best if I keep away. Maybe not forever, but at least until your pain has lessened.*

*Please don't try to find me. I feel so ashamed of my behaviour and couldn't bear to see your disappointment in me.*

*Kay x*

## July 13th

Kay's letter was on the table. Ruth had reread it so many times that she knew it off by heart. She hadn't told Janet about it at first, but the burden of the secret had proved too great. They'd talked about what to do but, like Kay, they decided to let fate lead the way. Ruth stood up but then grasped the edge of the table, suddenly dizzy. She knew she'd missed her check up with the hospital, but she couldn't face the place just yet.

Another thing she hadn't told Janet was that she'd written to Social Services not long after she'd heard about the abandoned little boy. She hadn't been able to get him out of her mind and, despite what Janet said, she'd needed to be sure. She'd had a lukewarm response saying they'd investigate it, but they never contacted her again, and Kay's letter had confirmed that her son was still living with her.

***

"Hey, Jack, how are you today?"

"Day." The little boy waved his arms and smiled at the speech therapist. He was almost unrecognisable from the scrawny, filthy waif who'd been abandoned almost eight months earlier. His speech development was slow, but the therapist was still convinced that it was more 'wouldn't' than 'couldn't'. The child had been so badly neglected and traumatised that she knew it was going to take a lot of hard work from his team of therapists before he could be considered for fostering or even being placed in a mainstream children's home. Still, he was proving to be a sweet boy and she had to remind herself not to become too attached.

***

Kay jumped off the bus and hurried towards Maisie's house. That was it. She'd done it! She'd completed the course with flying colours. Top of the class on the business element and a high grade on the practical. She stopped off at the corner shop and bought a bottle of fizzy wine. Time to celebrate and plan for the future.

## December 1st

Kay and Adam were looking out of the living room window. The heavy rain was running in rivulets down the panes. Adam laughed and tried to catch the silver streams.

"Rain. Mama. Rain."

"That's right." Kay smiled at her son. "Lots of rain. It's a good thing we don't have to go out today, isn't it? I hope it stops before tomorrow or else your friends will get wet coming to your party. Won't they?"

"Party. Lots of presents? Cake?" Adam's eyes widened. His speech was well advanced for his age, although he was sometimes a little lazy and used single words instead of full sentences.

Kay laughed and tickled him. "Yes, cheeky. Cake, and I expect you'll have some more presents. Do you like what Mama gave you?"

Adam ran over to the corner and sat in front of a toy garage, complete with cars, and a lift that worked by winding a little handle. He loved everything to do with transport. Kay had walked past the toyshop many times before she decided to spend some of her savings, and the look on her son's face made the use of the money so worthwhile. Besides, life was working out well for her. She had a part-time job in one of the better salons in a nearby small town, and together with the money she was making from her work with Maisie, she no longer had to watch every penny she spent. It meant she could afford to pay for two days at nursey for Adam, and Maisie looked after him for the other half-day. She worried a little about still claiming benefits, but until Maisie had completed her advanced course she was reluctant to formalise the business. Still, the way time seemed to be flying by, the next eighteen or so months would be gone in the blink of an eye.

\*\*\*

Where the hell is Jake? He said he'd only be half an hour. If he thinks I'm getting the bus in this weather, he's mad. Thinks he's Lord bloody Muck since he got that car. Trouble is, it makes it too damn easy for him to slip across town to the other house. He wouldn't want to be caught out here messing with the goods, but over there … Well, he won't be so happy when there's no food on the table tonight.

It's hard to remember what it was like before. This place is a dead end, but I can't complain about the house, or the money he hands over for the shopping. Still, I'd rather be back in Alderbridge. I wonder what Kay's doing now. Still hanging about with that Maisie, I expect.

It's the Twinnies' fourth birthdays today. I wish I hadn't been such a shit mother. If I hadn't got back together with Jake, things might have been all right, but he didn't give me much choice, did he? And what with Kay turning her back on me … Poor Lulu.

\*\*\*

The car engine spluttered several times before it fired into life. Janet switched on the wipers and cursed under her breath. She hated the rain. There was something about the dampness of everything and the shivers that she felt down her back whenever a droplet fell on her face or her hands. She was on her way to take Ruth to the hospital for a check-up. The dizzy spells had increased, and Janet worried that it might be something more serious than a blood pressure problem.

"Well, that's over with, thank goodness." Ruth slammed the car door shut. "See, told you there was nothing to worry about. All the tests were fine, they're going to adjust my medication, that's all."

"Better safe than sorry. You were a long time in the consultation room."

"Yes. They asked if I'd mind some students and junior doctors coming in for observation, so it took a bit longer. You'll never guess who one of them was – one of the twins I told you about. You know, the ones that Kay used to hang about with. He pretended not to recognise me, but I'm sure he did. He's probably finished at university now, hasn't he?"

"Yes, he's almost certainly on his first foundation year. He'll have to do another year after this one, then about five years to specialise. I'm surprised he decided to stay around here. It's a good hospital, but not many opportunities."

"Maybe there were other reasons …"

"Ruth! Stop it now. No good thinking like that. I shouldn't have told you what Paul said, about seeing Kay and the baby. Come on, let's go and do some Christmas shopping, then we'll go back to your place and put the decorations up. I know you don't feel like it, but Paul wouldn't want you moping about. Anyway, I'm not going to let you get out of cooking Christmas dinner!"

## December 2nd

"Happy Birthday, Jack!"

The little boy clapped his hands and blew out the candles on his cake. He had been moved from the special unit to a children's home two months earlier and after an initial set-back, settled in well and his speech had improved considerably. Most of the other children were older than him and, for a variety of reasons, all were deemed to be unlikely candidates for fostering or adoption. There had been no leads whatsoever on his identity, and it had been agreed by all concerned that he would be placed in care under the name of Jack Archer. Luke had disappeared.

# 1996

## December 1st

Jack stared out of the bedroom window. He watched as a few flakes of snow floated past. It was only a small flurry but something at the back of his mind flickered and he began to shake. He shut the curtains and jumped into his bed. He shared the room with two older boys, but they were allowed to stay up later than him. He didn't mind that as he liked being on his own: liked lying in bed looking at the nightlight. Safe and warm.

He knew it was his birthday the next day and it was a school day, but he was happy about that. The first few days had been hard because he didn't know anyone and he'd never had any friends, or even any kind of interaction with children his own age. Then he met a boy who seemed to like him and from then on Jack couldn't wait for the next school day.

The teachers thought they were a strange pair. Jack was so slight, with a pale, serious little face, and he rarely spoke without prompting. His friend, Adam, was the complete opposite. Sturdy, always laughing and a chatterbox. Yet the two became inseparable and gradually, under Adam's influence, they could see that Jack was developing well.

*\*\*\**

Kay stood over Adam's bed and hummed the *Winter Lullaby*. She watched him as he fell asleep, then she stroked his hair back from his eyes and smiled. They'd had a busy day. Maisie had invited them to Sunday lunch, and then they'd had a small party for Adam back at the flat. It was going to be difficult to wake him for school in the morning, but he was never any trouble. She'd been fortunate that the local primary school had a reception class and that both Holly and Adam had secured places in September. It made things easier for Maisie too, as she'd started the advanced course, so her mum or Jeff's looked after Callum, and picked up the little ones from school on her full day at college if Kay was working. Adam had made some new friends and was loving the challenge of learning.

Another Christmas was looming, and Kay anguished again about contacting her mother. Maybe it would be better to find Auntie Janet? She sighed and decided to wait a while before making a decision.

***

"Make yourself scarce for bit, Tia The boss is coming down. He wants to do a trial run with the selling. Thinks there's a lot more cash to be made than just with the houses. You'll have to get to know the area a bit better too, not just dossing about here or running to the shops."

"What's it got to do with me?"

"Don't act stupid. You'll be doing the drops, like before, only not so regular. One a month at first. You'll have to work out a system and then they'll check it out. Don't know who the contacts will be yet. That's why he's coming today. Here, take this and do a bit of scouting around. You know what to look for. Nothing boxed in or too obvious. Make sure you don't write anything down, and don't come back in if his car's still here."

Fifty quid! Bloody hell, he's feeling generous. Not happy about going back to the drops, though, especially in this kind of weather. It's freezing. I suppose they'll want the same kind of set-up as before, so I'll have to find at least four places, maybe a few more for back up. This place isn't as big as Alderbridge, but I should be all right. Haven't got the excuse of drawings for Lulu anymore, but I'll have to think of someway of remembering the rota.

Poor little Lu. Would have been five today. Probably have been in school as well. I bet he would have been a bright kid. Maybe I'll get a bottle of vodka to drink a toast to him. Just one or two can't hurt.

# 1998

## December 1st

Jake pulled back the curtain and cursed. It was raining heavily, and he knew Tia would kick off again about doing the drop. She was always whining these days, wanting him to take her everywhere in the car. He didn't usually mind for the shopping as she wouldn't have been able to carry all that was needed for the two houses, but she just wouldn't let up about using the car for the drops. No matter how many times he explained, or thumped her, she wouldn't see how risky it was. He sighed. To be fair, she'd found some excellent places and the routine was working well. The boss seemed happy and Jake didn't want to upset the apple cart. No, Tia had to be put in her place once and for all.

"There you are. What time's the drop today?"

"Six. Back of the community hall. Jake ..."

Slap.

"Don't even ask. Just get your stuff together and go."

Tia held her hand to her cheek, bit her lower lip, and her eyes filled with tears. She was at breaking point but couldn't see any way out. She turned and ran out of the room. Jake shrugged, then without warning, Luke's face formed in front of him and he shuddered. He followed Tia and caught hold of her arm. She tensed and put her hand in front of her face.

"No, don't do that. Look at me, Tia. I didn't mean to hit you, but you've got to get your head right. We've got a good number here, so why spoil it by taking risks. Eh? You have to see sense, girl. All right?"

Tia nodded. She looked so pathetic and downtrodden that

Jake almost hugged her.

"Look. Tell you what. I'll take you as far as the lane by the bus stop next to the playing fields, where you usually get off. It's not far then. When you've made the swap, head back to the bus stop. Get whichever bus comes along and get off after ten minutes. I know, I know. You're supposed to do an hour, but we'll skip that tonight. I'll come back to the lane about a quarter to seven and wait for you. All right? We'll pick up some fish and chips and have a drink when we get home, and then you won't have to do another drop 'til after Christmas."

Tia slid out of the car and hoisted the rucksack onto her back. She closed the door as quietly as she could and hurried along the lane. The playing fields were in complete darkness and Tia suddenly felt afraid. She knew the area well by now and never had any problem with moving about the town in the dark, but she couldn't shake the feeling someone was watching her, maybe even following her. She tried to speed up, but the rucksack was heavy, and the rain was gusting around her small frame, pushing her sideways. A crunch of gravel made rivers of sweat run down her neck and her back. Should she risk turning around, or keep moving as quickly as she could? She calculated that it would take about three or four minutes to reach the community hall, but what then? If someone was following her, she'd put the contact in danger as well. He could probably take care of himself, but what if it was the law behind her? On an impulse, when Tia reached the main road, she swung left towards the town centre. She knew there was a greater chance of hiding there than if she headed towards the hall. If she could give her pursuer the slip, she might still make the drop in time.

Tia heard a cough some way behind her and she tried to run. It was more sheltered in the town and she managed to speed up enough to reach the small shopping precinct and slip into the dress shop near the entrance. She picked up a few pairs of jeans and headed for the changing rooms. Her heart was pounding and her mouth was dry as she realised she'd fenced herself in.

The man who had been tracking Tia cursed when he entered the precinct. There was no sign of the woman. He knew that there was another way out and hurried along the central walkway. There was a sign pointing to the car park and another for the High Street. He cursed again and ran along the passageway to the car park.

Tia waited ten minutes before retracing her steps towards the community hall. She was careful to keep in the shadows as much as possible. The hall was usually closed at this time of night but as Tia crept along behind the wall on the opposite side of the road, she saw bright, flashing lights everywhere and heard men shouting and dogs barking. The law. It looked as though her contact had been picked up with his rucksack of drugs, and that she had also been a target for this evening's raid. She started to shake and felt sick, but she knew she had to get out of there and warn Jake.

Inch by inch, Tia moved backwards, never taking her eyes off the activity outside the hall. She kept one hand on the wall to steady herself and by the time she reached the corner, that hand was raw and bloody. She risked a quick look at her watch. Six forty. Should she risk the most direct route to the lane, even though it meant she needed to cross the road now, only a short distance from the hall? Hell, yes!

Tia ran as fast as she could, keeping her head low and trying not to make too much noise on the gravelled path around the playing fields. Thank God! Jake was already waiting. She opened the rear door, threw in the rucksack, then jumped into the front seat.

"Drive, Jake. Get out of here now. The contact's been busted. I was followed but gave them the slip. We've got to shift. Come on!"

Jake pushed his foot to the floor and the car leapt forward. Within ten minutes they were back in the house and shaking. Tia didn't think she'd ever seen Jake so rattled.

"What the bloody hell's going on? How did they get wind of us down here? Someone must have dropped us in it. One of the girls? You haven't pissed any of them off, have you?"

"That's rich, coming from you. Anyway, you see much

more of them than I do, don't you?"

"Don't start that again. We'll have to split. Get some stuff together. I'll tell Megan she'll have to look after the house for now, and she can tell Twiz to sort out the other place. Once we're far enough away, I can risk phoning Bones, or one of the others. They can let the boss know what's going down and maybe he'll sort us out."

"Why don't we just take the money and split? We could find somewhere quiet and I bet there's enough in there to set us up for quite a while." Tia looked at Jake and pouted. "Aren't you tired of running around for him all the time?"

"Don't be stupid. His arms are longer than an octopus. Don't you think I've wanted to disappear loads of times? But I'm not as daft as you. No. We play this straight. We've done nothing wrong. The leak's come from somewhere else. Maybe it's time we went back to Alderbridge, anyway. This might work out all right for us after all. Now move."

Tia scuttled up the stairs and began to throw clothes into black bin liners. *Home. Happy birthday, Lulu.*

\*\*\*

Adam was at the table drawing a picture of a train. Kay watched him and smiled. He was concentrating hard and screwed up his nose as he coloured in the carriages. They'd had a busy morning at the new play centre with Maisie, Holly and Callum, and then they'd had a small party for Adam at the flat. She was exhausted but it seemed as though Adam could go on for ever.

Kay thought about the past years and how quickly they had flown. Maisie had passed the advanced course, but only just. She'd struggled with the business element, especially the computer modules, and they'd agreed Kay would take responsibility for that part of the business. The main problem was accessing the equipment as the cost of buying and installing was high. She'd known there was a place in town that sold refurbished machines, usually from the local offices and even the college when they bought new. Maisie agreed to

198

pay for the computer and Kay would pay for a printer, but she'd had no idea of the price. She still had her 'Dad' savings box but was loath to take the money from there. She'd decided to check it out and the man in the shop had been helpful, but she was still about fifty pounds short. When he suggested selling or pawning her necklace, she'd laughed at him.

"But it's only from the market. It's not worth anything."

"Let me have a look."

She'd handed it to him, and he'd turned it over. "Look. It's hallmarked, and the chain as well. I wouldn't mind betting that the stones are real, too. Worth a trip to the jeweller down the road to check it out. He sells second-hand stuff, so he might give you a fair price for it."

Kay remembered that walk to the jewellery store vividly. She'd fingered the necklace all the way. Her heart was thumping when she went into the shop. What if she was trying to sell stolen goods? Would the jeweller be on the look-out for it? It had been six years since Tia had given it to her, and she'd never thought of it as anything other than junk but had worn it often.

A few hours later Maisie and Kay signed the forms, arranged for the equipment to be delivered and set up at Maisie's, and handed over their money. The business was on its way.

*** 

The shrill of the alarm clock shook Janet from sleep. She groaned as she thumped the clock into silence. She didn't usually mind the early shift at the hospital, but her night had been full of bad dreams. She couldn't remember the details but there had a been a lot of snow, and Kay and Ruth had been there, too. The *Winter Lullaby* had swirled around everything and still filled her head. Weird.

She hurried to the bathroom and pulled up short when she saw the broken glass on the floor. Ruth! Janet rushed into her spare bedroom. Her sister had stayed the night, after they'd been to see a play in town and had seemed fine when they went to bed, but now she was lying on the floor, unconscious.

The ambulance arrived within ten minutes. Janet guessed that it had been a heart attack rather than a stoke, and the paramedic agreed. She followed the ambulance to the hospital and paced along the corridor while Ruth was being assessed.

"Janet McElroy?"

"That's me. How is she?"

"Come through. She's stable and we'll be transferring her to the ward now. She's had a mild heart attack, but we'll have a fuller picture later. I want to run a few more tests and a scan. I see she's been on medication for high blood pressure for a while. Do you know if she's been taking it regularly?"

"As far as I know, yes. She hasn't complained of feeling unwell at all, just a little more tired than usual."

"All right. Well, you can see her for a few minutes if you like, but better to let her sleep. If it's what we think, then she'll need to rest for a while, but she should be back to normal in a few months. Does she have anyone living with her?"

"No, but I can arrange something. She'd hate to have to go into care – even for a short while."

Janet closed the door of her flat and dropped onto the settee. She was exhausted and worried about the future. There was no way Ruth could move in with her. A night or two was fine but, despite their shared parentage and upbringing, they were so different in their ways that living in a two-bedroomed flat would never work. Could she live in Ruth's house? Maybe, but she looked around at the place she'd called home for a long time and her stomach somersaulted. Perhaps their cousin, Rosemary, would be willing to help out for a few months. She was always looking for things to fill her time since her retirement, and her husband's death. Ah well. Needs must. Tomorrow was soon enough to think about that, but it was clear something had to change.

\*\*\*

"Hello, Jack. Had a good day at school?"

Jack nodded. There was no way he was going to tell anyone at the home about the fight he'd had with the class bully. He pulled his jumper sleeves down to cover the bruises on his wrists.

"Good. Why don't you get changed, and then you can watch TV for a while before we eat? All right?"

Jack nodded again and slipped out of the kitchen and up to his room. As he pulled off his jumper he winced. His arms were turning a strange colour and he could see that some of the scratches had been bleeding. He went into the bathroom to wash away the blood and bit his lip as the wounds began to sting. It was the first time he'd been in trouble at school. Usually it was Adam, but today had been different. It was Adam's birthday and the class had sung to him, and some of the children had brought him cards. Dean Maddox, or Mad Dean as most of the older pupils called him, had always been jealous of Adam's popularity, but today's celebrations had tipped him over the edge. Adam had ignored him for most of the morning, but at lunchtime, the taunts about Adam's heritage were just too much. Surprisingly, it was Jack who broke first, and he lashed out at the bully. Big mistake. Within a minute Dean had pinned him to the ground and was pummelling and scratching his arms and twisting his wrists. By the time Adam pitched in, Jack had been badly hurt but refused to cry. He smiled when he remembered the look of surprise and admiration on Adam's face. They really were best friends now.

# 1999

## December 1st

The boys were whispering together in a corner of the classroom. It was Adam's birthday and they were excited that Adam's mum had been given permission to take Jack to the cinema with them as a special treat. None of them realised it was actually Jack's birthday as well.

Over the past year Jack had grown a lot. He was not only taller, but his scrawny frame had also filled out and he now had some colour in his cheeks. He was still very quiet, unless he was with Adam, but able to communicate fully when he felt the need. He was also excited about the next day – his appointed birthday – as he knew he was to have his own room at the children's home.

That evening, Jack lay on his bed kicking his foot against the wall, thinking about his best friend. He often wished that he had a mum, and a flat like Adam. He wondered if his mother, whoever she was, ever thought about him. He tried not to think about her too often, ever since he learned about the day he'd been found, but there were the odd times when something prodded his memory that he tried to picture her. He ran the tip of his finger along the scar on his forearm. It didn't hurt anymore and he was so used to it that it didn't bother him. He'd tried to hide it at first when he started school but once someone spotted it, and he became the centre of attention for a short time, he just accepted it. Adam had been curious but not for long. It was just part of who Jack was.

He squeezed his eyes shut and tried to picture anything from when he was little, but all he could see was snow: all he could feel was the cold, and rough cloth against his face. There was no sense of a woman's presence. He tried to think why his mother would have left him the way she did but it was impossible for him to imagine any reasons at all. As he gave the wall an extra hard kick and punched the side of the bed, he knocked a book off the bedside cabinet. It fell open at a picture of a mother bird feeding its young. A sudden craving for chocolate pushed him off the bed and he crept down to the kitchen.

***

Well, that's it. Another bloody year nearly over and nothing seems to change. Different place maybe but my life's still shit. I thought when we got back to Alderbridge that we'd have a house like before, not this pokey flat. Can't say anything to his lordship, of course. Supposed to be grateful that I've got anywhere according to him. Wasn't my fault they got busted but who's the one to come off worse? Yeah, me.

"What're you doing in here? It's way past time you were out. Don't look at me like that or you won't be looking at all tomorrow. Now put something decent on and GET OUT."

"Don't shout at me, Jake. You can't blame me for wanting to stay in. It's freezing and it might snow. It's no fun being half-dressed hanging around the streets waiting for some disgusting bloke to paw me all over and shove me up against a wall. And if they've got cars it's even worse. You know how many times they've got what they wanted and then dumped me miles away."

"How else are you going to pay your way? You swig enough vodka to sink the Titanic. Not my fault that the boss didn't want you to do the drops anymore, and I'm not keeping you."

"Oh no. Perfect pretty Miss Shelley jumped in there quick enough, didn't she? Probably jump in here if she could, too."

That was too far and now I've got bruises on the bruises. I don't think I'll ever learn with Jake. Trouble is, he can turn so quickly, and I'm finding it harder to keep my mouth shut.

I'd cope better if I was in one of the houses but the boss wouldn't have that either. Said Jake could run me for himself if I kept my distance from his patches. This isn't the best part of town, but trade is rarely slow, unfortunately. Maybe the weather will keep them in tonight.

\*\*\*

"I'm off now, Maisie. You okay to lock up? I'll pick up the kids first and take them back to my place for an hour. It'll give Jeff's mum a break!"

"Thanks, Kay. I'll get Jeff to pick Holly up about six-thirty?"

Kay hurried down the road towards the school. Maisie's little boy had recently started in the nursery wing but only for a half day, so his grandmother looked after him the rest of the time. Kay and Maisie worked out a rota between them and took it in turns to either meet the children or lock up the shop.

Kay shook her head and smiled. It had been a whirlwind of a year. Jeff had found some information about small business set-up grants, operated by the local Training and Enterprise Councils. They also offered lots of business and other training courses, so the girls had made enquiries. Despite some competition, they'd been successful with their application and within six months had secured a small, rented salon. The previous owner had died suddenly and, as there was no family to take over, the property had been empty for some time. A thorough clean and a lick of paint courtesy of some of Jeff's mates, as well as a complete check of the equipment, and they were ready to go. The TEC supported Maisie through the official process of setting up the business and helped Kay to negotiate the best way to handle her earnings and benefits.

Business was a little slow at first but many of their former clients from the estate starting booking appointments and Kay agreed to do some home visits for those who couldn't make the journey. It was working well, and Kay was confident that she'd make a decision about her mother and aunt very soon. Just not yet.

# 2000

## December 1st

"Happy birthday, Adam." Kay smiled at her son and ruffled his hair.

"Muuum! Stop it." He flattened his hair with his hands but couldn't help grinning at his mother.

"Nine years old today. Do you think that deserves a present? Mmmm? Well, maybe if you look behind the settee …"

Kay didn't have time to say another word before Adam leapt out of bed and rushed into the living room. She heard him squeal and then there was a lot of ripping and rustling. She peeped around the door and when she saw his face, she knew she'd got it right, even though she thought he might be a bit young for it.

"*A Game Boy*! *A Game Boy*! You got it. It's great. Wait until Jack sees this."

"Hold on a minute, Buster. That's not going anywhere outside this flat. If you're good, I'll see if Jack's allowed to come over at the weekend for a few hours, or if not, maybe you can go to his place. We'll have a look at the instructions later."

Adam hugged his present and Kay smiled. He was too young to realise that this wasn't the latest colour version that had been released recently, and heavily advertised everywhere, but the first version launched almost ten years earlier. Still, it was in good condition and she'd been lucky to find it. She watched as he fiddled with the buttons and thought, not for the first time, how impatient he was. She grinned – she knew the feeling only too well! A picture of Kal flashed across her mind and she caught her breath. She hadn't thought about him in a long time. It was obvious that Adam now looked very much like her, but anyone who knew Kal well would see his imprint clearly. She'd worried if the other children at school would pick on him for being a little different from them, but apart from one incident some years earlier, Adam was a popular member of the class. She'd been as surprised as the teachers when she found out Jack had defended her son. She'd heard a lot about the boy from Adam, but she'd never met him until that time. She'd bought him some chocolate to say, 'thank you', and waited after school for the lady from the home who came to meet him. There was something vaguely familiar about the child but no matter how hard she tried, she couldn't think where she might have seen him before.

She mulled over the past year and felt immensely proud of what she and Maisie had achieved. The business was doing well, and they were keeping their heads above water. She thought about how her dad had built up his business but that led her to the memory of the stolen money, and then to Tia and Luke. She shook her head: she wasn't ready to go down that road again.

As she stood at the window, a sudden, sharp pain in her stomach took her breath away. It wasn't the first time it had happened, but this was the worst it had been.

*** 

"Come on, slowcoach! The mob'll be here soon and we haven't even got the soup on."

Janet jumped. Mary was right, she had been dawdling. She wasn't trying to avoid doing anything, she'd just been distracted by the snow.

"Sorry, Mary, I was miles away. I love watching the snow."

"Not so nice if you're out in it, though. Especially if you've nowhere to go."

Janet agreed. She knew she had the luxury of a warm

home to go back to. The people waiting outside didn't. They were society's cast-offs, drifters, drop-outs: the homeless. But however they were labelled, she still saw them as people. Maybe needing a little more help, a little more guidance, but still people. She couldn't pretend that she'd particularly want to call them all friends, or take them home with her, but she did feel sympathy for all of them.

"I expect we'll have quite a crowd tonight. The snow's really coming down now. Poor devils come in for a warm as much as for the food. Can't blame them but I always think it seems cruel to let them in here for a while then expect them to go back out into the cold. Might be better just to have a serving hatch at the door. What do you think, Janet?"

"I'm not sure. At least when they come in we get chance to talk to them. It's the only conversation some of them have."

"Few and far between, though - the ones that can hold a sensible conversation. Mostly, all I get are grunts and nods. Some of them can't even be bothered to say, 'thank you'. There's the odd one or two, I grant you, that have a bit more about them, but I can't say I find a lot to talk to them about."

Janet knew that Mary meant well, and was a hard worker, but often wondered why Mary had chosen this type of volunteering. She'd have been great in one of the shops, or in the hospital or hospice but she didn't seem able, or even want, to try to connect with the poor souls who trudged along to the church hall three nights a week for a cup of soup and a few sandwiches. They used to be open five nights but over the past two years that had been cut down. Money was tight but it was so hard trying to explain to the 'customers'. Some of the residents were glad, though. They didn't want the charity there at all. Said it gave the district a bad name: lowered house prices. They argued that it was encouraging the drunks, the drug addicts and other unsavouries into the area and that there ought to be a mobile unit somewhere else.

Mary unlocked the hall door and let in the first group. They were mostly the regulars, the ones who knew which nights and what time to come. Others would drift in later, but they had to take their chances that there would be any food left.

"Come on you lot. Shift yourselves. Let's keep the snow out." Mary raised her voice against the shouts of the crowd. "Anyone who's new, wait over here next to me. I'll show you where everything is as soon as everyone's in. The rest of you know what to do."

Mary made sure the big light was on in the porch, so that the stragglers knew that they could come in. Then she closed the door with a bang and shivered. She sighed and began to talk the 'newbies' through the drill.

An hour later the hall door creaked open and Tia slid into the room. She pushed back her hair, wiped the snow from her face and began chewing the skin at the side of her nails. The sudden heat of the hall and the smell of the soup made her feel dizzy and sick at the same time. She didn't know what to do or where to go, and no one was looking at her. She started to walk backwards and put her hand behind her to open the door when Janet caught sight of her.

"Oh no! Don't leave. Come in, come in."

Tia stopped.

"It's all right. Everyone's welcome here. Haven't seen you before, have we? My name's Janet and that's Mary over in the kitchen. You're a bit later than most of the others, but I'm sure we can find you something hot. Would you like that?"

Tia nodded.

"Come on. Come and sit over here. It's a bit quieter and I can tell you how we work. Is that all right?"

Tia nodded again and followed Janet to a table on the far side of the hall. She sat down and began to shiver so hard that the table rattled.

"Good grief, you really are cold, aren't you? Listen, why don't you take off that wet coat and I'll find you something else to wear for a while. OK?"

Janet went through a door next to the kitchen and a few moments later she returned with a towel and a quilted jacket.

"There. Now dry your hair and put this on. It's probably miles too big for you but at least it's warm. I'll put your coat in the kitchen to dry off. You must have been outside for ages. I'll bring you some soup and whatever else I can find."

Tia took the towel and mopped her hair. It wasn't long before the towel was sodden as well. She struggled into the jacket and wrapped it around her. For the first time that night, she smiled. She looked like a sausage roll! The warmth of the jacket and the hall made her feel sleepy and her eyes closed. When Janet came back with the food, she stopped for a moment before waking Tia. The young woman was so thin and pale that Janet wondered how she'd even managed to walk here against such a strong wind. Her hair hung to her waist and needed a good wash, but Janet could see that it would look beautiful if it was properly cut and clean. She put down the food and was just about to wake Tia, when she noticed the bruises along her cheekbone and around her neck. Janet sighed. Another poor soul, another sad story.

"Hey, wake up. Come on, try to eat this while it's hot."

Tia opened her eyes wide and jumped up, knocking over her chair.

"It's OK. It's OK." Janet caught hold of Tia's sleeve. "You're safe here. No one's going to hurt you. Sit down and eat. You don't have to pay for it, and no one will bother you. You don't even have to talk to anyone if you don't want to. If you want me to go away, I will, as long as you promise me that you'll eat. When you want to leave, come to the kitchen and I'll give you your coat. All right?"

Tia nodded and sat down.

"Do you want to tell me your name?"

Tia shook her head.

"All right, that's fine. Maybe another time."

Half an hour later, Tia sidled up to the kitchen hatch. Most of the others had gone – just a few hopefuls waiting to clear up any leftovers. Mary had gone as well after Janet had agreed to lock up. She wasn't supposed to be on her own in the hall, but she wasn't worried.

"Oh. Are you going? I won't close up for another half an hour yet if you want to stay a bit longer. No? All right. Here's your coat. It's not completely dry but it's a bit better than when you came in."

Tia handed back the jacket and pushed her arms into her coat. The sleeves were soggy and as the collar touched her neck it sent shivers right through her. Janet frowned. There was something about this young woman that touched her more than some of the others, but she couldn't quite figure out what. She seemed oddly familiar, but Janet couldn't put her finger on where she might have seen her before.

"Do you have somewhere to sleep tonight? Somewhere out of the snow? You could try the shelter down near the station. They sometimes keep emergency beds. We'll be open again the day after tomorrow if you want to come again."

Tia half-nodded and managed to croak, 'Thanks', then she left. Janet watched her close the door and wondered if she'd even make it to the next open-hall time.

"Come on, you lot. I've wrapped up what's left and you can take it with you. One each, now."

Ten minutes later the kitchen and the hall were clean. Janet switched off the lights and locked the inner doors. Before she put out the porch light, she glanced up the street. The snow was gusting along and piling up in drifts against the walls. At the end of the road she saw someone who looked like the young woman with the long hair. Janet locked the porch door and decided to walk home. She could pick up the car when the weather was better. She plodded through the snow, making deep imprints with her boots. She pushed her hands further into her pockets and wriggled her fingers in her woolly gloves. It was hard to keep her eyes open with the wind in her face and her breathing was becoming ragged. She stopped for a moment and leaned against a garage door. The woman was still under the lamppost and Janet was just about to call to her when a man came out of the lane and crossed the road. He stopped to speak to the woman and then they left together. Janet shook her head and moved on.

# 2001

## March

"It's pouring down, Jake. Do I have to?" I should know better than to ask. Slap in the face, punch in the kidneys and shoved out the door. What the hell am I doing? All for what? Some cheap booze and a bed for the night. But what's the alternative?

Bloody hell, it's cold. Blokes must be desperate to come looking for it in this weather. Just a few punters, please. Then I can go back inside.

There are people going into the hall. Must be soup night. I could go in for a while – what's the harm? There's no one about. Just ten minutes. One cup of soup. I can bring a sandwich out with me.

I need to be more careful around Jake but it's getting harder and harder to make up the money. I could go out earlier but there's not much traffic then. Not the sort that I need, and the last thing I want is to get picked up by Plod. I can't even charge more 'cos that would get back to Jake somehow, even if they were willing to pay it. Got nothing else to sell, either.

I didn't think I'd go back to the hall, but I couldn't help myself. I don't go too often 'cos Jake would notice that my 'wages' have dropped. It wouldn't matter why, although he'd probably be angrier about me going to the hall than the fact that even the punters don't want me anymore.

I like Janet. It was weird at first. Apart from the Summers, and Kay, I'd never really had anyone in my life who'd listened to me. Plenty of people told me I wasn't worth listening to, so I guess I never bothered trying. Janet's different. Not much shocks her, although she did laugh when she found out about my name. It had been so long since anyone had used my real name that I just accepted being called Tia, but it was only a nickname. I was registered as Maria, but when I was about six, there were lots of adverts around for a coffee-flavoured liqueur. At first, that's what everyone started calling me, but after a while it became just *Tia*.

I have no idea if my mother chose my name or if it was the people in the home. Can't have been easy for her I suppose. It's still hard now but lots more girls keep their babies on their own and manage all right. Strange to think that there could be a woman close by who shares my blood and genes but that we wouldn't know each other if we were sat next to each other on the bus. As for my father... no point even trying to think about him. Was it from him I got my liking for the booze, or her?

Janet wanted to know what happened after my mother left me and I told her that it was just a series of different houses, different people. Some nice, some not so nice, but I wasn't an easy kid and it always ended up with me going back to the home. They called me the bad penny. She laughed at that, too.

It didn't take too long for me to realise who she was once she mentioned the charity shop. Luckily, she hasn't recognised me. I don't think that's a road I want to go down for the moment.

## October

Janet poured herself a cup of tea and sat down in the kitchen. She wondered if Tia would come in tonight. She hadn't seen her for a few months – not even at the end of the street. She felt she knew the girl a lot better now. That's how she thought of her – a girl. Despite all she'd been through and everything she did, she still seemed like a lost child.

"Skiving off again, Janet?"

Janet jumped and spilled her tea on the floor.

212

"God, Tia, you frightened me to death! How are you? I haven't seen you for a while."

Tia frowned. "Naw. Had to do a bit of work somewhere else." She looked down at her chewed fingernails. "Got any soup left?"

Janet smiled but she was becoming increasingly worried about Tia and the man she called Jake.

"Of course. Want to sit in the hall? It's a bit quieter now. Mary's talking to some people from the Council, so she won't bother us. Have you thought anymore about what I said last time you were in?" Janet leaned forward and looked Tia right in the eyes, but Tia looked away quickly.

"Yeah, I have, but I don't know if I can do it. Trouble is, I feel like a caged bird. Trapped, but even if the cage door was open, I'd be too scared to fly. I've stayed dry for a while before, but as soon as I get knocked around again, I go back. It helps."

"But Tia, if you cleaned up you wouldn't need to work for Jake anymore. He takes the money to pay for your drink, yes, but he takes far more than it costs him to buy it, I'm sure. Would he really miss what you bring in?"

Tia shrugged. "Probably not, but the money's for my keep as well. I have somewhere to stay and food and stuff."

Janet sighed. "Look, I know I'm not supposed to tell people who come in here what to do, but sometimes it's hard not to. You need to cut all ties. Move out. Clean up. Make a new life for yourself. Does he mean that much to you? After all he's done? All he's put you through?"

"I don't know, Janet. It's scary. I've never really done anything on my own before – except – well …"

"What?"

Tia shook her head. "I can't tell you now. Maybe another time. I did leave him once and it felt good for a while - making my own decisions."

"Why did you go back to him, then?"

"Not now, please. I've got to go. I will think about what you've said. Honest."

"And I'll help you all I can with meeting the people who

can support you, I promise. One step at a time."

Tia stood up and tilted her head to one side. "Why?"

"Why what?"

"Why would you want to help me? I'm no one special. No different from a lot of these that come into the hall. Why me?"

Janet bit her bottom lip. "Long story as well. Next time, eh?"

Tia nodded and left.

## December 1st

Kay glanced at the clock and began the process of shutting the salon. Maisie had left earlier to pick up the children from school. She hoped Adam would behave himself tonight. He'd started resenting the days Maisie met them, and the Saturdays with Jeff's mum, but that was the arrangement they'd agreed on, and there was no way Kay could jeopardise their friendship or the business now. She looked around and smiled. The place was so different from when they first moved in. They'd done well enough to invest in some new equipment and were even taking on placements from the college. Jeff had persuaded Maisie to buy a mobile phone, and Maisie wanted Kay to do the same, but she was unsure. She'd saved enough to be able to pay her mother back, although she realised that what she had didn't reflect any kind of interest on the money, and she didn't want to use it for anything else. She'd decided that after Christmas she was going to make plans for reconnecting with her family.

Kay paused for a moment before flicking off the light and looked out onto the snowy street. There was a woman on the other side staring at her. She knew that it was Tia right away. What now? Hang back and hope she went away? Or go out and confront her? Kay shrugged. She'd changed a lot over the past few years and she'd had enough of Tia turning up out of the blue or stalking her, so she picked up her bag and stepped outside. The door shut with a loud click and Kay double-locked it. When she turned around, Tia had gone.

***

"Tia! Oi, Tia, stop fuckin' daydreamin'. Get off your fat arse and get out to work!"

Jake's voice really grates on me. There was a time when I thought he was the only person in the world who cared for me, who really knew me, but that was a long time ago. A long time ago that I'd thought it – I mean. Now, all I hear is *Tia do this, Tia do that, fetch me, give me.* No point whingeing about it, I suppose. I got myself into this mess and I've been too weak to get myself out.

Jake's right, though. I have been daydreaming. I can't stop thinking about Lulu. It's his tenth birthday today. Or it would have been. It's the snow. It always makes me feel this way, especially when it's windy and the snow creeps up the walls and swirls around the windows. That's when I remember. Or at least, I think I remember. When it happened, I thought I'd never forget, but now it's blurred. That was seven years ago and apart from Lu, nothing much has changed. Even when I'm totally pissed I don't think about him much. Maybe if I eased up I could remember a bit more, but whenever I try to dry out, I never get far with it. Maybe if things had been different since then I'd remember it better. Who knows? It was funny seeing Kay today. I hardly recognised her. She looked right through me. Like I didn't exist. Too good to mix with the likes of me, now. Her and that Maisie, too. How the hell did they get enough money to have a shop of their own? She'd have been able to help me plenty if she'd wanted to.

"Tia, if you don't shift off that chair and get out in the next five minutes, I'll bleedin' drag you out there myself."

Another bruise to add to the collection. Wonder what shape this one will be. "But Jake, it's freezing. Can't I give it a miss? Stay in with you?"

"What for? You know what, Tia, you're gettin' to be a fat, lazy cow. I've been thinking for some time now - you should move on. Carla or Shelley would be more than willing to fill your knickers."

I know he means it. It's not just talk with Jake. He did it to

215

me last year – put me out on my own. Thank God I still had Kay's keys. They'd changed the locks on the flat but the entry door was the same and the storage room was safe, at least. I managed to worm my way back in after a week, though. Some little tart had moved in, of course, but I soon got rid of her. Trouble is, I'm older and look it. Time's taken its payment. But do I care what he says? I'll miss the flat more than I thought. It isn't brilliant but at least it's fairly clean and usually warm. I'm not sure I can take it, being in a squat again, but where else can I go? Maybe I'll go see Janet. I don't know why but it just seems kind of easy to talk to her. I've never told her the complete truth about Luke, though.

"Right, I'm off."

"Good. And if you don't make any money, don't bleedin' come back."

"No, Jake. I won't."

I really won't.

# 2002

## April

Janet watched as Tia went around the church hall clearing up. She'd been helping out quite a lot since she'd left Jake. She was looking a lot better, too. She was still in the hostel, but at least she had somewhere to live and someone keeping an eye on her. If she could keep her head above water a while longer there was the possibility of her having her own bedsit, or even a small flat. Janet had supported her as much as she could, organising meetings with social services, the council and a local charity and it seemed that the effort was paying off. Tia had asked about helping her in the charity shop as well, but Janet was undecided about that.

The door banged and a latecomer slipped into the hall. Janet didn't recognise him and was just about to greet him and do the newcomers talk, when Tia approached him.

"Binny! Fancy seeing you here. Didn't know this place was on your patch. How are you?"

"What? Oh, it's YOU. You stay away from me. Don' wants another run in with tha' bloke o' yours. Three weeks in 'ospital the last time. Never 'ad many teeth in the first place, now I got none thanks to 'im. "

"I didn't know that, Binny. Honest. Sorry he hurt you. I'm not with him anymore."

"You said tha' before. I don' wants nothin' to do wi' you. Clear off an' leave me alone."

"Binny!"

Janet frowned and watched the man rush out of the hall. There was still so much that she didn't know about Tia and her previous life.

***

The letterbox rattled and Kay picked up the pile of mail from the floor. She glanced through the envelopes and sucked air through her teeth when she saw the one with the health board logo on the front. She checked that Adam was still in his room before she opened it. Even though it was expected, the confirmation of her operation date came as a shock. She thought back over the past sixteen months and the countless doctors' and hospital visits before she was finally told she had gall stones. She'd managed well for some time but when the attacks became more frequent and vicious the consultant said she would need an operation. Maisie had been brilliant about it and offered for Adam to stay with her, but Kay knew it wouldn't work. Adam was growing up fast and lately he had become more challenging and difficult to manage.

When Kay knew that she would have to spend some time in hospital and would need at least two or three weeks to recover, she'd approached the home where Jack lived and asked if they could help. They'd been brilliant and had organised everything with social services. The big problem now was to tell Adam. Even though he loved spending time with Jack, she didn't know how he would react to being away from her. Still, it might do him good. Might make him realise how lucky he was to have his own home.

## July 13th

Kay smiled at her son as he came out of his bedroom. He'd taken the news of staying with Jack quite well, although he'd certainly been a little more clingy over the past few weeks. She picked up his bag and they left the flat. Two hours later she was back and packing her own bag for the hospital. Jeff was giving her a lift and Maisie said she'd visit that evening. Surgery was scheduled for the next morning, and she was glad it was going to be the keyhole type. She'd be home in a few days and Maisie's mum said she'd come and stay until Kay felt able to manage on her own. She knew how lucky was to have such good friends and it strengthened her resolve to sort things out with her own family.

The next afternoon, Kay opened her eyes and quickly shut them again. She felt so tired and her stomach was very painful.

"Kay? Kay Jones?"

Without even opening her eyes again, Kay knew who it was.

"Come on, Kay, I know you're awake."

She took a deep breath and opened her eyes. "Hello Kal. Fancy seeing you here."

Kalan smiled and caught hold of Kay's hand. For a full minute, neither of them spoke.

"How are you feeling, Kay? Your notes say that everything went well. I wasn't on duty yesterday or I would have seen you sooner."

"I'm okay, I guess. Still feel a bit sore. But what are you doing here? I thought you'd have moved on long ago."

"No. Decided to stay local. Kay…?"

"What is it?"

"It says in your notes that you have a ten-year-old son. It also says that you don't have any other next-of-kin listed, so I guess you're not married?"

Kay shook her head. She'd pictured this meeting a million times, although maybe not in a hospital, but she was suddenly very afraid.

"Kay. Look at me. Is he mine? I know what we did was stupidly irresponsible and after you left, I actually thought I hated you for a while, but I knew I was only kidding myself. I've thought about you such a lot and I often wondered if you'd become pregnant. I tried to find you but didn't know where to start. I saw your mother here once, but I was too scared to ask her."

"My mother? Here? Why, what was wrong?"

"I can't tell you that really, but she was all right. You still haven't answered me."

"Yes, Adam is your son, but I don't expect anything from

219

you, and I don't want to cause any trouble between you and your wife and family. Honestly. We're doing fine."

"Oh, Kay. I never married. There was a lot of pressure from my father, but I couldn't do it. Jazz conformed but it didn't turn out quite like he expected. He thought he was going to have it all his own way, but Amira is much tougher than she looks. She could run the business single-handed and she made it quite clear she wasn't taking any nonsense from him. I think he still strays from time-to-time, but they seem to be making it work now. No kids, unfortunately. After my father died, my mother changed a lot as well. She told Jazz he could have the house if they bought her a little bungalow. Shocked us all but it's good to see her so happy."

"Sorry to hear about your dad."

"All in the past now, but we could be in the future. No matter our differences, I know my mother would welcome her grandson."

Kay stiffened. This was all too much, too soon.

"Hang on, Kal. She might welcome him, but not me, I think. Anyway, what makes you think I want him to get to know her? Or you, for that matter."

Kalan's face fell and he stood up suddenly. "I'm so sorry, Kay. I've botched things again, haven't I? It's just that when I read your notes, I felt that this was meant to be. Sorry. Too fast, but will you give it some thought? I'll leave you my number and you can call me whenever you're ready. Or not at all if you feel that's best. Do you have a phone number?"

Kay kicked herself for not following Maisie's lead and buying a mobile phone. The only phone in the flats was in the entrance hall and no-one really used that for incoming calls.

"No, but I can give you the shop number if you like. I won't be back for a few weeks and I can't really take personal calls there, but at least it's a means of contact. I need some time to think, Kal. Please don't rush me. I'm going home tomorrow, and I really will think about what you've said, but it's been a long time and I don't know if I want my life to change."

220

# July 20th

"Oi, Jack, wake up."

"What? What's happening? What time is it?"

"Shhh! Don't wake everyone up. It's half past five. I found something out about you."

Jack sat up in bed and rubbed his eyes. It had been fun having Adam share his room for the past week, but his friend always seemed to be looking for trouble these days.

"What are you talking about? Found what? Where?"

"Look." Adam was waving a letter around. "You have a grandmother. I found this in the office."

"In the office! What were you doing in there? You'll get us into trouble, for sure. I thought it was locked at night, anyway? And how can I have gran if I don't have a mother, stupid?"

"Watch it! I couldn't sleep and I wanted a drink. I must have tried the wrong door and it was open. Honest. Just thought I'd have a nosey about and there was a cupboard full of old boxes so I just sort of opened a few and I saw a file with your name on it. This …" he waved the letter around, "was right at the bottom. From some old dear who thinks she's your grandmother."

"What! Let me see." Jack grabbed the letter from Adam and quickly scanned the single page. His jaw dropped. Adam laughed.

"Mad, isn't it? Know what we should do? Go and find her. Her address is there and her name. We could go now. I've got some money for the bus. We could just go and have a look."

"But this is years old. She might have moved. And anyway, if it's right, why have I had to stay here?"

"Who knows. Maybe your mother was a murderer or something and they think your gran is mad as well and you'd be safer here."

"Don't be so daft. And if she is mad, why would I want to find her?"

"Aww, come on. It'll be an adventure. We always said we'd do more exciting things when we were older. This is just a chance to do something now. Come on!"

Reluctantly, Jack climbed out of bed, dressed himself and followed Adam downstairs. Five minutes later they were running down the road to town. When they reached the outskirts, they found a quiet spot behind some big wheelie bins at the back of a fast food place. It stank and Jack started to gag. He could see Adam looking at him out of the corner of his eye.

"It's not too late to go back, Adam. They won't have missed us yet."

"No way. This is too exciting. And if the old lady turns out to be your Grandma, she'll help us. She might even be filthy rich and give you loads of money. Just think, we could end up with the same surname!"

Jack shook his head. He was beginning to think it was his friend who was mad.

"Adam. I'm going back. I'm sorry. I'm scared. Adam? Adam?"

But it was no use. Adam was fast asleep with his head against the wall. Jack knew he couldn't just leave him there, so he tried to get comfortable and eventually dozed off. He woke when a binman kicked him in the ankle.

"Oi, what are you kids doing here? Clear off now before I call the law. Go home."

The boys jumped up and ran to the bus station, not that there was any rush, but it warmed them up a little. The timetable showed that the first bus to Fieldslea left at seven thirty - half an hour to wait. There was nothing open, so they pushed some coins into a machine and breakfasted on cola.

When the bus pulled in to Fieldslea they hopped off and looked around for some way of finding the district called The Meadows. They saw a woman pushing a pram and decided to risk asking her. It wasn't far. Just a few streets away.

"Adam, what are we doing? We can't just turn up at her door and say, 'I might be your grandson, and this is my friend and, by the way, we've just run away from a children's home.' She'll freak out."

Adam grinned. "Don't be daft. She'll be so excited she'll

do anything you ask."

Jack had never seen this side of Adam before, and he didn't like it.

The rest of that day was a bit of a blur. They hung around the end of the street, then outside number ten, for so long that someone had come out and shouted at them. They didn't stop to think but ran as fast they could back to the bus stop. There was a bit of trouble at the home, but they said they'd just gone out early to play. A few days of being grounded seemed a small price to pay.

***

Janet's sister has a nice house. Must be hard to leave a place like this. I bet she got a good price for it, though. Seems a waste having all that money and no-one to spend it on. I hope they're not too long at the solicitors. I know I said I'd help with the packing, but I need to get back by four for my meeting. I can't believe I've got my own place at last. Not very big but I have a key and I can come and go as I please. Janet's been great. I couldn't have done it without her. Probably would still have been with Jake. But it's time to forget all that. Put it behind me. I wonder if Kay's still at that shop with Maisie. Maybe when I get settled, I can ask her around. Straighten things out. She can't hold a grudge for this long, surely?

I don't know what else Mrs Jones wants me to do. She only said about the glasses and the kitchen stuff and that didn't take too long. Maybe I can do something in the living room.

Weird. Those two kids were hanging about at the bottom of the road when we got here this morning. They can't be more than about ten. Doesn't look as though there's anyone with them, either. Hang on, they've just come into the front garden. What the hell are they up to?

"Hey. You two. What're you doing? Clear off or I'll call the law. Scarper!"

***

"Well, that's it, Ruth. All signed and sealed. A few more days and you'll be in your new home. Excited?"

"Sort of. It's going to be hard leaving the old house, but it's time. I need to make the most of my life now and the house is getting to be too much. I know I wasn't too keen having Rosemary stay for so long, but I certainly missed all she did for me after she left."

"Right. Well a bit more packing, then I'll take Tia home and pick up some fish and chips on the way back. Naughty, I know, but it'll save pulling things out to cook. I'm glad I've got some time off work. It makes it much easier."

"Thanks Jan. It's good of you to give up your time."

"That's all right. It's been handy having Tia around too."

Ruth didn't reply and Janet gave her a sideways glance. She knew that look.

"Come on. Spill the beans. What's the matter?"

"Nothing really. I'm just not too sure about the girl. Can't take to her. What exactly do you know about her?"

Janet gave Ruth a brief, potted history for Tia and her involvement with Jake.

"I think he must have been some kind of odd-job man – she said he managed a couple of houses for some fellow. Think he's always been handy with his fists but between that and the drinking, she'd had enough and finally left him."

"Nice. And how come you're so involved with her 'recovery'?"

"Don't be like that, Ruth. She's had a rough life and just happened to cross my path. I suppose in some ways she made me think of Kay and I just wanted to help. I had the contacts, so what was the harm? Once I can find her a job, she'll be less dependent and hopefully, she'll start to make some decent friends."

"Has she ever worked?"

"I don't think so, although …"

"What?"

"I think she might have been on the game for a while."

"What! You're kidding me?"

Janet pulled the car into Ruth's driveway and as they

stepped out, Tia opened the front door.

"Everything okay?"

Janet nodded. "All done. How about you?"

"Yeah, fine. I've done what you asked. Funny thing happened though. Two lads were hanging about for ages and then I saw them sneak into the garden. I shouted at them and they scarpered. Cheek!"

Half an hour later, after tea and biscuits, Ruth and Janet went into the dining room while Tia cleared up.

"We can do in here next. I'm not sure about leaving the globe for the removal men or putting it in our own packing cases. I know it's only a hairline crack, but I'd cry if it broke. What do you think?"

Janet examined the globe. "See what you mean. Best not to take chances. Tell you what, I'll get Tia to find a box and we'll pack it carefully. When I take her home, I'll drop it off at my place and then you can have it back when you've settled in. All right?"

"Makes sense. Thanks, Jan."

Janet called Tia. When she walked into the dining room, she stopped dead in her tracks. The blood drained from her face as she saw the globe and her insides felt like ice. She started to tremble, and the two women stared at her.

"What's the matter?" Janet caught hold of Tia's arm. "Sit down for goodness sake before you fall down."

Tia dropped into a chair and looked from one woman to the other.

"That's the snow globe. I know about that. How have you got it?"

"What do you mean?" Ruth glared at her. "It's mine. How do you know about it?" She looked at Janet, who shook her head.

"It plays music, doesn't it?" Tia began to hum the *Winter Lullaby* shakily.

"How …" Ruth moved forward and as she did, Tia caught sight of a photograph on the sideboard.

"Kay."

When Janet returned with the promised fish and chips, she headed straight for the kitchen. She smiled when she saw that her sister had laid out plates and cutlery. No paper bags for her! Still, it was good she cared enough to make the effort. Things had been tough for her since Paul's death and the bombshell Tia had just dropped was enough to make anyone crack up.

## September 11th

Kay switched on the news and was transfixed by the reports from America. A whole year had passed by since the awful events at the Twin Towers in New York, but the pictures being flashed on the screen were still powerful enough to make her cry. Such a loss. So many families torn apart and grieving.

"What's wrong, mum? Why are you crying? Are you ill again?"

Kay held Adam close and rocked him.

"It's all right. I'm fine. I've been watching something sad on the television. Nothing for you to worry about."

As she hugged her son, she knew she was being unfair to him by denying him his father and both grandmothers, but her stomach knotted at the thought of all the possible complications such contact might bring. They had a good life. Yet the hurt expression on Kalan's face at the hospital still haunted her. She'd almost called him several times but held back. He called the salon once and Maisie had answered. Of course, as soon as she knew the full story, she'd been badgering Kay to make a decision. One thing she'd insisted on was that Kay bought herself a phone.

The scene on the television shifted and an interview, with a young girl whose father had died when the second tower collapsed, finally convinced Kay it was time to face the consequences of her earlier mistakes. She knew she'd changed a lot over the past ten years and hoped her mother could at least see that and forgive her, even if she wasn't prepared to welcome her back into the family fold. As for Mrs Khatri, well, that remained to be seen.

## October 13th

Janet helped Ruth to clear away after their Sunday lunch, then they sat down with a glass of wine. Ruth had settled into her new home quickly, and Janet was pleased to see her looking so well.

"You've done wonders with this place, Ruth. Really brought it back to life."

"Thanks. It was a bit tired, wasn't it? Good thing that chap who did yours last year was available. I miss the old house but I'm glad I moved. Never thought I'd find a bungalow near you, though. It's lovely to still have a garden, even if it is small."

"Just don't try to do too much on your own."

"Yes, bossy boots! I'm feeling fine, honestly. Oh! There was one thing I've been meaning to ask you. You remember the bags I gave you for the charity shop?" Janet nodded. "Well there was a box with some bits and pieces of jewellery – nothing fancy –costume stuff, mostly brooches."

"I remember. To be fair to Marge she said they were too nice to put in with all the others, so she made up a stand, covered it with a piece of black velvet and pinned all the brooches on it. Why? What's the matter?"

"I think I might have put one in that I didn't intend to. Do you remember the brooch that looked like the snow globe? Kay bought it for me one Christmas. Well, she chose it and Paul paid! I'm sure it was quite expensive and there's no way I wanted to part with it, but I think I must have put it in the box by mistake. I've looked everywhere but I can't find it. Can you check in the shop, or ask Marge? I know it's been a while, but I have to try."

"Sure. I don't recall seeing it, but I'll double check. Tia's coming in tomorrow for a few hours, so I'll ask her as well. What? What's that face for?"

"Sorry. I don't mean to be judgemental but there's something about her I don't like. I know it's none of my business, but I do wish you'd ease off a bit now. It's really not like you to get so involved."

227

Janet shrugged. She knew Ruth was right but every time she tried to sound out Tia about work opportunities, or some kind of training, she evaded the issue or looked so terrified that Janet backed off. She allowed Tia into the shop on the odd occasion, but the girl was pressing for a more permanent arrangement. In one way it felt good to be able to help someone to pull themselves out of a bad situation, but she hadn't intended to become so enmeshed.

## October 14th

Kay stepped off the bus in Fieldslea and looked around. It had been a long time since she'd walked along these streets and she could feel her stomach somersaulting and her knees beginning to shake. She was glad they didn't open the salon on a Monday. It gave her the chance to make this journey on her own. She couldn't face Adam's questions and his disappointment if things didn't work out the way she hoped.

Ten minutes later she stood at the gate of her old home. She noticed the new curtains and that the garden wasn't as neat as it had been. She took a deep breath, walked up the path and rang the bell. A boy in his late teens opened the door and stared at her.

"Umm, is Mrs Jones in?"

"Dunno any Mrs Jones."

"But she lives here. She's my mother."

"If she's your mother then you should know where she is, shouldn't you? We've been here since the summer. Dunno where the old lady who lived here went."

He slammed the door and Kay stepped back quickly. She hadn't expected that. She thought about waiting until the boy's parents came home but decided against it.

When Kay entered the charity shop, Marge was on her own at the counter.

"Hello. Is Janet in today, please?"

"She's in the back room. Why do you want to see her?"

"I'm Kay. Her niece."

"Not the one who …"

"I guess so. Can I see her, please?"

Marge pointed to a door at the rear of the shop and Kay moved swiftly forwards. The door opened quietly and she saw her aunt emptying clothes out of a black bag.

"Auntie Janet." She could barely get the words out.

Janet spun around and her jaw dropped. "Kay!"

"I've just been home but they said that Mum had moved."

"Yes, that's right. Near me. Oh Kay, you've no idea how long we've waited for this. Come here."

Janet moved forward to hug her niece and Kay caught sight of a figure kneeling on the floor. She pulled back suddenly from her aunt's embrace.

"YOU! What the hell are you of all people doing here. I thought I'd seen the back of you."

"Don't be like that Kay. Can't we talk?"

"Talk? Talk? Are you mad?" She turned to her aunt. "I don't know what she's doing here, but I hope you haven't fallen for her bullshit stories. She's trouble, through and through."

"Hang on a minute, Kay. Tia's told us about how you met and how you helped her but she's had a rough time. I've been helping her to straighten out …"

"Us? Us? You mean she's been with Mum too? Well, I hope you've checked all the silver because little Miss Tia here is quite light-fingered. You know, it's ironic that the money I took from Dad was stolen from me – "

"Yes, your mother told me. You put it in the letter you sent."

"Yeah, and guess who it was that nicked it? Oh, you can look away, Missy. There's no-one else it could have been. You know what, this was a big mistake. If I'd thought even for one minute that she'd be here, I'd never have walked in the door."

Janet put out her hand. "Stop for one second, Kay. You've obviously worked hard and you look really well. Tia hasn't had it so good, but she's been trying to deal with her problems. Why don't you at least listen to her for a few

229

minutes and then you can decide if you want to walk away. I'll go into the shop and you two can talk in here."

She closed the door and Kay glared at Tia.

"You might have fooled her and wormed your way in as usual, but you'll never change. You're rotten through and through. Why did you lie about the hostel place that Mrs Connor sorted out for you? Why on earth did you steal that money? You knew it was all I had. After everything I did for you. Risking losing my home, sharing all I had with you. Helping you with Luke. Why? Just why?"

"Sorry." Tia flushed and looked at the floor. "I didn't mean to hurt you and I was grateful that you spoke to Mrs Connor for me, but I couldn't face the Social people and all the questions, and I knew you didn't want me to move with you to your new flat, so I made it up about the hostel. When it sank in what I'd done I panicked, and I took the money at the last minute."

"And what about Luke? Did you give any thought to him? Is he all right?"

Tia hesitated. "Luke's dead."

"WHAT?"

"He had an accident when he was three. He fell and cut his arm badly. He lost too much blood. It was snowing really heavily but Jake got him to the hospital – "

"JAKE? Bloody Jake? You don't mean to tell me that you took that poor little boy to live with that psycho bastard. What in heaven's name were you thinking of?"

"No. I didn't go back straight away. We had a couple of months in a caravan."

"Blagged that off someone else, I suppose?"

"No, I paid for it."

"With my money. You know what? I'm sorry about Luke but you deserve everything that happened to you. You're a leech, and nothing's ever your fault, is it? If my aunt's determined to let you stay around then that's her decision, but I don't want anything to do with you."

Kay ran out and made for the shop door. Janet caught her sleeve but Kay just shook her hand away.

230

"Sorry. I can't ask you choose between us, that's not fair, but if I never see her face again, it'll be too soon. Please don't tell Mum you've seen me."

"Wait. Take this. It's her new address. Just in case. I'm still in the same flat. Please think about this."

Janet hadn't meant to eavesdrop, but she was curious about the relationship between the girls and wanted to learn more about Tia. What she heard confused her. When Tia had told her the story of how she'd lived with Kay, Janet had realised that she'd lied about giving up her son for adoption soon after his birth. She hadn't pressed her on that and had assumed that it happened after she'd got back together with the Jake character. So why would she tell Kay that the child was dead? There was something else about the story nagging at the back of her mind, but she couldn't capture it. She knew that she wouldn't discuss any of this with Ruth as her sister would be sure to blame Tia, and perhaps Janet, for preventing Kay's return.

Kay ran all the way to the bus station. She had to bite the inside of her cheek to stop herself from crying. By the time she reached her flat, she'd worked herself up into a frenzy and spent ten minutes pounding the cushions and catapulting every swear word she could think of at the wall. The tears followed very quickly, and she cursed the day she'd met Tia. When she thought about Luke, she cried even harder. She could well imagine the conditions the little boy had been living in. At least, she thought she could, but she didn't even come close.

By the time Adam was home from school, Kay was calm and gave him no indication of the kind of day she'd had.

*** 

Well, that was unexpected. Kay of all people. I thought she could have been a bit more friendly. I mean, it's been ten years since she kicked me out and she seems to have done all right for herself. Fancy her begrudging me getting some help from Janet. Think she'd be pleased I was trying to do something to better myself. I don't know why I told her about Luke – I didn't mean to; it just came out. I hope Janet didn't overhear. Don't want her asking questions or poking about in the past. I do like her but it's still hard to trust anyone completely. I guess I came the closest with Kay and look how she stabbed me in the back. I couldn't have managed without that money and at least she had a place to live and regular benefits. It wouldn't have killed her to let us stay for a little while. The kids didn't really need their own rooms right away and nobody at the new place would have known anything about me. Preferred her new mate though, didn't she? Too good for the likes of me. Snooty cows, the pair of them! I can see where Kay gets it from, too. That mother of hers is the same. Happy to have me skivvying around for her, but then it's *'Ta ta Tia, clear off now'*. Janet's different. Still a bit cautious around me, but I think it'll be okay. I need to keep sweet with her. She's the only one helping me now. I suppose I could tell them where Kay's living – if she's still there. Or tell them about the shop, but if I do that they'll want to go after her, especially her mother, I bet, and where will that leave me? Out in the cold again. No, I think I'll keep that to myself for now.

## December 1st

Another birthday. Kay could hardly believe Adam was eleven years-old and in his last year at primary school. She hoped when the time came that he'd settle into comprehensive school. He'd been quite disruptive over the past year and she'd had several notes from the school about his behaviour. On an impulse she picked up her phone and looked for Kalan's number.

"Hi. I'm not disturbing you, am I? Good. I'm sorry I haven't called before, but it's all been a bit much to take in. I've thought about what you said and if you promise that we can take things slowly, then I'd like to see you again. It might not work out but at least you can meet Adam and get to know him. After that, it's up to him. As for our mothers, well, let's wait and see about that for the moment. All right? How about coffee some time? I'm almost always free on a Monday. Okay. See you there."

\*\*\*

"Come on, slowcoach. Everyone's waiting."

Jack grinned and followed the home's manager into the dining room. There was a cake in the centre of the table and piles of sandwiches, sausage rolls and other party food on plates around the edges. On the table near the window there was a small pile of cards and some brightly wrapped parcels. They were having the party a day early, or so they thought, as it was Monday next day and too much of a rush, but Jack didn't mind. He looked around and felt glad that he lived here. He liked the orderliness of every day and of knowing that there would always be clean clothes for him; always be food on the table, and always be someone here in the house with him.

\*\*\*

Janet and Ruth were just about to start their Sunday lunch when the doorbell rang. Ruth opened the door to find Tia clutching a bunch of flowers.

"Hello Mrs Jones. I'm really sorry to disturb you but I went to Janet's and she was out, so I guessed she might be here. Do you think I could speak to her?"

Ruth didn't answer and left Tia on the step while she fetched her sister. Janet didn't need to ask how Ruth was feeling.

"Tia, come into the hall. What's the matter?"

"Sorry. It's just that it's Luke's birthday today and I can't stop thinking about him. I thought you and Mrs Jones might be the same, what with it being Adam's as well. Seeing Kay the other month brought it all back to me. I'm sorry if I got in the way."

Janet pulled a face and put her finger to her mouth, but it was too late. There was a clattering in the kitchen and Ruth burst into the hall.

"What's she talking about, Jan? How did she see Kay? Did you know about it? Don't lie to me, please."

Fifteen minutes and many tears and angry words later, Tia left the bungalow: smiling.

# 2003

## February

After the upset when Ruth overheard Tia's comments about seeing Kay, Janet had been quite cool with her. Tia had protested that she didn't hear Kay asking Janet not to tell her sister, but Janet didn't quite believe her. Tia had been wise enough to keep her distance for a while but then the old neediness crawled back. She struggled to avoid the temptation to buy vodka, but when it became a daily urge, she sought out Janet at the church hall. After the tears and self-recrimination, the promises and pleas, Janet relented and agreed that Tia could return to the shop, but not on a regular basis. She was still hurting from some of Ruth's comments and it had taken a lot of grovelling and promises to keep looking for Kay, to even come close to appeasing her sister. She didn't want to rock the boat again, so she decided to keep the arrangement with Tia to herself.

***

The phone rang and Kay caught her breath. She knew it would be Kalan. She glanced across the room at Adam but he was engrossed in the latest episode of *Grange Hill* and didn't notice her slip into her bedroom. She'd met Kal a few times since their first phone call and they spoke at least twice a week. She realised she'd never known him properly and that he was far from the introvert she'd first thought him. He was bright, funny, caring, and considerate and he made her feel good about herself. He didn't pressurise her into talking about anything she didn't want, and he didn't force the issue of meeting Adam, but she knew if they wanted to date properly, then Adam would have to know the truth. But how to tell him?

## July

"Adam?"

"Mmm?" Adam looked away from the television and raised his eyebrows.

Kay hesitated. "Do you remember some time ago you asked me about your father?"

Adam frowned. "Yeah, so what?"

"Did you ever wonder what he was like? Or why you never saw him?"

"Not really. You said you were both too young to be together so you kept me with you. Why? What's going on? Why are you asking me all this stuff?"

"Well, the thing is, I bumped into him a little while back and he'd like to meet you, if you want." Kay crossed her fingers behind her back.

"Eh? What for? Why didn't he want to see me when I was little? Why now?"

"Don't scowl like that, Adam. I said I'd ask you, that's all. He couldn't see you before because, well, it's complicated. His family expected him to finish university and then do his training, and we lost touch even before you were born. It's not his fault, Adam. I didn't tell him about you. I'm sorry, but I thought it was for the best."

Adam took some time to process the information, then turned back to the programme he'd been watching. Despite Kay's attempts to open up the conversation again, he wouldn't answer her.

After days of receiving the cold-shoulder treatment from Adam, Kay was afraid that any plans of a relationship with Kalan were doomed. She decided to let things lie but to continue their meetings whenever possible.

\*\*\*

Another boring day. I'll go mad if I have stay in this flat much longer. Maybe Janet's right and I should be thinking about a proper job, but what can I do? Cleaning's about my limit, I suppose, but why should I be scrabbling about for some hoity-toity bitch who's too idle to look after her own place? Naw. I just need to find myself something to do. I thought that Janet would have softened up a bit more by now. I wish I could persuade her to let me work at the shop properly. If I take her up on any of her other schemes then she'll cut me off, I know, and then there won't be anybody to sort things out with the social and council and whatever for me. And I'll miss out on all the extras she gives me. Pick of clothes from the shop and bits and bobs for the flat. Leftovers from the soup-kitchen. Not sure why she's been cooling off a bit lately. That sister of hers, I'll bet. You can tell she's Kay's mother all right. Probably checked her purse after I helped when she was moving. The soup kitchen's all right but a bit too close to Jake's flat for my liking. I don't mind when Janet gives me a lift but if she goes to that sister of hers, I have to walk. God, I could murder a drink.

\*\*\*

Jack was growing increasingly apprehensive about the end of term. It would be the last in the primary school that he had grown to love, and the thought of moving to the local comprehensive filled him with dread. He knew it was much larger and that he'd have to travel on the school bus instead of walking. Although Adam would be transferring with him, there was no guarantee they'd be in the same form and they definitely wouldn't be on the bus together. Despite the beautiful weather he began to have the old nightmares about the cold, and snow, and frequently awoke shivering and afraid.

# December 1st

The boys were chatting over their lunch and Adam was

telling Jack about his plans for the following weekend. He'd asked his mum for money for his birthday and Maisie had given him the same. Jack wasn't so lucky but he didn't begrudge his friend anything.

"Do you think you'd be allowed to come into town with me, Jack?"

"Dunno. I can ask. What do you want to buy?"

"A present for my mum. For Christmas. I've been a pig to her for ages but I don't know how to say sorry. I can't get the words out. She's not cross with me but she seems sad."

Jack nodded. Adam had told him about the conversation with Kay about his dad and they'd spent a long time imagining what he looked like, where he lived and what he did. Jack thought it would be good to have a dad as well as a mother, although he sometimes thought that he'd settle for either. He also knew Adam well enough to know not to push him on the subject. The stubbornness trait certainly ran right through the Jones family!

"What kind of present? What does she like?"

Adam grinned. "I know just what to get. When she was little there was a snow globe at her house and she was scared of it but she's always going on about it whenever it snows and she's always humming the song that it played. I want to get one just like it if I can."

Jack looked puzzled. "What's a snow globe?"

Adam poked him in the ribs and laughed. He described Kay's childhood globe and tried to draw it as well. He had no idea where to look, but he was sure if he could find one, then it would help him to make friends with his mother again. He realised Jack had become very quiet and wondered if all the talk about parents had upset his friend.

"You all right? Sorry, got a bit carried away then. Do you ever think about her? You know, your mum?"

"Not really. It's the not knowing anything, mainly."

"How do you feel about her?"

"Don't feel anything. I used to hate her for dumping me like that, then one time all I wanted to do was find her. Just to have someone in my life that I was related to, but then I thought perhaps that's not the point. Having people in your life who really care about you and how you are is more important than someone who shares your blood but couldn't give a monkey's. Right? The worst thing is being scared that I'll turn out like her – you know? That I'll become someone who always puts themselves first or runs away from problems."

"No way, mate. That's not you at all. Listen. Just keep doing what you're doing, and if you want to talk anytime, you know where I am, and I know my mum would help too. Sounds a bit soppy but, you know …"

"Thanks."

## December 25th

"Happy Christmas, Mum." Adam laid the present on the table in front of Kay.

"Oh, Adam, thank you. Whatever can it be?"

"Open it, quick!"

Kay unwrapped the gift and laughed out loud when she saw what Adam had bought. It certainly wasn't the globe from her childhood, but it was still beautiful. Inside was a miniature forest with robins perched in the trees and tiny foxes sitting on the ground. There was no music but when the globe was shaken, glittery snow covered everything. She thought back to the winter days when she was small and her parents had tried to convince her that the icy Jack Frost didn't mean her any harm, and her eyes filled with tears. Then she smiled.

"Is it all right? It was the best I could find."

"It's perfect. Thank you so much. Are you too big for a hug?"

Adam threw himself into her arms. "I'm sorry about before. When you talked to me about my dad. I do want to know more and to meet him if he still wants to. Is that okay?"

Kay hugged him even harder. This was going to be a great Christmas, and who knew what the new year would bring.

\*\*\*

The dishes had been cleared away and the sisters sat on the settee enjoying a glass of wine. The tension that had built up between them earlier in the year had gone and they were comfortable with each other again. Ruth had guessed at, and still disapproved of, Janet's continued support of Tia but kept her opinions to herself. As long as Janet didn't expect her to become involved, that was fine. She wondered what Kay and Adam were doing today and couldn't help sighing.

Janet knew only too well what her sister was thinking. She'd been thinking along the same lines and kicking herself for not trying harder to persuade Kay to stay in the shop. It only took a slight thought-shift to bring Tia into the picture and Janet wondered what the girl was doing today. It had crossed her mind briefly to ask Ruth to invite Tia for Christmas dinner, but common sense prevailed. Still, it must have been lonely in the little flat, with no family or friends.

Janet shook her head.

*** 

Fine bloody Christmas this has been. Almost as bad as last year but at least Janet had me around to her place on Christmas Eve. Her sister's calling the shots this year, though. Organised it all so Janet's with her all the time. Bitch! I expect Kay's over at that Maisie's place as well. She doesn't know how many times I've watched her back and fore there. Adam's certainly grown. I wonder what Luke would look like now. If she hadn't been so mean about letting us stay, I'd know, wouldn't I? What would he have been this year? Twelve? Poor kid. All Jake's fault, really. If he hadn't found us at the station, it would never have happened. We'd have found our own place and I know I'd have got help eventually.

Shit, I'm so pissed off. It's only eight o'clock and the telly's rubbish. I think I deserve a treat. I mean, warmed up dinner, no real presents – what kind of holiday is that? I've been off the drink nearly two years now and that bottle's been in the cupboard since the summer so I know I can control it. I'm sure a small one won't hurt.

## December 31st

When the doorbell rang, Tia didn't bother checking who was outside as she was half-expecting Janet. They'd met for coffee earlier in the week and Janet had promised to try to call in for an hour.

"Hi, come in."

"Don't mind if I do. Don't mind at all."

Tia gasped. "Jake! What are you doing here? How did you find me?"

Jake pushed her back into the room and kicked the door shut behind him.

"That's no way to greet an old friend. Not difficult to find you, girl. Not difficult at all. Couple of the boys have seen you about town. Thought I'd see what the champion blagger was up to. How d'you manage to score this little place then? Who'd you con this time?"

"It's not like that. It's my place. I went into a hostel at first and then I got this. Look, you have to go. I don't want any trouble and there's someone coming soon, anyway."

Jake sneered. Tia could tell he'd been drinking. She edged towards the front door but Jake caught her by the wrist and forced her onto the settee.

"Not so fast, bitch. You owe me. Running out like that left me out of pocket, you know."

"I don't have any money, if that's what you're after. I've got about ten quid, that's all."

"That'll do for starters. Now what about a drink or has the slut become a saint now?" He stood up and dragged Tia into the kitchen area. He held onto her arm while he flicked open the cupboards with his free hand. "Ha! Thought so. Going to have a little new year party with your visitor, eh? So, who is he? Another poor sucker?"

"No, it's a woman …"

"Oh yeah. Changed sides, have you? Silly cow. Now sit down and we'll have a nice chat and a few drinks. Civilised, like."

He drank a glass of neat vodka and forced Tia to do the

same. She resisted at first but her own demons had awoken and the second glass went down easily, as did the third. When Jake grabbed her neck and started to kiss her, she froze. She moved her face away and he lunged at her shirt, ripping off the buttons. She screamed and wriggled onto the floor but before she could move away, she felt a thump on her arm and heard the crack of a bone breaking. Then a kick to the head and all she could feel was warm blood running down her face and onto her white rug.

# 2004

## January 15th

The whirr and clack of machinery were the only sounds Tia could hear but she couldn't quite place what they were. For some reason her eyes wouldn't open properly no matter how hard she tried, so she gave up and drifted back into an uneasy sleep filled with red and white flashes. As the dawn light filtered through the blinds, she moaned and tried to turn over.

"No, Tia, keep as still as you can. Can you open your eyes for me?" Janet placed a hand on Tia's shoulder and leaned over the bed. "It's all right, you're safe now."

Very slowly Tia opened her eyes a fraction. Everything was blurred but gradually she was aware of Janet standing next to her. She tried to speak but couldn't.

"No, don't try to talk. You're in hospital. You're going to be fine but you'll be here a while. I'll get someone to come to you and I'll see you soon. Don't fret – just try to rest."

Janet looked down on Tia's blackened face and shoulders, and at all the tubes and wires attached to various parts of her body. She felt such a rush of pure rage against the man who had done this, against Tia for being so stupid as to let him in, and against herself for not going to Tia's flat earlier that night. Still, at least she had gone, otherwise the girl could have lain there until it would have been too late to save her.

## December 4th

The sisters had been shopping and were unpacking before making a pot of tea in Ruth's kitchen.

"Do you think we'll have snow this year, Jan? I don't think we've had any since I moved here."

Janet shook her head. "The forecasters say not, but I never believe them. The bushes have been full of berries this year and that's supposed to mean a hard winter, isn't it? I just hope I'm not working if it does snow."

"Are you going to keep on with the shop and the soup kitchen as well as the nursing? Seems an awful lot for you."

"I think I'll give up on the kitchen after the winter, although I do enjoy it. If it was in the daytime, I'd do that rather than the shop, but I'm finding the nights a bit hard."

"Mmmm. Still, probably better in the shop. I do worry about you with all that riff-raff."

"Ruth! That's not fair. Poor devils. Just need a helping hand, most of them."

"Talking of helping hands, what happened with that Tia after she was attacked? You never said much."

"Didn't think you'd want to know. She was in hospital for ages. Couple of operations to sort out her broken bones. Head scans and goodness knows what else."

"Did he …?"

"What? Oh. Yes, but no real damage there. Well, not physically. She's been moved to a psychiatric and rehabilitation unit over in Ivygate. It's got a good reputation. After that she'll probably be relocated by the council and social services. She can't stay around here. She wouldn't name him, so there's nothing much the law will do now. Shame really. She seemed as though she was finally letting go of her past."

"Ah well. You know what they say about leopards and spots. And it seems like her past doesn't want to let go of her. Best to let her get on with her life and let others take care of her now."

Ruth refilled their cups and Janet shook her head. Sometimes she wondered how they could have come from the same parents and grown up in the same house.

\*\*\*

"Come on Adam. Hurry up. The car will be here soon."

Adam looked in the mirror, flicked back his hair and grinned at his mother.

"You look cool! Is Dad coming here or meeting us there?"

"Meeting us. Jeff is picking up the hire car, then coming here. Maisie and the others will go with her folks. All set?"

Four hours later, Dr and Mrs Kalan Khatri, and their proud son, Adam, waved goodbye to their friends, closed the front door of Kalan's house and collapsed onto the settee. They'd decided to postpone their honeymoon until the spring but Adam and Kay would move out of their flat the next day. The past year had been a blur of major events and Kay found it hard to believe all that had happened. Kalan and Adam had hit it off right away and it had been a joy to watch Adam get to know his father and interact with him so naturally. Kalan's mother had welcomed Adam unreservedly, although it had taken a little while longer before Kay was accepted. There was, however, a realisation that Kalan's mind was set and it was better to gain a grandson and daughter-in-law than to lose a son. When Kalan proposed, Kay had a moment of pure fright mixed with ecstasy, and a million reasons why she should say no jumped up at her, but Kalan chased them all away. The expression on Adam's face when they told him was one she would remember for the rest of her life.

***

Jack lay on his bed and watched the clouds scudding across the sky. He was now officially a teenager, although he wasn't sure whether that was supposed to be important or not. He thought about Adam and what was happening right at that moment. He was pleased for his friend but incredibly jealous at the same time. A dad and a big, new house on the same day. It meant Adam would live further away from him, but that didn't really matter. At least his mum had agreed he should stay at the same school for now. Adam's grades had been slipping and Jack was afraid they'd be split up for some of their subjects. They'd been lucky to have been put in the same form when they started and had continued to stick together. Jack knew he would have had a much harder time with the school bullies without his friend to look out for him.

He rolled over, opened the bedside cabinet drawer and pulled out an envelope. Even after all this time, he still had the letter Adam had taken from the Home's office. Not for the first time he wondered what would have happened if they'd stayed a bit longer at the house or spoken to the woman who'd shouted at them to go away. Maybe when he was older, he might try again. Who knew – he might have some family after all.

# 2005

## December 3rd

Kay and Maisie walked the short distance from the salon to the car park. It was Saturday night and both women were tired. Kay wanted to get home as quickly as she could as Kalan had booked a table at a local restaurant to celebrate Adam's fourteenth birthday.

"Do you have time for a coffee, Kay?"

Kay grimaced. "I'm sorry Maisie. Not tonight. Is there something you want to talk about? You've been quiet all day."

"Yes, but it can wait. Can you call over tomorrow for an hour?"

"Of course. Eleven all right?"

"Fine. See you then." Maisie let herself into her car and waved as she drove off. Kay frowned. She hoped Maisie didn't have anything too serious to discuss.

Next morning, Maisie made coffee and sat at the table with Kay. She fiddled with her mug for a while and then sighed.

"Come on, spit it out." Kay reached across and touched Maisie's arm.

"Sorry. There's no easy way to say this so I'm sorry if it sounds blunt, but I'm thinking of selling the business. Jeff has had a fantastic opportunity but he can't move on it without the money from the salon."

"Oh, I see, but it's your business, Maisie. You shouldn't feel bad about me."

"But I do. We've been in it together from the start and I know I'd never have done it on my own. I wanted to talk to

247

you first because I have an idea. I wondered if you'd like to buy me out? Now that you and Kalan are together it might be possible. What do you think?"

"It's certainly worth considering. What's Jeff thinking of doing?"

"His boss is retiring and there's no-one to take over so he asked if Jeff was interested. He's been with Mr Rivers since his apprenticeship and they're quite close. It seems to have come at the right time too, as we're thinking of moving to that new estate over Fairfield way. Do you know it? It's not far from you. Mum's going to sell up and come and live with us. I'm hoping to swap my car for a little van and maybe go back to home treatments. Jeff says we could probably ask the builders to make a double garage as well, so I could set up a home-base like before. If you don't want the salon, you could always pitch in with me again, if that's enough?"

Kay smiled. "That's wonderful news. We've certainly come a long way since the kids were babies, haven't we? About the salon – thanks for the offer but I can't take it up. I wasn't going to say anything just yet, but I would have needed to take a break next summer for a few months, or even longer maybe."

"Are you and Kalan going away?"

Kay shook her head and blushed.

"Oh! You don't mean…? You are, aren't you?" Maisie squealed. "That's fabulous. I'm so happy for you. Do Kalan and Adam know?"

"Kal guessed almost right away but we're holding off telling Adam just yet. I think it's going to be a bit of a shock for him. He's been the centre of my world for fourteen years and besides, he's started playing up again. After Kal came on the scene he settled down but I think the novelty's worn off. He won't focus on his homework and he's getting bad reports at school, too. Kal wants to transfer him to a private school before he starts his GCSE programme but I'm not sure."

"How about some private tutoring? At least to see him through his exams."

"Yes, we'll see. So big changes for all of us."

## December 19th

Kay looked at her watch for the tenth time. The bus was late and she was feeling cold and a little bit sick. The salon was closed for the day and she'd made a spur of the moment decision to go out after Kalan had left for work. She looked at the piece of paper in her hand and sighed.

Half an hour later she stepped from the bus and crossed the road. She looked at the paper again and walked along a wide street until she arrived at the place she was looking for. She rang the bell.

"Hello Mum."

# 2006

## July

The letterbox rattled and Janet opened the door to the hallway just as a small package was pushed through the door. She turned it over and frowned. She didn't recognise the postmark and couldn't remember ordering anything. Inside the package was a small box and a letter. She set the box to one side and unfolded the paper.

*Dear Janet,*

*I know it's been a long while since we spoke, and I know I can't see you anymore, but I wanted to write to clear up a few things that have been playing on my mind. You were so good to me and I don't think I ever thanked you properly. In fact, I caused more harm than you and your family deserved.*

*Let's start with Kay. She was right. I did blag my way into her life and put her whole existence at risk. I was so selfish and convinced myself that I had no other choice. But of course, I did. I lied and cheated all the time I was with her. Even at the end she tried to help me find somewhere safe to live but I threw it back in her face and stole her money. She was so kind to me and I paid her back in the most despicable way. I blamed my mother, my background, other people – anything for my behaviour – anyone except myself. Maybe there were things that influenced how I thought; how I behaved, but I had choices. The therapist told me that I have to learn to overcome the bad experiences; to look forward. I have to stop hating myself. I'm trying but it's still hard not to think of myself as evil.*

*If you see Kay, please tell her that I'm truly sorry. When she stormed out of the shop that day, I could have helped you to find her but I chose not to because I was jealous. I don't know if she still lives in the same flat but I'll write the address at the end of the letter, and the place where she was working.*

*Please give the little box to Ruth. I hope she can forgive me. I won't say that I didn't mean to steal the brooch, because I did. As soon as I saw it, it made me think of the snow globe and I had to have it. It wasn't for the money it might fetch; I just wanted the memories it brought to me. I can still hear Kay humming the Winter Lullaby. I have goose bumps just thinking about it. I'm sorry about telling Ruth that we'd seen Kay, as well. I really was a spiteful cow, wasn't I?*

*And that leaves you. I don't think that there are enough ways to say sorry or thank you. You helped me so much, when others would (and did) turn their backs on me. I don't know if you ever remembered, but you helped me on the day Luke was born. I was the one who dropped down outside the shop in the snow and you rescued me. You always said that I reminded you of someone! Maybe it would have been better for everyone if you'd left me there, but I'm not supposed to think like that now.*

*I have a nice place to live, although I'm not allowed to tell you where. My care worker knows I am writing this and will check that I've not said anything I shouldn't. I have lots of support and later in the year I'm hoping to give my education another go and I'll try to find a job, as well.*

*My biggest regret is Luke. If I hadn't been so selfish, he might still be here. Not with me, obviously, but he might have had a good life. I can't change that, I know, but it will haunt me forever. No amount of therapy can dull that level of guilt.*

*Goodbye, Janet. Maybe one day I'll be able to see you and, if I do, I hope you'll at least say hello.*

*Thank you again for everything.*

*Tia x*

Kay sat with her mother and aunt in the park. They took it in turns to peer into the pram at the new baby.

"She's so beautiful, Kay. Look at her little fingers." Ruth stroked the baby's hand gently. She felt so blessed that she not only had her daughter back in her life, but also two grandchildren and a son-in-law. She'd been a little shocked when Kay told her about Kalan, but as soon as she saw them together, she'd known all was well. They'd taken some time to work through their feelings but they'd made it.

Janet looked at the baby and smiled. They'd been given a second chance. It was lovely getting to know Adam but they'd missed all his baby years. This time nothing was going to separate them.

"I had an interesting letter this morning..." She told them what Tia had said and gave the brooch back to Ruth. Neither mother nor daughter were keen to discuss Tia but at least they didn't express any anger. Janet sighed. Maybe it was best to leave the past behind. Baby Hope would be occupying a lot of their time in the future, she was sure.

\*\*\*

I can't believe it's been almost two and a half years. Most of it's been a blur. Hospital. Psych unit. Rehab. Hostel. Here. It's good to have my own place again. Never thought I'd make it. Part of me wanted to let go after the Jake episode. There didn't seem much point in anything. I'd messed up so many people's lives, as well as my own. There's so much that I still feel bad about, though. The therapist has helped but I know there's a long way to go. It was such a relief to be able to open up to someone, but it wasn't easy. I miss Janet a lot but I know I have to stay away from Alderbridge.

# 2008

## September 8th

Jack was feeling sick. He'd signed up for an engineering course at the local technical college, and today was the first day. The past two years had flown and he'd decided he didn't want to stay at school for A levels. He'd worked steadily for his GCSE examinations and had done well in Science, Computing and Maths. He'd struggled a little with the other subjects but had managed to scrape a pass in English and History; all of which allowed him to apply for a place at the college. He wished that Adam would be going with him, but their paths had finally split. Adam had continued to mess about at school but had still managed to pass most of his exams. Even so, his parents had decided to transfer him to Willow High, a private school where his dad had gone. Jack thought it would be a waste of money if Adam continued along his destructive path, but maybe a change of environment might help him. His passes were good enough for him to be accepted to study at A level, although Jack wondered what Adam would do, as he had no idea about a career. At least he had a good family behind him. If he did manage to settle down, he had the option of university ahead of him.

A quick glance at the clock, then Jack grabbed his rucksack and set off.

\*\*\*

"Come on, Adam. Don't be difficult, please. Just try it for a term and if you hate it so much then we'll consider something else."

"Really? You mean it? All right, but just a term."

Kay sighed. The past two years had been a struggle and she wasn't sure that she could take another two. It had been hard enough coping with Hope. Although she was an easy child, it had been such a long time since Adam's baby days that Kay had forgotten how tiring it all could be. Kalan was good with both the children but he worked long, and often unsocial, hours so most of the parenting fell to Kay. If the promise of negotiations with Adam ensured that he went to school today, she'd take it!

"Yes, but you have to promise that you'll try. Don't think you can simply turn up and turn off. Try to get involved with things that are going on. You always loved sports when you were younger so try joining some of the teams or think about some of the after-school clubs. Promise?"

Adam grinned. "Okay, and thanks."

He hugged her and she smiled at him. *Little rogue!*

***

"Hello, Jan. Come in. Kettle's on."

"Hope you're not in the middle of anything, but there's something I wanted to talk to you about."

"Fine. Nothing serious, I hope?"

"No, not really. It's just that I've been thinking over what you said last month about work and I've decided to hand in my notice at the hospital. I know I've only been part-time for a while now but I'm finding it harder and harder. It's not so much the actual work but all the changes, the management, and the petty in-fighting. Maybe if I'd quit the soup kitchen a few years back, like I thought about, I wouldn't feel so worn down but there again …"

"I wasn't expecting that if I'm honest. I thought you'd give up the voluntary stuff before the nursing. Still, if you're unhappy there's no point pushing it. Will you be all right for money? I can help a bit if you need it."

"Bless you, but I'll be fine. My pension won't be huge but

I have savings. After all, it's only been me all these years."

"What about the shop and the soup kitchen?"

"Not sure. I can't stop everything at the same time or else I'd go mad. I'm used to being busy. I think the soup kitchen would be next on the list but I'll wait a while before making that decision. Thanks, Ruth. It feels good to get it out in the open."

"Anytime, you know that."

# 2010

## August

Kay and Maisie walked through the town centre and sat on a bench outside a coffee shop. They chatted for an hour about their families and reminisced about the children's early days and the salon. After Maisie and Jeff had moved to their new house, the women hadn't seen quite so much of each other. Kay was busy with the baby and with adapting to running a new home and Maisie was re-establishing her manicure business.

"What are you going to do now that Hope's in nursery? Any thoughts about going back to work? You could always start off with me if you want. Be like the old days!"

"It's a thought, but I haven't decided yet. Kal doesn't really want me to go back to hairdressing but I told him he's being snobbish! I know he'd like to have more kids, but I don't think I could face that."

Maisie groaned. "Me neither. Things are comfortable for us right now and working at home suits me. I do the odd house call but I prefer it when they come to me. If you change your mind, let me know. Always glad of your company."

Kay smiled. She'd been lucky to find a friend like Maisie. Not so lucky with some of her other choices but she didn't want to think about them. Especially not Tia. She still couldn't bring herself to forgive her, and when she thought about little Luke, she often cried.

\*\*\*

Jack looked around his new room one more time. It was strange how quickly he'd become used to it. After he'd finished school, and like many of the children in care, he'd moved out from the home into one of the half-way houses scattered across town. It was a big change for him but he'd surprised himself by settling in quickly and even making friends with some of the other lads who lived there. The wardens were helpful but encouraged the boys to develop the practical and social skills they'd need for the future. Jack had worried about money for a while, but Social Services and the council had explained to him how he'd be supported and he was gradually becoming used to managing his own finances. He glanced at his watch for the tenth time. He had a special meeting this morning and he didn't want to be late.

Jack glanced up as the coffee shop door swung open and he grinned at Adam.

"Hello mate, how's it going?"

"Not so bad. What about you?

Half an hour later the boys had exchanged the news of their exam successes and their plans for the future. Jack was staying on at the college for the advanced engineering course but was also applying for apprenticeships. Despite Adam's insistence that he would have quit Willow High by Christmas, he'd enjoyed being there and had settled in very quickly. Unfortunately, he'd enjoyed the social aspects rather more than the academic ones and had only managed bare passes in Chemistry, Biology and Maths, and had decided that he was going to go travelling for a year to think over his options.

"Bet that didn't go down well at home?"

"Naw, not at first but I agreed that I'll either resit for better grades when I come back and apply for Uni, or find a job. They made it clear I can't expect to doss about at home and sponge off them."

"When will you go, and where?"

"Leaving in September. A couple of guys are taking a gap year so I'm tagging along with them. We're going to start off in France and work our way across Europe. Pick up casual work if we can."

"Oh, right." Jack rattled the spoon in his saucer. Even though the boys had gone their separate ways two years before, they'd kept in touch and had met up regularly. This was going to be different.

"Listen, I know you don't have a computer but if I email you, you can use the college library to pick them up, can't you? That way, we can still keep in touch. Okay?"

Jack nodded. He guessed that was better than nothing.

# 2012

## July

*Hello mate. How's it going with you?*

*Thanks for all your news. Hope you'll get the exam results you need and that the apprenticeship interviews go well.*

*Sorry I haven't been in touch before now – ages, I know, but I've been working on a farm (don't you dare laugh) and technology isn't something they're too familiar with!!!!!! After the lads left last summer, I couldn't face coming back so I blagged a lift to Greece and mucked around for a bit. I met up with a girl (nudge, nudge) and she told me she was travelling to Skyros (little island) to work on a horse breeding farm, so I tagged along. Man, it's been fantastic. They breed this funny little pony called The Skyrian Horse (bit obvious, yeah!) and it's supposed to be one of the rarest and oldest breeds in the world (stop me if I'm getting too technical for you!). Anyway, I got real caught up in the lifestyle (and the girl) but she's moving on to Australia so I'm thinking of heading home. Haven't told the folks yet. I need to figure out what I want to do first. Got an idea but I don't know if I've got the stamina.*

*See you soon, mate. Need a decent beer!*
*Adam.*

Jack smiled. Typical Adam. He'd kept in touch quite a bit the first year but after that it had been almost total silence. Jack was hurt initially but then he'd met his girlfriend, Alys, and his mind was taken up with thoughts other than his wandering friend. Still, it would be good to see him again.

Kay opened the door of Adam's room. Funny how she still called it that even though he hadn't set foot in it for almost two years. His absence had hit her hard, even though she knew the experience would do him good, but his almost total silence over the past year was worrying her more than she wanted to admit. For the first time she completely understood how her parents, and especially her mother, had felt when she had disappeared out of their lives. She prayed that history wasn't repeating itself and that Adam wasn't in trouble and too afraid or too stubborn to let them know. She sighed, closed the door and picked up her car keys. Time to meet Hope from school.

As she waited at the school gates and chatted to a few of the other mums, she shuddered suddenly.

"You all right?"

"Yes, thanks. Had a strange feeling that someone was right behind me. I'll have to stop watching those late-night movies!"

***

That was so wrong of me, but I just couldn't help it. No, that's not true. I've been wanting to see her for ages. Wasn't too difficult to track her down. I guessed Janet might lead me to her eventually. Fancy Kay and Kalan Khatri getting back together. And another kid, too. I was so close today I could almost have touched her but she didn't give me a second glance. Can't blame her. I was a shitty friend. Wasn't even that, really. I just latched onto her and expected her to sort out my life. And then I did the same with Janet. It was hard not to talk to her the other week but I'm glad I didn't. I've come a long way since … yeah well, I don't want to think about that now. Only two more weeks before I get my results and then I can look for a proper job. If someone had told me six years ago that I'd have completed English, Maths, History, and possibly Home Economics GCSE by now, I'd have laughed in their face. Can't pretend it's been easy but

I've had so much support from everybody. Even my minor fall off the wagon didn't faze them. That new woman at the job centre is great. I hope she can find me something, then I can apply for a better place to live. Maybe when I'm settled, I can get in touch with Janet again.

I still miss Janet, and Kay if I'm honest, but I know I must let all of that go. Every day that passes makes me a bit stronger and I can't waste it all. Now I have to decide what to do next. Back to college or try to find a job. Still the same problem as before, though. I'm not qualified to do anything except cleaning or basic shop work and with my record …

# 2013

**August**

"Mum! Muuuuum! Where are you?" Adam slammed the front door.

"In the kitchen. What's all the noise about?"

"I did it! I bloody did it, Mum! Look."

He waved a piece of paper in front of Kay's face and when she realised what it was, she grabbed it, read it quickly, then she screamed and hugged Adam so hard that he groaned.

"Brilliant. I'm so proud of you and I know Dad will be, too. Well done."

Adam grinned. After his return home he'd told his parents he wanted to be a vet and that he was prepared to resit his A levels at college if they'd help him. His results of three A grades meant he'd secured his place at veterinary school, starting in September.

# 2014

## August

Adam's jaw dropped.

"Say that again."

"Alys and I are getting married. In December."

"God, she's not …"

"No! You know we can't afford anything fancy, so what's the point waiting. It's what we both want so we're just doing the registry office thing. If you're home from uni by then, will you be a witness? We'll need someone else as well but one of Alys' friends will do it, I'm sure. What d'you think?"

"Of course I will, if I can. Bloody hell, didn't expect that but congratulations, mate."

"Thanks."

Adam told Kay about Jack's news and she was pleased for the lad. She'd not had much contact with him over the years but she was glad Adam and he had remained friends.

"Neither of them has any family? That's sad."

"Yeah, I know. Alys has been fostered on and off most of her life but not with anyone who'd be interested in her now. She met Jack at the college. Can't remember what he said she'd been doing but they got together in the second year and stayed together."

"Listen. This might sound a bit mad but what if we put on a bit of a party for them here after the wedding? Nothing fussy, but we could ask mum to help, and maybe Jack and Alys have a few friends they'd like to invite. What do you think?"

"Sounds great to me. I'll have a word with them. I've checked my term dates and I might have to miss the last week but that should be okay."

## December 6th

Kay put up the tree and Christmas decorations a little earlier than usual to make the house look festive for the small wedding party. Jack and Alys were so delighted at her offer and couldn't stop thanking her. Kay helped Alys to choose her dress and bought her shoes and a few other things as a small gift. Kay and Kalan went along to the registry office as well as Adam and six of Alys and Jack's friends. It was a quiet but joyful affair and Kay was so pleased to see how the young couple supported each other. Thankfully, Adam liked Alys and was pleased for his friend. Kay had seen Jack much more in the past few months than she had (or so she thought) in his whole life and from about the second meeting, she felt there was something familiar about his features and some of his mannerisms, but no matter how hard she tried, she couldn't create a definite shape from those shadows.

"Thanks again, Mrs Khatri, and thank your mum as well. This has been so wonderful. We'll never forget it."

"You're both so welcome. I can't believe how long you and Adam have been friends, Jack. Seems like only yesterday that you met and look at you now. Come on, Mum, say hello properly to the happy couple."

Ruth beamed at them. She'd heard a lot about the young man who had stuck so closely to her grandson and she felt sorry he had no family of his own.

"You're welcome. Just pleased I could help. Where will you two be living?"

"We have a flat in Riverglade. It's not huge but we'll be fine for a while. As soon as I finish my apprenticeship, I'll be better paid."

"Riverglade?" Ruth smiled. "That's not so far from where I live, and my sister, too. If you're ever in need of someone to talk to, give me a call. Kay can write my number down for you. I mean that, you know."

"Thanks. It's not an area we know very well, but it seems cool. Have you always lived there?"

"No, I used to live in Fieldslea. Do you know it? Village called The Meadows, but after my husband died, I found it too much for me. Whatever is the matter?"

Jack and Adam were staring at each other with their mouths open.

Two hours later, Ruth, Kay, Kalan and Adam sat in the living room. The bombshell that the boys had dropped was still reverberating. Ruth kept shaking her head and Kay couldn't stop crying. To think that Adam had almost come face-to-face with his own grandmother and hadn't even known it.

"If only that girl hadn't chased them away. You know, that Tia. We'd only left her there to start packing up while we went to the solicitors. If we'd been a bit quicker maybe we would have seen the boys."

"No good thinking like that, Nan. The letter made out that you thought Jack was your grandson. I wouldn't have had a clue."

"No, but I think if I'd seen you, I might have been a bit suspicious. After all, you look so much like your mum, and your dad. And if we'd spoken to you, well, I knew your name was Adam. Wait 'til I tell Janet. Shame she couldn't come today but she couldn't get any cover for the shop."

## December 7th

The sisters had spent hours going over the same ground once Ruth had shared the news from the previous day. In the end they'd agreed to drop the subject. Nothing to be gained by wishing for things in the past. When the doorbell rang, they jumped and Janet was surprised to see Kay.

"Hello, love. What brings you here today?"

Kay kissed her aunt. "Hi, Auntie Janet. Kal's looking after Hope for an hour or so. There's something that's been niggling me all night and I thought it was better to come and talk to you both rather than 'phoning."

"All right. Out with it then." Ruth patted the settee and Kay sat down.

"That letter you wrote, Mum, to the Home, or Social Services, about the child they'd found – Jack. What made you think he was your grandson?"

Ruth looked a little shamefaced. "Well, we heard what had happened to him and I knew he was about the same age as Adam would have been –"

"But you can't have thought I'd leave him like that?"

"Not really, Kay, but I didn't know how things had turned out for you or anything. When Janet told me she'd been working the night he'd been brought in, I just started imagining all sorts. I had a very lukewarm response from Social Services – just that they passed the letter to the Home - and then I forgot about it. When I found out your Dad had seen you and Adam and he'd guessed who Adam's dad was, I just pushed the letter, and the boy, out of my mind. Janet, whatever is the matter? You're as white as a sheet."

"There's been something flickering at the back of my mind for ages – well, several things really, but I think I've just joined up the dots. Yes, I did hear about, and see, the little lad that was brought in that night, and what I'm connecting it with is something I overheard a few years ago, but it can't be."

"What are you rabbiting about, Jan? What can't be true."

"Before I go on – Kay, do you know anything more about Jack?"

"No, but I think I know where you're going. That's what's been bothering me all night. I've always felt there was something vaguely familiar about him and, well, you overheard what Tia told me in the storeroom that day, didn't you?"

Janet looked a little shamefaced but nodded. Ruth looked from one to the other and frowned.

"Is someone going to let me in on the secret?"

Janet turned to her sister. "We're both thinking there could be a chance that Jack is actually Luke, Tia's son. She told

266

Kay the boy had cut himself badly and that bloke of hers had taken the child through the snow to the hospital but that he'd died from loss of blood. Jack was found in the snow, dumped on a doorstep with his arm sliced open. No name, no identification. You know the rest."

"So, she never looked for him because she thought he was dead? And the boy was too traumatised to give the police or anyone any clues. What a mess, but do you think it's possible? Are you going to do anything about it?"

Janet and Kay looked at each other for a long time.

"Nothing." Kay shook her head. "What good could possibly come from it? Jack knows the basic story but thinks it was his mother who left him. He's not kindly disposed towards her. I don't think finding out what really happened, or the conditions he was living in, would make a positive difference. She thinks he's dead. If we find her and tell her he might not be, she'll probably make his life hell, and he'd never be free of her. Why don't we just agree to keep a friendly eye on Jack and Alys and help them out if we can? And we should make sure that Adam doesn't find out either."

# 2016

## November 30th

*Dear Janet,*

*It's been such a long time but I hope you'll at least read this letter as I'd like to try to explain a few things and apologise again for the hurt and trouble I caused. I continued my therapy sessions for a few years and I think they really helped. As I told you in my last letter, I have realised how destructive I was, not only towards others but also to myself. I won't bore you with the details but I learned that I couldn't go on blaming 'bad genes' for everything and, even though my upbringing was varied, I can't excuse myself totally from all of the horrible things I've said and done. I used to switch from one extreme to the other – from blaming my mother or background, to blaming myself, but I think I've reached a place where I can just about be comfortable in my own skin. I can't change the past, I know that, but I can try to like myself a bit more and to atone for the damage I know I caused.*

*I've stayed sober and I did return to my studies and, over the years, I've gained a few GCSEs. Nothing wonderful but it's marked a big turning point in my life. I've had a lot of support, for which I'm truly grateful, and I've been working in the office of a small supermarket for the past few years. Nothing grand but at least I am earning some money for myself. I have my own little flat and I try to take care of it the best I can.*

*I read in the papers last year about Jake. I don't know if you saw it? They found his body in the river and it took some time for them to formally identify him. Who would have thought that his name was Jacob Gabriel Cross! This means that I'm free to let people know where I'm living and even to move back to Alderbridge or Crompton if I want. I'm not rushing those decisions, obviously, but I would like you to have my address, if that's all right? I don't have any next-of-kin so I listed you as a person to contact if anything happened to me. I know I should have asked first – sorry, but I don't expect anything of you, it just felt good to have someone to put on the form.*

*I won't go over all the apologies I made last time. I meant them then and I still do. It doesn't really matter if Kay or Mrs Jones, or even you, don't believe me. It's enough to know that I have recognised what I did and have finally taken responsibility. My biggest regret was, is, and always will be, Luke. I let him down so badly and no amount of recrimination will help. It's a scar I'll carry to my grave. I tried to find out where he would have been buried but no one wanted to help and I decided to let it go.*

*If there's any way you could bring yourself to write to me, I'd be eternally grateful, but I'll understand if you want to keep your distance. I won't trouble you, I promise, but I hope you won't mind if I write the occasional letter.*

*Thank you for everything that you did for me; for setting me on the long road to recovery and to valuing myself as a human being and not a monster.*

*Yours,*

*Maria x [Decided to reclaim my name – new start!]*

## December 1st

"Are you sure you want to do this, Jack? You had that dream again last night, didn't you?"

Jack leaned across the table and patted Alys' hand.

"It'll be fine. Honest. I just want to have look in the window. I only had a quick glance when I walked home last night, and it didn't register then."

"What if it's not the globe that Adam told you about?"

"Then no harm done, is there? If I think it is, I might go in and ask about it."

Alys frowned. She thought it was better to let go of the past but knew Jack well enough not to press the issue.

"Okay, but I'm coming with you. No. No arguments. Anyway, it's time you did some Christmas shopping!"

An hour later, Jack and Alys stood outside the charity shop and gazed at the globe in the window. Snow was drifting down quietly from a grey sky and Jack shivered. Alys caught his arm and propelled him into the shop. Although Jack had become quite friendly with Kay and her mum, he'd not had that much to do with Janet. When the couple entered the shop, Janet had her back turned to them. She was sorting through the post that she'd picked up from the mat when she'd left her flat. She frowned when she saw Tia's letter. Even after all this time, she recognised the writing. She pushed it to one side and tutted. When she turned around, she was startled to see Jack and Alys.

"Hello. What brings you to my little domain on this snowy day?"

"Hi Janet. We didn't realise it was this shop where you worked."

"Well, not for much longer. I'm thinking of finishing after Christmas. One last effort. What do you think of the display?"

"That's why we came in. Years ago, Adam told me about a snow globe that used to frighten his mum when she was a kid and he wanted to find it for her. The way he described it made me wonder if it's the same one that's in your window. Now I know you put it there, I guess it is. Does it play some spooky music too? Adam said his mum used to sing it to him whenever it snowed."

Janet laughed. "I wouldn't call it spooky exactly, although to a child it might seem that way."

"Can I look at it?"

"Sure. Just be careful. It's got a little crack near the base."

Janet unplugged the globe, lifted it and handed it to Jack. He stared at the glittering crystals and held it out towards

Alys. As he did, the palm of his hand caught on the fracture in the glass and small drops of blood splashed onto the cotton wool snow of the display. He trembled and Alys caught the globe before it hit the ground. Janet ran into the back room to fetch the first aid kit and she pushed back Jack's sleeve: she tried hard not to stare when she saw the long scar on his forearm. A movement outside the window caught her eye. She glanced between the pale face in the glass and Jack's and her hands shook. His gaze followed hers and he looked into his mother's eyes for first time in over twenty years.

Janet moved away from the window quickly. "There we are. No real harm done. Okay? If you want to listen to the music, come over here. It's easier if I plug it in from the counter."

"Yes, please. I heard so much about it that I can't let this chance go."

On the pavement, Tia stood transfixed. She hadn't meant to travel to the shop but after writing to Janet the day before, she hadn't been able to settle. She promised herself that even if Janet was there, she'd simply watch for a while, then leave. Just seeing her would be enough, but what she saw shook her very soul. Luke. It couldn't be anyone else, surely? Right here where it all began. Why had Jake said that he was dead? More importantly, why had she been so willing to believe him?

Tia put her hand on the door, then stopped. Three deep breaths later; a thousand scenes flashing through her mind, and her heart pounding like racehorses on the track, she dropped her hand, bit the inside of her cheek, and turned away. The falling snow quickly filled in her footprints: within a minute it was as if she had never been there.

# Fantastic Books
# Great Authors

darkstroke is
an imprint of
Crooked Cat Books

- Gripping Thrillers
- Cosy Mysteries
- Romantic Chick-Lit
- Fascinating Historicals
- Exciting Fantasy
- Young Adult
- Non-Fiction

Discover us online
**www.darkstroke.com**

Find us on instagram:
**www.instagram.com/darkstrokebooks**

Printed in Poland
by Amazon Fulfillment
Poland Sp. z o.o., Wrocław

64364411R00157